DECKED WITH HOLLY

Also by Marni Bates

AWKWARD

Published by Kensington Publishing Corporation

DECKED WITH HOLLY

Marni Bates

KENSINGTON PUBLISHING CORP.
www.kensingtonbooks.com

K TEEN BOOKS are published by

Kensington Publishing Corp.
119 West 40th Street
New York, NY 10018

All Kensington titles, imprints, and distributed lines are available at special quantity discounts for bulk purchases for sales promotion, premiums, fund-raising, educational or institutional use.

Special book excerpts or customized printings can also be created to fit specific needs. For details, write or phone the office of the Kensington Special Sales Manager: Kensington Publishing Corp., 119 West 40th Street, New York, NY 10018. Attn. Special Sales Department. Phone: 1-800-221-2647.

Kensington and KTeen Reg. U.S. Pat. & TM Off.

ISBN-13: 978-0-7582-7485-4
ISBN-10: 0-7582-7485-8

First Kensington Trade Paperback Printing: October 2012
10 9 8 7 6 5 4 3 2 1

Printed in the United States of America

This book is dedicated to my loyal readership.
You're all rock stars, in my book!

I owe a lot of people *big-time* for making *Decked with Holly* possible. Specifically, my amazing editor, Megan Records, and the talented team of people at Kensington-Teen—thank you! This book has been an absolute pleasure for me, and I'm so grateful for both the opportunity to write it and for your tireless support behind it.

My incredible agent, Laurie McLean, deserves a medal for laughing at my jokes, putting up with my pranks, and helping me realize my dreams. I'm so fortunate to be navigating the perilous waters of publishing with her by my side!

Thank you, Mom, for loving both me and this book so freaking much. Not necessarily in that order. You're the best!

Thank you, Dena Bates, for taking me on so many incredible adventures by land, sea, and air. I love you, Grmma!

Julie and Abigail Dock—ducklings are still cuter than bunnies. But you ladies tend to be right about everything else. I love you both!

Pam van Hylckama, Shanyn Day, Julie Kagawa, Laura Fraley, Brigid Kemmerer, Erica O'Rourke, Nina Berry, Jenn Rush, Emily Guasco, Diana Rosengard, Wes Parker, Olivia Kelly, Jennifer Carolyn—a special thank you for using your immense powers for good . . . at least when directed toward me!

And last but not least, I'd like to send out a super-sized hug to the writing community that has welcomed me with such warmth. Authors. Writers. Dreamers. Bloggers. Reviewers. Readers. Tweeps. Friends. All of you have filled my life with laughter and joy. Thank you!

Chapter 1

Holly

I looked like a skank.

I tugged down the green bit of monstrosity wrapped tightly around my waist so that it brushed mid-thigh and tried to remember why I put up with Jennifer Lawley as my best friend. This time she had gone too far.

"I can't do this!"

It wasn't the first time I had tried to mutiny, but given that I was now *wearing* the aforementioned green bit of monstrosity instead of staring at it on a hanger, I guess she was justified in believing that I'd back down.

But never again.

She plumped up her already cherry-red lips and rolled her eyes at me in the mirror.

"Come on, Holly. It's not so bad."

"Not so bad!" I sputtered. "We look like mutants! Worse than that! We look like slutty mutants whose clothing went through a wood chipper!"

"We look like Santa's helpers. Get into the spirit of things, already. 'Tis the season, you know!"

Right, because nothing perks up a girl more than hearing Christmas carols for hours on end while being forced to ask little children if they've been naughty or nice lately. And while I hadn't actually asked any kids about their naughty-to-nice ratio, it was only because I had yet to join the crowds in the Westside Pavilion and serve my time as "Santa's little helper." I still knew what was coming. Crying babies and overprotective parents who snapped orders and bitched into their cell phones about their stupid yearly Christmas cards. And given the very short nature of our "Santa's little helpers" skirts, I had a feeling that Jen and I would be on the receiving end of more than a few crude suggestions about how we could help certain boys fully enjoy their Christmas season.

Let me tell you: You have to be desperate to agree to become an elf in Los Angeles. Or anywhere else, for that matter.

But that's exactly what I was: desperate. Maybe if I had an allowance, or a regular source of income, I wouldn't have been taking a Christmas cruise to the Mexican Riviera with my grandpa and (wince) my cousins with absolutely nothing appropriate to wear. But my grandpa believes I need to know the true value of money, and I know it, all right . . . it's the difference between being mocked and being accepted.

Under normal circumstances, Jen would tell me how lucky I am to have a grandpa who wants to celebrate his seventy-fifth birthday in paradise. She would be envious of me for trading in smoggy Los Angeles for sunny beaches and fruity drinks. Under normal circumstances, I would be thrilled to go myself . . . if it weren't for my cousins. To be fair, Andrew and Jacob are okay. I mean, they're teenage boys who would be more than a little interested in noting the length of Jen's short skirt. But they're relatively harmless.

Allison and Claire, on the other hand, are like the Olsen twins on bitch steroids.

I don't think I'm exaggerating here.

Allison and Claire are an amalgamation of all the twenty-first-century social problems: They are self-entitled, materialistic jerks who enjoy online bullying, teasing, and general unpleasantness as hobbies. They also have a talent for detecting every crack in someone's self-esteem, which they then hammer away at until the tormented person breaks into a million shattered pieces.

And I'm lucky enough to share a gene pool with them.

Which is why I know from firsthand experience that if I show up for the cruise wearing the same jeans I've had for the last two years, they'll start calling me Annie again. As in Little Orphan Annie. Because ever since my parents died in a car accident that's exactly what I've been—an orphan.

Real nice, right?

But it's not all bad. I mean, it's not like I ever knew my parents in any meaningful way. Apparently, I was a fussy baby, so at the nine-month mark they asked my grandpa to watch me for a weekend while they took a much needed mini-break.

And when my exhausted dad fell asleep at the wheel and crashed into a tree, what started as a two-day visit turned into a permanent living situation.

My grandpa was great about the whole thing. There were never any parental duties that he skipped out on. He supported me when I became a Girl Scout, helped me sell boxes of cookies, and then hugged me tightly when I told him that none of the other girls liked me. He told me they just didn't appreciate my chutzpáh the way he did. And even though he went to synagogue every week, he never pressured me to have a Bat Mitzvah or go by Rachel, my Jewish-sounding middle name. Grandpa understood that after a brutal ten hours of labor on Christmas Day, his Jewish daughter and her Catholic-raised husband thought the prickly name Holly was appropriate.

If only they could see me now—dressed up like a tarty elf.

I tugged down my skirt once again.

"I mean it," I told Jen. "You said I only had to try on the costume and then I could back out. Well, I tried it on. I look like a holiday hooker. Can we go now? I need to start handing copies of my résumé out to department stores."

Jen tugged her own costume down, only she was adjusting the low-dipping green shirt so that it flashed a cheery bit of red bra under the cleavage.

"Like you have a résumé!"

She had a point.

"Then clearly we need to get out of here so that I can make one up and *then* I can start handing it out to department stores."

"The economy, as always, sucks. No one is hiring, Holly. It's a Christmas miracle that we found this job as it is. Now we are going to go out there and spread some holiday cheer!"

I didn't know how she could manage to say that last bit with a straight face.

"A Christmas miracle that has me sluttified and asking people how 'naughty' they've been?" I squawked. "If we were outside we could get arrested for this!"

"It's not indecent exposure on an elf." She flicked back the red streak in her bangs. "Look, there are *kids* out there and they expect us to make them happy. Are you really going to disappoint the *children?*"

Jen knew I had a soft spot for kids, and if it got me out of the dressing room and into the mall where she could try out her flirting technique in her green elf skirt, then she was going to play the *you can't disappoint the children* card for all it was worth.

"Fine," I grumbled, "but you—"

"Owe you big time," she finished for me. "Yeah, Holly, I know. Whatever. Now let's boldly go where many elves have gone before."

"Fine. Let's just get this thing over with then."

Jen grabbed my arm and thrust me out the door of the employee bathroom like she didn't trust me to actually leave.

She knew me way too well.

The outside world was an absolute madhouse. Shoppers in December should be forced to take a sedative before trying to purchase presents for loved ones. One particularly frazzled mother was yelling at her daughter, "No, I'm not going to buy you any plastic ponies, Krystal! And if I hear one more word about them, Christmas will be canceled!"

Jen and I were shoved and jostled by strangers who madly searched for just the right gift that says, "I love and appreciate you. Also, I'm sorry about that stupid thing I did last week. Forgive me?" With the pressure to be thoughtful, creative, generous, and sweet all tied into a present, it was a wonder that more people didn't off themselves during the holiday season. It's not so much that I really *minded* Christmas . . . just the way it eclipsed my birthday. My grandpa did his best, but I never had a real party since no parents wanted to schlep their kids around the day after Christmas when they could gaze, bleary eyed, at the fake plastic tree sitting in the living room. But when Grandpa told me his plans for this year—that in celebration of his mid-December birthday we were spending the holidays on a family cruise with my aunt and her picture-perfect nuclear family—I really wanted to ask if I could stay with Jen in LA instead.

Hence the need for new clothes and the job that forced me to spread holiday cheer. And act jolly. And all that other nonsense.

So I plastered a big ol' smile on my face as Jen and I walked up to the special area where Santa was evidently enjoying the last of his lunch break with a cup of eggnog in his hand.

It wasn't until we were right next to St. Nick that we realized eggnog wasn't the main ingredient in his drink.

Apparently, I wasn't the only one having trouble getting into the holiday spirit.

Although he seemed to become significantly more chipper when he spotted Jen and me in our outfits. "C'mere!" he suggested. "Sit on Santa's lap!"

Then he cackled as if he had said something incredibly clever instead of creepily attempting to hit on a pair of high school girls.

Jen clutched my hideous green tunic sleeve. "Oh, my God!" she breathed in horror. "Not Santa!"

Jen was one of those kids who resolutely believed that the big man came down her chimney all through elementary school. She also wanted to give other children that some feeling of magic each year. I didn't care. I mean, I *like* kids, but it's not like they aren't *eventually* going to figure out that they sat on some weird guy's lap every year.

"Yep. It looks like good St. Nick has been a bit on the naughty side this year."

Santa lolled back in his huge chair, apparently oblivious to our whispered conversation.

"Should we report him?" I asked Jen. "Or better yet, can we leave now? The man reeks and if he spews we don't want to be the ones cleaning it up."

I might have been hired to prance around in this ridiculous outfit, but no one said anything about vomit duties. I checked.

"Holly!" Jen practically growled my name. "We don't have time to search for someone! We can't let a pervy Santa near these kids! We have to *do* something now!"

"Okay. I'm not disagreeing with you, Jen. I'm just not sure how you expect us to fix it."

Santa chose that moment to ask me blearily, "So tell me, have you been *naughty* this year?"

Another happy round of cackles followed that witticism.

"Just stay here and try to cover for me." Jen marched over to the long line of kids who had been tugging on their parents' sleeves and asking if it was time yet. "Um, I'm sorry, folks, but Santa just got an urgent message from his toy shop, so he needs to head for the North Pole straight away. But he's really sorry for the inconvenience and he wishes you all a *Merr-y Christmas!*"

"But he's sitting right there!" an indignant mother snapped. "We've been waiting in this stupid line for over two hours and my son is going to see Santa!"

And that's when all hell broke loose.

The disgruntled parents, children in tow, charged past Jen and headed straight for the highly inebriated Santa, who was so smashed he didn't recognize the danger in a stampede of determined parents.

"Holly!" Jen yelled. So I did the only thing I could think of—I stood right in front of pervy Santa and waved my arms in the universal signal for *please don't crush me! Please!*

For a brief moment it looked like it might work too. The mob slowed and I cleared my throat to make some inane promise of a replacement Santa right away, when Santa lived up to his pervy reputation by reaching out and copping a feel of my short, green-clad butt.

And that's why I slapped Santa across the face in front of a whole line of impressionable young children.

Hard.

One second I was seeing red and mentally cursing the stupid commercial holiday and its tacky decorations and repetitive music and the general *crappiness* of my situation, and the next a little boy was yelling, "You can't hit Santa! You're a bad elf!" at me.

Then he charged.

The blow to my stomach knocked the air out of me. I stepped away from the little maniac and promptly tripped over the stair of the Santa platform and went crashing into St. Nick, who was the one who had started this whole nightmare. But everyone in line apparently seemed to think that I was trying to commit Santa-cide, and what started as a minor tussle turned into a full-on brawl with Jen screeching for mall security while attempting to shove her way over to me. Santa, half a dozen enraged shoppers, and I were all rolling around the floor, scrambling, and struggling to breathe given the number of elbows we had received (on purpose and accidentally) right in the gut.

And things only got worse as I went crashing into the mall's fake Christmas tree, which tilted, then toppled over, causing dozens of shiny glass ornaments to shatter upon impact. Everyone: Santa, shoppers, Jen, and I all stopped moving and absorbed the wreckage we had created in a matter of minutes. I was still staring in horror when I felt a firm tug on my arm as mall security started dragging my skanky elf-clad posterior away while Jen trailed behind us chattering the whole time.

"Well, good riddance! I never really wanted that job in the first place. Too many crazies." Her face brightened. "And now we get to enjoy the holiday without ruining it with work!"

I just glared at her. "I've got a security escort. I'm wearing a slutty elf costume, and Santa just groped me. Now might not be the best time to tell me *it was all for nothing!*"

I knew murder was against the law and that killing Santa at Christmas was wrong. But I didn't remember any regulations against elf-icide.

Jen turned her puppy-dog eyes on me. "I'm sorry. Let's go to my house, get out of these stupid clothes, and see if I've got something you can wear on the cruise. I'm really sorry, Holly. I'll make it up to you."

Except we both knew that she couldn't when I heard an all-too-familiar voice yelling out my name.

My grandpa. With my whole family: aunt, uncle, cousins, the lot of them staring at me as if . . . I had just gotten into a fight with Santa.

He shook his head and I knew it wasn't because he was admiring my chutzpah this time. "We wanted to support you on your first day of work."

Well, that plan had definitely backfired.

It was only then that I noticed Allison and Claire both had their iPhones out and had obviously taken photos of the whole thing.

Allison grinned at me maliciously, flicking her eyes over my barely-there skirt. "Ho. Ho. Ho."

'Tis the season, all right.

To make me want to crawl under a rock and die of mortification.

Chapter 2

Dominic

I love being a rock star.

Sure, it has its share of disadvantages—a lack of privacy being one of the biggest issues—but overall, it's a damn good career. I'll always choose speculation over which starlet I might be dating over spending my days crunching numbers in a cubicle. Especially since I could never hack it as a corporate drone, sitting in a cubicle, fastidiously shuffling papers from one side of my desk to the other. I would drive all my colleagues insane by incessantly drumming on anything and everything nearby. A four-hour drum solo that features a number-two pencil thwacking away on a stapler and a paper-clip dish would justify someone walking over and stabbing me with my makeshift drumsticks.

Dominic Wyatt, rock star drummer, also has an excellent ring to it.

So I'm perfectly aware of just how lucky I am to have a job working with my two best friends and doing what I love the most: playing music. Truthfully, Tim and Chris aren't just friends—they're family. That's what happens when you travel across the country together in a tour bus . . . you connect with your band . . . *unless* someone "accidentally" takes the last can of Coke in the minifridge on the hottest strip of road between Las Vegas and Los Angeles, denying you a caffeine rush that you desperately need, and you snap.

Unless bodies are dumped in Middle of Nowhere, Nevada, it's not possible to spend that much time with two other guys and walk away as casual acquaintances or people who can be described merely as "coworkers."

But as much as I love my job, it's still work. Grueling work where the hours bleed into each other until you can't tell one eighteen-hour day from another. It's a grinding job where you can never rest and you can never look as tired as you feel. Nobody wants to see an exhausted rock star rubbing blearily at his eyes and croaking about how if he is expected to handle a photo shoot, a rehearsal, an interview, and a recording session before noon, so there *damn* well better be Starbucks within arm's reach. Nobody wants to hear that performers work *damn* hard to look laid-back or that there's a point when it becomes impossible to tell just how little energy you have left since you've been running on empty for so long. That's the scariest part: when you've deluded yourself into thinking that if you can just have one more double-shot espresso, it'll be fine.

Because at some point, most people crack. If you're lucky, that won't include shaving your head and attacking parked cars with umbrellas or going on weeklong benders that result in a long series of stints in rehab. But that aching, gnawing pressure that comes from working single-mindedly for a nebulous concept called *success* . . . it can't keep building forever without some sort of a release. Eventually, there has to be an outlet for the pressure, which ironically is what music used to be for me before it became my job. My foolproof method of relaxation now keeps me up at night with the guys, pacing recording studios, and obsessing over every minute detail of our careers.

Which is why when Tim called out, "Okay, let's take it

from the top, everyone!" instead of nodding and leading into the song on the drums, I found myself setting down my drumsticks and massaging at the pounding headache beneath my temples.

"Tim, I'm calling a group meeting."

That got his attention fast. Something that doesn't happen often when Tim goes into full work mode. In fact, the only thing that can consistently break through Timothy Goff's famed concentration is a call from his boyfriend, Corey O'Neal. But since they're still in the happy, chipper stage of a fresh relationship, despite the long-distance challenge, it's hard to know how long even that will work.

Tim set down his guitar and Chris rubbed his left eye, a sleepy gesture that he always makes when we've been pushing too hard for too long. Not that he'd ever admit it. Tim's a workaholic and Chris refuses to say anything because he doesn't want to slow anything down or hold anyone back. Maybe that's why we work so well as a band: All of us are paranoid that we're not pulling our weight. Except it also meant that Chris was never going to set down his guitar and demand some time off. Which left it up to me.

"I need a break."

I blurted it out before I could convince myself to keep my mouth shut. One moment of hesitation and the part of me that had busted my ass for years would point out that the higher you rise the harder you fall. That I should keep my head down a little longer, slog through just one more brutal week laying down tracks for our upcoming EP . . . then the promotional period before the release . . . and the concert tour after.

My stomach twisted. I couldn't back down. Not again. Not this time.

"I need a break," I repeated firmly.

Tim blinked at me in confusion. "We can take five if you want. Starbucks is on me."

That's the way Tim works; someone's having an off day and he steps in and tries to fix it. Even though he's usually oblivious to the problem.

Chris eyed me and shook his head. "I don't think he's talking about a coffee break. What's going on, Dom?"

"I think that we should take a break for a while . . . try something new."

Tim frowned. "I don't understand."

Christ, I felt like I was trying to spit out the dreaded "It's not you, it's me" breakup line.

"I can't keep working at this pace! I want to get out of the recording studio at a decent time for a change. Get a full eight hours of sleep. Have a day to relax. Go out on a date. I want to enjoy what we've got going! Take a well-deserved break. And who knows? Maybe I'll even try my hand at songwriting."

The guys nodded silently while I spelled out exactly what I wanted; neither of them looked the least bit fazed, until I mentioned that last part. At least they hadn't seen that one coming.

Chris stared at me as if I had just announced I wanted to go to all our interviews in drag. "You want to *write?* I had no idea. Since when, Dom?"

I shrugged uncomfortably. "I've considered it for a while, but . . . we've always been rehearsing or performing or giving interviews and . . . I never found the time."

Pathetic excuse. "My dog ate my lyrics" would have probably sounded better. Sure, being a member of ReadySet left me with little time to sleep, let alone to do anything else. But as the photogenic band frontman, Tim had to do even more of the publicity stuff than Chris or me combined—and he always came through with fresh material.

Then again, not everyone could be like Hollywood golden boy Timothy Goff.

If it weren't for the fact that the guy was my best friend, I'd have a hard time keeping my competitive nature in check.

Still, I wasn't lying when I said that I had considered composing songs. I just couldn't seem to do it when I knew that one of the best lyricists in the U.S. would be breathing down my neck the whole time. It was kind of like a high school student working on writing his first horror story with Stephen King reading over his shoulder. Not exactly the most conducive atmosphere for a first timer to create something great, or even halfway decent.

Tim nodded cautiously. "Look, Dom, if you want to write songs I think that's great. Hell, it'll ease up my workload." He flashed his famous grin, the one that had landed him on *People*'s Most Beautiful list for two consecutive years; Chris and I had teased him mercilessly about that. "But now just isn't the time for a break."

"Now is the perfect time," I argued. "We're a week out from Christmas. If we split up our existing obligations—and don't add any new ones—we can actually enjoy the holidays. Relax for a change. Maybe even get real social lives!"

Chris and Tim exchanged looks, and I forcibly shoved my hands back into my pockets before I could rake them through my dark brown hair and make it look like I'd recently shoved a fork into a light socket. That's how a photographer had once described the look I'd accidentally created when I'd gotten frustrated near the end of his photo shoot. Everyone hanging around had a good laugh except the hairdresser, who scurried over to fix the damage.

"Uh, you don't seem like yourself right now, man," Chris said finally.

Which was absolutely true. I couldn't maintain the easygoing, laid-back drummer persona I had carefully packaged for the public. Even knowing that everyone wandering in and out of the recording studio could surely see that I was at my breaking point, I couldn't force any of my muscles to lose their rigidity. Dominic Wyatt, casual rock star, had left the building. In his place was a shell of a musician, exhausted yet restless, drained yet jumpy, like an insomniac who had just downed a triple-shot espresso after a sleepless night.

But I wasn't about to admit as much to my friends. My pride had some limits. So I deflected instead of answering. Even at my most ragged, my Hollywood training in the art of changing the subject had turned it into a reflex.

"Look, if we don't take a break now we'll just keep pushing it back. And soon we'll have the MTV awards, or maybe a movie sound track job, or a concert tour, and it'll be another night on the road or in a hotel room, scarfing down food between sound checks and performances."

I turned to Tim. "You've got a boyfriend, Tim. Don't you want to be able to see him instead of texting between interviews and appointments?"

I had him there and all of us knew it. He had been trying to schedule more visits to Portland, but it's not exactly on concert tour routes with the regularity of bigger cities like LA and NYC.

"You could surprise him for Christmas. You remember Christmas, right? That's the holiday we've worked through for the past two years. And, Chris, weren't you dating an actress not too long ago? What happened with that?"

Chris grimaced. "We started living in this studio. That's what happened."

I could sense the two of them slowly coming around to my point of view.

"Tim can handle that *Cosmo* shoot by himself and then fly to Portland. Chris, you didn't want to leave LA, did you?"

He shook his head and I found the tension in my back easing a little.

"Great! Then you can take that movie sound track meeting. That'll take a day, max. Which should give you plenty of time to pay a certain celebrity a visit. Although, what she sees in a guy like you . . ."

Chris feigned a punch to my arm and when I moved to block it he smacked me upside the head. But he was grinning the whole time and seemed more relaxed than I had seen him in ages. I might have been the first to admit exhaustion but that didn't mean I was the only one feeling it, which made me feel slightly better about being the first to break.

"And what will you be doing, o mastermind?" Tim wanted to know. "Partying it up in a club?"

I smiled, glad that the time I had spent poring over our group obligations and upcoming events had paid off.

"Remember that deal we were considering with Famous cruise line? Three nights of concerts and complete freedom the rest of the time? Well, I called up the owner, Jeff Ridgley, and he's very interested in hiring us. Best of all, he's open to our provision for limited fan access. So I'll meet with him and check it out on his eight-day cruise to Mexico and then catch up on my sleep."

"Right," Chris replied, his grin growing wider. "With all those girls on board wearing skimpy bathing suits and throwing themselves at you, *uninterrupted sleep* is exactly what you'll be looking for at night."

"I might be interested in other means of relaxation," I admitted, thinking more about putting my dive certification class to good use in clear tropical waters than girls in swimsuits. Air tanks don't have a tendency to squeal and ask for autographs.

Tim raised an eyebrow. "What about all that songwriting you wanted to do?"

"I'm sure I can squeeze in time for that between drinks and dives. Or I can hold off and do my writing back in LA after the trip. After all, if you can do it, it can't be *that* hard."

He shook his head but laughed all the same. "Okay, so we take one week off and—"

"Two," I corrected.

Tim looked ready to mutiny at that.

"Two full weeks," I repeated. "Starting immediately. And by the time we meet up, we'll be well rested and working on the best songs ever produced by ReadySet. And those songs will be written by me."

That last part sounded pretty damn cocky, especially when you consider that I didn't have any experience stringing more than a single sentence together or tweaking Tim's words in collaboration with Chris. But it felt good to pretend like I was actually the laid-back, confident drummer most people expected, now that things appeared to be going my way.

Tim looked skeptical. "And when are you going to get all of this writing done if you're relaxing with a swarm of female fans?"

I hadn't thought of that, but I merely shrugged it off. "I'll lay low for a while then. I'm not *you*, Tim. Girls recognize lead singers, but drummers . . . not so much. And I can always go by Nick instead of Dominic. It's close enough that it won't trip me up."

"Well, if you're sure—"

"Oh, he's sure," Chris interrupted.

"I am."

"Then I guess . . . I'm in too."

I almost couldn't believe my luck. Tim hadn't put up much of a fight at all. Not that I was complaining, but I had expected him to flip through his planner, call up our manager, check out airfare prices online as well as the availability of the recording studio, before agreeing to anything. Either Tim was starting to feel the burnout too, or he missed Corey badly enough to jump on the opportunity I was offering—frankly, I didn't care which reason had him acting like a normal human being. Although maybe "normal human being" was a bit of a stretch, considering that Tim reached into his backpack and tossed a can at me with a quick "Think fast!" as my only warning.

I bobbled it once. "What the hell!"

"Pepper spray," Tim explained, then snickered at my surprised expression. "To fend off female admirers so you can actually get that writing done."

I briefly considered tossing it back or handing it over to Chris, but then I shoved it into my bag. "Thanks, but I'm not going to need it."

I only wish that had been true.

Chapter 3

Holly

Most girls don't get grounded right before Christmas because they slapped Santa in a mall, in front of a mob of little children.

Then again, most girls don't get escorted out of the aforementioned mall by security guards and depend upon their seventy-five-year-old grandfather to bail them out.

I felt so guilty about the whole thing. Well, not so much the slapping Santa part, since pervy St. Nick had it coming. But the rest of it, *that* I regretted. Especially since my cousins had obviously gotten pictures of the whole thing.

There was also the little problem that since I was grounded (rather unfairly, I might add, since I did *not* start the skirmish) I couldn't try on any of Jen's more cruise-ship-appropriate wardrobe. Allison and Claire would *definitely* be making their snide Little Orphan Annie references to me when nobody else was around to hear them. And since Aunt Jessica and Uncle Matt were sharing a room, Andrew and Jacob were paired up, and my grandpa had booked a cabin for himself . . . I'd be sharing a room with the Twins from Hell. So that would give them an infinite number of opportunities to make me feel like crap.

Oh, goody.

Still, there was nothing for me to do about it. It was my grandpa's birthday cruise and even though I was rather miffed that he hadn't bothered to listen to *my* side of the story, he was still the only real family that I had.

Which was why I had a big, stupid smile plastered on my face as we went through the time-consuming process of boarding the ship surrounded by a throng of excited vacationers. Half of the crowd was already wearing enormous tropical shirts, as if they couldn't wait another second to defy office-wear convention with big palm tree prints. None of them looked as harried and harassed as I already felt. In fact, I was getting the distinct impression that some of them even *enjoyed* the awful tinny wail of Christmas carols à la Bob Marley blaring from the nearby deck of the ship. I really hoped that once we actually got out to sea someone with good taste would take over the role of playing DJ.

But I was determined to stay upbeat, or at least to do a good job pretending. I imagined Jen's reaction to the scene. She'd probably be glowing with excitement as she brushed her long auburn bangs out of her eyes. And then Jen would have said something ridiculous like, "Aren't you just *so* excited! This is going to be the best vacation ever!"

It's always sunshine and rainbows for Jen. Except around Christmas when she trades them in for Santa and reindeer.

Me . . . not so much.

Still, I kept that stupid grin in place even while the employee in charge of checking passports struggled to identify me as the girl in my hideous passport photo. Of course, I had been having a bad hair day and my head was surrounded by a scraggly, dirty-blond mess, which, combined with the glazed look in my green eyes and the noticeable sheen of sweat on my forehead, made me look both unintelligent and ill. The only person I had ever willingly shown that picture to was Jen and she had laughed before assuring me that I usually looked much better. Then again, she had also once informed me that my hair was the color of burnt honey and that my nose was decidedly aristocratic. After which I had politely informed her that she was full of it.

I don't even know where she gets that nonsense. Aristocratic nose? If she meant that I had a rather distinctive schnoz (thanks to my Jewish ancestry, I guess) she could have just come out and said it. No amount of sugar coating was going to change the situation.

Still, remembering Jen's earnest expression almost made me smile for real as my passport was returned to me. But Claire caught a glimpse of it and instantly said, "Oh, my God, hideous photo much!"

"Claire!" her mother reprimanded. "You know that not everyone is naturally photographic like you and your siblings."

That's my aunt Jessica for you: Well intentioned, maybe, but her cutting words leave no doubt as to how her daughters have become so well versed in the art of insults.

"But why does she have to room with me and Allison?" Claire whined, tossing back her pale blond hair that was decidedly *not* the color of burnt anything. And apparently she didn't care in the least that I was standing *right there*. "Why can't Little Orphan Annie stay in Grandpa's room instead?"

"Because it's his birthday and he deserves a break!" Aunt Jessica snapped. "He has to live with her year-round as it is!"

Ouch.

It's times like these when I occasionally indulge in a daydream about what life would be like if my parents were around. I particularly like the version where my effortlessly cool mom marches over to her sister, calls her a self-involved bully with monstrous children, and then takes hold of my hand and orders me to "just ignore them" since they "aren't worth worrying about."

I always try to take my imaginary mom's advice, but it's never easy.

Especially since the moment Claire, Allison, and I reached our cabin, both of them looking cruise-ship stylish in their short shorts and strappy tank tops, they instantly started unpacking into the dresser that was intended for all of us to share. When I mentioned that, however, they just pointedly eyed me in disgust, letting their gaze linger on my scuffed Converse shoes, ordinary jeans, and favorite ReadySet band shirt (gray and worn to the point of maximum comfort).

So I liked to be comfortable. That wasn't a crime.

Except in Los Angeles, apparently.

"Okay, here are the rules, *Annie*," Allison told me, when she finally deigned to acknowledge my presence. "You don't speak to us. You don't speak to anyone near us. You don't follow us. You don't ask us stupid questions. Actually, you don't ask us *any* questions. You stay out of our way and in return we *might* not send those pictures of you as a skanky elf to everyone at your high school."

My mouth fell open. It's rather hard to forget that my cousins made a pact with the devil to become both gorgeous and evil, but each time I think I understand their slimy interior they do something even more despicable. You'd think that at some point I would realize that they don't have any redeeming qualities. But I guess a really stupid part of me keeps hoping that the little family I have might eventually try to make me feel like less of an outsider.

Like I said: *really* stupid part of me.

"You look even dumber than normal with your mouth open like that," Allison told me sweetly. "Just so you know."

I snapped my jaws shut and said, "Fine. No problem," through clenched teeth.

"Excellent. Then Claire and I will share the bed and you can take the roll-away cot." Allison put on her fakest smile. "Our room arrangements are going to stay between the three of us. If you were to squeal about any of this to Grandpa, that might ruin his birthday trip. And you wouldn't want to do something so selfish to an old man. After all, how many birthdays does he really have to look forward to? Not many, I bet."

I didn't know how they could be so cavalier about my worst nightmare, my biggest fear, the terror that was more real to me than rapists or serial killers or weapons of mass destruction: watching our grandpa feel the weight of each one of his years until they crushed him into dust.

Knowing that it's coming and not being able to do anything to stop the process.

For them, it was just another way to manipulate me.

Evil. So evil.

"Of course not," I said stiffly. I snatched up my backpack, which held my journal, my camera, my iPod, and a sketchpad as well as a nice pack of colored pencils, and left the room. All of that stuff had kept my babysitting money from ever earning interest in my bank account, but it had been completely worth it. At that moment all I wanted was to sit out on the top deck, listening to the playlist Jen made me for my birthday and breathing in the salty air while it whipped through my hair.

The reggae Christmas tunes were still playing in an endless loop, but I cranked my music up louder and let myself relax for the first time in days.

I could do this. I could avoid ninety percent of my family for the next eight days. Jen would tell me to work the situation to my advantage, and the more I thought about that the better I felt. I was headed for a tropical location: sand under my feet, sun heating my skin, soothing waves lapping against the ship as we pulled out of Los Angeles.

A few pesky relatives couldn't get me down.

Except the waves didn't seem to have the intended soothing effect on me. If anything, they made me feel a bit queasy.

But I had everything under control. I drank some water to counterbalance any dehydration from my time out in the sun and tried to convince my body that I wasn't actually on a floating chunk of wood in the middle of nowhere. This was a *luxury* chunk of wood, making it an entirely different story.

By dinnertime, I had drawn two sketches of my delicious fruit smoothie, I had ranted in my journal, my iPod was in serious need of a recharge . . . and my stomach still felt a touch unsettled. Still, I made my way over to the dining area where my family, so to speak, was already waiting at table eighteen. Jen would have tried to convince me that since I was almost eighteen, the table number was a good omen. But not even Jen would have been able to convince me that it wasn't embarrassing for me to slink into the fanciest dining room the ship offered, five minutes late, in distressed denim with a band logo splayed across my chest.

I didn't stand out too much in a sea of formal skirts and dresses.

Oh, wait, yes I did.

Next time, I was changing in the cabin. Avoiding the Twins from Hell wasn't worth this kind of social mortification.

But my failure to meet the dress code was just the beginning of my problems. The menu appeared to be created entirely so that I would have no idea what I was ordering. It was all stuff like "Cascadia Fideua," which appeared to have too many vowels to me. I decided to play it safe and just go with basic Alfredo noodles, but that only inspired my aunt to ask, all concernedly, "Are you sure that's best, Holly? That's awfully fattening, you know."

"Yeah, it's not like you need the extra padding," Allison chimed in snarkily.

This is when my imaginary parents would smash a lemon meringue right into the twins' stupid, perfectly-made-up faces, before hauling me off somewhere.

Instead, my grandpa gave me a slow, knowing wink and ordered his lasagna.

None of the other guys, Uncle Matt or Andrew or Jacob, appeared to notice anything unusual in the shift of topic. Maybe because they were so accustomed to those kinds of jabs in their own household. Considering that Aunt Jessica then passed the bread basket to her husband, maybe they were fine with the way things worked.

Boys got the bread rolls and the girls got water refills.

Because that's fair.

"You really need to be going to a gym on a regular basis," my aunt informed me. "Otherwise your tummy will pooch . . . more than it already does."

I glanced down surreptitiously to my lap and even though my loose band shirt hid it, I knew there was a slight belly roll. It wasn't like my (sigh) muffin top was noticeable most of the time. And okay, maybe I bought roomier shirts specifically so that they wouldn't showcase my middle, but everyone has *some* physical area that they critique in the mirror. I just have an aunt who likes to confirm my fears by vocalizing them in public.

"You didn't actually pack a bikini, did you, Holly?"

I shook my head, unsure if I could keep my words civil if I opened my mouth.

"Oh, good! Maybe if you avoid all starches and sweets and work out *really* hard you might be ready for one by the time we get back to LA." She looked pretty doubtful. "Maybe. If you lose . . . a pound a day."

So, I'll never be mistaken for a movie star or a model. Living in LA, I see plenty of girls at school who look glossy and perfect every day—and Jen and I will never be among them. Because no matter how many articles I read on the best way to dress with an apple shape (or was it a pear? Some kind of fruit), I can't seem to pull it off. Whatever bizarre skill Allison and Claire had been born with that made them effort-lessly stand out in a crowd, it wasn't hereditary.

And I didn't exactly need a reminder from my aunt that I was deficient in essentials.

"Wow, hottie incoming," Allison muttered to Claire under her breath as she refilled her glass, which was already getting quite the workout.

I glanced up partly because I needed the distraction and partly because I wanted to see if we shared the same aesthetic when it came to boys.

Apparently, there was one thing the three of us could agree on.

He had wind-tousled dark brown hair that contrasted nicely against a green-collared shirt and a black suit jacket, which lent him an air of casual formality. He looked com-fortable as he crossed the dining room, shook hands with a middle-aged man, and took his seat at the table. Not com-fortable in a slouched, sweatpants, *eating popcorn in my La-Z-Boy chair* kind of way. It was more like he knew that he was untouchable so he didn't have to try to act tough. He could just take it easy.

Which was really attractive, actually, and I couldn't help envying Hot Guy for his self-assured handshake. If I were that smooth in my dealings with other people, I would've talked Jen out of her elf plan long before Mr. Claus tried to get his hands on me.

"That's him," Allison breathed. "My vacation fling. Right on time."

I rolled my eyes but thankfully no one noticed. She hadn't so much as waved to the guy and already Allison was calling dibs on his social calendar. Just because he was hot and she needed a juicy story to share with her friends back home.

Typical.

Claire scrunched up her nose in thought. "There's some-thing about him that seems familiar to me. I just can't place it."

"Maybe he's the face behind a cologne ad or something. I wonder if he smells as good as he looks."

"I'd buy whatever he's selling." Claire giggled but the sound stopped abruptly when the waiter moved and the rest of Hot Guy's dinner companions came into view. There was already a girl leaning coyly toward him from across the table.

"Looks like you have competition," I pointed out.

Allison tossed her hair back in a way that was obviously calculated to be sexy. "She doesn't stand a chance."

This time I couldn't help snickering. "And if he has real feelings for her, you'll what? Attack her with perfume?"

Claire and Allison both glared at me in disgust. "He's talking mainly to the old guy so he's obviously not into her. God, could you be any more dense?"

Maybe I was dense, but they were delusional if they thought it'd be easy to have a fling with the hottest guy we had yet to see on the ship. What did they expect? Him to take one look at Allison and blurt out, "I need you to be my girlfriend"?

Doubtful.

For all we knew he could have a serious girlfriend back home. Or a boyfriend, for that matter.

I've always enjoyed imagining strangers' personal lives when bored, restless, or uncomfortable, and Hot Guy . . . well, he was providing an excellent distraction. He'd probably been superpopular throughout high school and had dated half of the cheerleader squad his freshman year. His lazy, confident demeanor made me doubt if he had ever been insecure about anything. Which meant he was way out of my league.

It's funny that I was just thinking that the only thing I probably had in common with Hot Guy was that we were stuck on the same ship, when he scanned the room as if looking for his waiter . . . and his eyes landed on me.

I could have sworn I saw him grin, but as I continued making eye contact (and feeling like I should probably look away because how awkward is it to be caught staring) his expression turned . . . distrustful. Almost nervous, even, because of *me*.

But that couldn't be right.

Then, just as abruptly as he had smiled, he hunched over the table and angled his body away, leaving me with an excellent view of his back. And nothing else.

"He smiled at me." Allison's pouty lips tilted into a smirk. "Oh, yeah, he's interested."

Well, that explanation made more sense to me than what I thought had just happened. Guys look at Claire and Allison all the time.

And by "look" I mean they usually drool.

Except it was hard for me to shake the impression that I had been the one to somehow rattle the laid-back Hot Guy.

Weird.

Chapter 4

Dominic

She was staring at me.

Normally, I would be fine with some female attention—more than fine with it, actually. I'm usually too busy for relationships and while I've been able to meet all sorts of attractive girls, the hard part is always juggling schedules. Half of them are in the music business or actors or comedians or somehow involved with the celebrity scene. And that comes with photo shoots, filming on location, interviews, product endorsement obligations, and studio time laying down tracks. It also doesn't help that girls always see me with two other rock stars, both of whom seem to do better with them.

Especially Tim, and he isn't even interested in girls.

And even though there are tons of girls who would love to be seen with the band, none of us want to date our fans. They have a tendency to squeal at decibels that cause permanent damage to dogs' hearing. And while we do love and appreciate our fans, we still have to be careful to avoid some of the crazies who follow us on Twitter and constantly request that we friend them on Facebook. The three of us jokingly checked out one of Tim's fan sites once and we swore never to do it again. It was disturbing to see his life laid out like that: his every move documented and photographed, from landing in LAX to drinking coffee to having business meetings.

The hardest part is that you can never tell just by looking who is among the crazies.

I usually try to give people the benefit of the doubt.

So when I spotted the girl wearing our ReadySet shirt in a sea of formally attired diners, my first impulse was to laugh. She was a mess, and not just because she was the most under-dressed person in the place. Her disheveled light brown hair framed a face that might not have been unattractive if she hadn't been sandwiched between two girls who were undeniably hot: tan, toned, and displaying their assets nicely in tight, stretchy little dresses. Frankly, The Mess resembled a grungy pigeon trying to blend in with two peacocks. She was also scrutinizing me with an intensity that quickly turned my amusement into unease.

Chris and Tim usually get the lion's share of attention when the three of us go out, so I had assumed it would be easy for me to fly under the radar on my own. Apparently, I stood out more than I thought if I already had three pairs of female eyes trained on me. In a different situation I might have enjoyed the ego boost. But I was in no position to be discovered during a business meeting on my relaxing cruise getaway.

If I was identified, it would be good-bye vacation, hello screaming fans.

I couldn't let that happen.

Shifting in my seat so that the girls could only see my back, I tried to focus on cruise owner Jeff Ridgley and his daughter, Cynthia, both of whom were working way too hard to impress me. Mr. Ridgley kept saying stuff like, "You can always expect impeccable service like this on Famous cruises," and "I hope you like your suite! It's rather 'sweet,' don't you think?" before chuckling at his own pun.

Hilarious.

Meanwhile Cynthia Ridgley, who looked to be fourteen years old under the pounds of makeup she had slathered on, kept leaning toward me as if hoping to inspire pounding lust through a glimpse of her developing figure.

Again, not so much.

I felt like an idiot, sitting there and smiling at the kid while trying my best not to lead her on. It might have been a while since I'd last been in a relationship, but I still had my standards. Young girls with stars in their eyes and hero worship written all over their faces were to be given a wide berth whenever possible.

So I did my best to keep the conversation focused on the cruise contract. Of course, we would have our manager and lawyer go over it before we signed anything, but there were plenty of times when it was best to hash out the details yourself.

"I discussed the matter with the guys," I told Mr. Ridgley and he froze with a piece of lamb halfway to his mouth. "They're very interested."

He let out a quick sigh of relief and put the fork down on his plate with the meat still speared on the prongs.

"That's great! Famous wants to promote our new celebrity line in February, right in time for Valentine's Day. We were thinking something like 'Fall in Love with the Single Men from ReadySet!' What do you think?"

"Well, we're not all single. Tim is in a relationship, and Chris and I aren't looking to be set up on blind dates, here."

Mr. Ridgley just waved his hand at that. "None of you are married. That's all that counts. And since no one knows who Mr. Goff is involved with, well . . ."

"That's Tim's business," I said coolly. "Not mine, not yours, and not anybody else's."

"Of course." Mr. Ridgley backpedaled wildly. "I just mean, well, who knows what will happen to relationships two months from now. Isn't that right, Cynthia!"

She smiled coyly and then said in a voice that was clearly meant to be husky but just sounded hoarse, "You can never predict or plan for true love."

"Quite right!" her father chuckled. "That promo is still subject to change, of course. 'Cruise into Love with ReadySet' might be a better sales pitch."

Just listening to all of this crap had me feeling stressed all over again. This was supposed to be my vacation, and between dealing with the Ridgleys and worrying that any second The Mess might jump up, point at me, and start shrieking, I felt about as relaxed as the captain of the *Titanic* when it hit the iceberg.

I needed to get out of that dining room. Fast.

But business came first.

"As long as the band's privacy is respected, we shouldn't have a problem."

Mr. Ridgley beamed. "Excellent." He promptly continued munching on his lamb while Cynthia peppered me with questions about the upcoming album. I answered the ones I could and merely smiled when she touched upon something confidential. In Hollywood, you learn pretty quickly that the best way to keep a secret is to keep your mouth shut.

I kept wondering if The Mess had identified me, but I controlled the urge to check until dessert. I leaned back casually and glanced over. The Mess appeared to be too preoccupied with stabbing ferociously at her slice of pie to notice me.

Strange.

I finished my chocolate cake and made mindless small talk just long enough so that I wouldn't seem overly eager to leave. Normally, I was good at acting casual. That's the image of myself I personally branded: the rumpled but unflappable rock star.

Too bad it wasn't even close to the truth.

I made my escape from the dining room and headed straight for the tackiest-looking gift shop on the ship. At least three girls had been staring at me over the meal and I found that fact more than a little disconcerting. I wasn't ready to lose my newfound anonymity. So after only a few minutes of deliberation, I bought a tacky Hawaiian-print shirt with enormous palm trees on it and a baseball cap with *Mexico* scrawled across the brim. I forked over some cash before slipping back into the dressing room so that I could wear my disguise out of the shop. The outfit would probably be enough to throw even superfans like The Mess off my scent.

After all, no one would suspect a rock star to be dressed like a geeky tourist.

I could finally relax. And there was no better place to do that than in my luxury suite, something I took advantage of by sinking into one of the plush sofa chairs and propping my feet up on the nearby coffee table. Damn, but it was nice to have the place to myself. The cramped living arrangements on the tour bus get old. Fast. But I wasn't going to have any trouble adjusting to traveling in a deluxe suite. It's one of the perks of being a celebrity: Every now and then you get to really kick back in style. Which in this case meant an enormous bedroom, a spacious bathroom, a "living" area, a walk-in closet, and a wet bar. And attached was my personal verandah, which offered a spectacular view of the ocean from the privacy of my room.

Oh, yeah, I could definitely get used to having all this space to myself.

I was about to lazily flip through the catalog of activities to do in the various ports of call, when my iPad started ringing.

Tim. The guy couldn't go fifteen hours without checking in to make sure everything with the band was going smoothly. Most of the time I appreciated his compulsive need to be on top of everything. But it also made it hard for anyone to so much as breathe around him.

Still, I answered the call, knowing that if I didn't pick up he would only call me again fifteen minutes later. And fifteen minutes after that, too.

"Dude, you really need to get a life," I told him, by way of greeting.

" 'Dude'?" he echoed. "I leave you alone for less than a day and you already sound like an idiot."

I grinned and lifted the iPad to give him a good look at my room. "Yeah, well, at least I'm relaxing in style."

Tim whistled. "Nice room! Wait, is that a balcony out there? Holy shit, you've got a suite?"

"Yep."

"I hope the band isn't paying for this thing."

"It happens to be comped. They really want us to perform for the cruise line, and I don't see any downsides to the deal from where I'm sitting."

"Which would be a master bedroom, I see."

"Of course."

"Well, don't enjoy yourself *too* much. I expect to hear those new songs you promised when I get back from Portland."

My stomach clenched. It was easy to talk a lot of game in LA, but it was going to be significantly harder to actually produce the damn things.

"What is that?" I made loud, crackling noises and waved the iPad around a little. "We seem to be going through a tunnel. I mean . . . rough seas. I'll call you back later, Tim."

"Very funny . . . I mean it, Dominic: I want to see what you write. And if at any point you need my help, just call, okay?"

I stopped moving the iPad. "Got it. Now get a life."

He grinned back at me. "Oh, and one more thing."

"Yeah?"

"Nice outfit. You look like a demented fisherman."

And with that he disconnected . . . leaving me to pace the empty room as I tried to think lyrical thoughts. Tim's stupid work ethic is infectious; that's why Chris and I push ourselves so hard when the three of us are together. Apparently, it could still get me moving in a guilt-inspired frenzy on a cruise ship moving toward Mexico. I hadn't thought any more about songwriting since I had opened my big mouth about it the day before.

I wanted to get all of my responsibilities out of the way so that nothing would be hanging over my head when we finally docked near the sandy beaches of Puerto Vallarta. That gave me a window of two days at sea to hunker down in my suite, order room service, sit out on the verandah, and write.

A shower to wake me up and I'd be good to go.

Well, then a game of solitaire.

And then my guitar would need to be tuned since I hadn't played it in months, if not years. I was never all that good at playing it and since I could never tolerate being second-rate, I had dedicated myself to the piano and drums instead.

Unfortunately, you can't write a song on drums, and I couldn't exactly pack a baby grand into my suitcase.

I was still plucking at the guitar two hours later, no closer to musical genius than I had been when Tim had called me. My eyes kept wanting to close and I fought the urge to just call it a night. Clearly, my shower hadn't worked. I needed coffee, stat. So clad only in my boxers, because it was *my* suite and I could wear whatever I wanted, I called room service to request more towels and two extra hot cups of coffee.

Then ditching the guitar, I pulled out my drumsticks from my backpack and started experimenting with rhythms outside on the verandah railing. The familiar feel of them in my hands, the consistency of the beats, allowed me to believe that if I just mainlined enough caffeine eventually the words would come.

But the muse didn't appear willing to join me.

At least, not in the form I expected.

Chapter 5

Holly

If I had to hear one more crack about my weight, I was going to lose it.

I was going to scream in the fancy restaurant and I didn't care if the waiters forcibly removed me. It wouldn't be the first time I'd been dragged off in shame in front of my family. At least this time I wasn't dressed like a slutty elf. That had to count for some improvement. And really, the humiliation of getting escorted to the door might be worth it if it liberated me from the presence of certain family members.

But then my grandpa asked what I thought of the pie that I was currently butchering instead of eating. Well, he didn't mention the fact that I was clearly venting my frustration by stabbing the helpless dessert repeatedly with my fork, but I'm sure it was pretty obvious. Of course, I *had* wanted to eat the damn thing when I ordered it. But then my aunt had calculated the number of calories and the number of hours I would have to spend on a treadmill to burn them off. That promptly killed my enjoyment of the treat.

But it was still my grandpa's birthday cruise and I didn't want to spoil any of it for him. So even though my stomach felt tight and queasy, I took a big bite.

"Delicious."

I don't know if it was that last small act of defiance that made me feel decidedly sick forty minutes later, but regardless of the reason, I had to make excuses to go straight to the cabin instead of a juggling performance. The boys headed for the teen center, while their sisters picked a different socializing technique: drinking at the bar. At least that's where I thought they were going with their casual, "Oh, just hanging out in the lounge for a while" response.

Yeah, more like *Oh, Grandpa, we're going to flirt with any guy who can buy us a drink.*

Sometimes I seriously wonder if I could have been orphaned *and* adopted.

At least I had the tiny cabin to myself while I tried to sleep off my nausea. I closed my eyes and said, "It's okay, Holly. You aren't moving at sea. Oh, no, you are actually lying still on something very stable like . . . a mountain. That's right, an enormous mountain with no water anywhere nearby."

I sounded like an idiot and my stomach wasn't buying a word of it.

But at least Allison and Claire weren't around to make fun of me.

So I turned onto my side, thrust my head into the pillow, and tried to think happy thoughts. Only two more days at sea before I would have my feet on dry land. That was only forty-eight hours. Or . . . a lot of minutes. The exact number eluded me and I wasn't about to force myself to do math when I needed to focus on not throwing up.

I started mentally listing activities I might enjoy tomorrow, occasionally muttering them into my blanket. Sit out on the sundeck, listen to my music, do some more sketching. Maybe I'd even take some photographs and people watch. I could do all of that while avoiding everyone but my grandpa.

It could happen.

I was just lulling myself into a false sense of comfort when the light flipped on and the thoroughly tipsy Twins from Hell stumbled in, clinging on to the arms of two boys who didn't appear to be of legal drinking age but must have gotten the girls drinks somehow, since they all were reeking of alcohol and laughing like hyenas.

The smell had my stomach clenching as if the boat had just rolled. I rubbed my face tiredly, sat up, and told them the truth.

"Listen, guys, I'm sorry but I'm feeling sick. Do you mind hanging out somewhere else? I'd really appreciate it."

"It's only eleven!" one of the sleazoids informed me, as if that should make a difference to my churning stomach and the tightness that ached in my chest.

"And I'm sorry." I apologized even though *hello, it wasn't my fault that I was seasick!* "But I'm trying not to puke and I really just . . . I need to sleep it off."

"Oh, we understand," Claire said as she collapsed onto the bed in a giggling drunken heap. "You don't want to party because you're a loser." She snorted then dissolved into laughter. "Even the girl getting us free drinks was cooler than you!"

Allison giggled. "God, she was trying *so* hard. There's no way she's actually dating someone famous. Desperation was written all over her."

Claire tossed back her long blond hair. "So pathetic. What was I saying again? Oh, yeah, we're going to have fun. You can do whatever you want."

The smell was unbearable and the longer eau de tequila wafted over me the harder I had to work to suppress my gag reflex. I couldn't stay in that room. Especially not with one of the guys leering at me. Mustering up the effort to change into pajamas had been beyond me when I had first entered the cabin, and now I found myself incredibly grateful to be fully dressed. Just lurching to my feet felt like a Herculean task. Apparently, I was just not built for long periods of time on water.

Or any time on water.

I just wish that I had known that *before* I had boarded the ship.

"Fine," I said, even as my body tried to mutiny against my every movement. "Enjoy your private party. I'll figure out something else."

Scooping up my backpack and my iPod, I paused for a moment before snatching up my blanket for good measure. I might end up sleeping out on deck but I still required a modicum of comfort.

"Enjoy your night, girls, because eventually karma is going to catch up with you. Oh, and try not to get too many STDs."

And with a cheery wave I made my exit.

Okay, maybe not the best of parting lines. It lacked, well, class for one thing. But no matter how many times my imaginary parents tell me to "rise above" my cousins there are times when I can't resist stooping to their level.

And this time I felt sick enough that I didn't even care.

Wrapping the blanket tighter around my arms, I meandered blindly down the hall and into an elevator.

"Nowhere to go but up." I pressed a button at random, leaning heavily against the cool metal control panel as it began to rise. All I needed to find was an unoccupied couch in a corner somewhere. That should also be significantly closer and warmer than any deck chair, which would be good because not only was I sweating like I'd just bitten into a hunk of jalapeño, I also couldn't stop my body from quaking. Every last ounce of my spunkiness was officially drained.

But it had to be better than staying with Allison, Claire, and Sleazoids #1 and #2.

And to remind myself of that fact I kept repeating, "This is better, way better, it gets better," with each step. My body didn't believe that any more than my mountain fantasy. Something in my chest squeezed tightly and I had to fight back a rising tide of bile.

I was going to throw up.

It wasn't a question of *Oh, maybe the sensation will pass* anymore. It was *Holy shit! I'm going to spew like Mount St. Helens! I need a restroom! NOW!*

But all I could see in either direction was a long expanse of white hall. It was going to be off-white if I didn't find a trash can or a toilet in a hurry. But I didn't have time to run around, searching for public facilities. My body felt so utterly drained I wasn't sure I was capable of moving at a pace faster than a crawl.

I really hoped that whoever had booked room 327 wouldn't come out to inspect what was going on outside their door, because I wasn't going to make it.

Except . . . the door to room 329 appeared to be slightly ajar with a room service trolley waiting right outside of it.

I bolted inside.

Which was honestly the most daring thing I had done since . . . slapping Santa. Okay, bad example, because I am a good, rule-abiding citizen. Honestly. That had just been an instinctive—and justifiable—response to uncalled-for grope-age.

It was a knee-jerk reaction, which ended with me kneeing a jerk.

This time, at least, my instinctive response was unlikely to incite a minor brawl in a public area. That ought to count as even more progress. I was just doing a little bit of breaking and entering.

Oh, yeah, I had definitely earned myself a spot on Santa's naughty list this year.

A startled room service guy who appeared to be wringing the life out of a towel, or maybe turning it into one of those swans fancy hotels leave for decoration, tried to stop me with a horrifed "Ma'am!" but I just waved him off.

"It's fine. I'm supposed to be here!"

Which wasn't a total lie, strictly speaking. Getting sick in a bathroom was definitely preferable to having it happen in a pristine hallway. Although at that point, I honestly would have said anything for bathroom access.

I made it just in time. Clinging to the toilet, I let loose a muffled roar that sounded distinctly prehistoric, like the mating call of a dinosaur, which echoed dully around the room.

Then it all came back up and a distant part of myself that was observing in a state of calm detachment just shrugged and said, "Well, at least now you won't have to work off *those* calories. Aunt Jessica will be so proud."

Because that was a healthy way to put things in perspective.

Not.

All I wanted was to hear the captain announce over the loudspeaker, "There has been a change of plans, folks. We're pulling into Cabo now and staying here for the full eight days of the cruise. We hope this isn't an inconvenience."

That would be perfect. Although anything that would get me off the damn ship would sound like heaven to me. But the silence in the room remained unbroken for such a long time that I wondered if I really was all alone. If I could curl up and fall asleep right beside the toilet with no one the wiser.

That little fantasy fizzled out when I dimly heard a sliding door shut before the room service guy said, "Here's your coffee, sir. Will that be all?"

"Yep, that's it. Have a nice night."

"Thank you, sir."

Just my freaking luck.

The door clicked shut, and it should have been silent in the room again except I thought I heard . . . tapping. It sounded like there was a deranged woodpecker nearby, but that wasn't possible. Not on a cruise ship. My brain felt inundated with a wave of static as everything momentarily became pixilated and fuzzy. I rested my forehead in the palm of my hand and waited for the feeling to pass before trying to focus on the bright colors by my feet. It appeared to be a garish Hawaiian-print shirt, crumpled on top of dark jeans, which only exacerbated my headache.

The clothes appeared to be male in origin. Which also made sense given that I distinctly remembered the room service guy calling The Resident of Room 329 "sir."

It had taken me way too long to figure out that little puzzle.

But at least now that my stomach was empty it couldn't churn quite so viciously and I could focus on the important stuff. Like whose room I had, ahem, *borrowed*.

Okay, so it belonged to a guy. Probably a nice, conservative corporate drone who fantasized about being a fisherman and leaving his cubicle far behind him. Although he might not be alone. If the room was anywhere near as nice as the bathroom, that guy had spent some serious money for these accommodations. Something he'd probably done in order to get Mrs. Corporate in the mood. I squeezed my eyes shut. I had no idea how I had gotten myself involved in this farce but I had to get out of there before they decided to hit the sheets.

So I wrapped the blanket around myself once again, hiked up my backpack on my shoulder, and stood on trembling legs. So far so good. Maybe I could slip out of the room without them even noticing. Cautiously, my heart pounding out a fast tattoo, I flushed the toilet, wincing at the loud gush and gurgle.

Nothing.

I turned to the sink and washed my hands as silently as I could, fearing that at any moment the bathroom door would jerk open and an irate lawyer would yell about slapping me with a lawsuit for breaking and entering. Or at least entering under false pretenses, since technically I hadn't broken anything.

But all I could hear was my unsteady breathing. Feeling almost prepared to barrel my way out the same way I had barged in, I opened the door and took my first step toward freedom.

Freedom was blocked by a boxer-clad hottie. *The Hot Guy from the dining room!* My jaw dropped open. Yeah, he definitely looked as good without clothing as he had in his collared shirt and business jacket. Better, even. Okay, so maybe I was leering even worse than the skeazoids currently residing in my cabin, but it's not every day that a geek like me gets such an up-close-and-personal view of hotness. And after the hellish day I'd just had, I figured there was nothing wrong with appreciating what was right smack in front of me.

But the admiration must not have been mutual since he jerked back, yelled "Zombie!," and sprayed something into my face.

That's when the world dissolved into a sea of pain and everything went black.

Chapter 6

Dominic

The distinctive sound of flushing interrupted my impro-
vised drum solo.

Well, that wasn't supposed to happen.

I stared at the closed bathroom door, coffee in hand, wondering if I had lost my mind. I'd heard of other celebrities
snapping but I'd never expected it to happen like this. Not to
me.

Maybe this is what it was like to truly crack under pressure.

Which was shit timing, really, since I was about to embark
on a vacation. In fact, I'd have already begun relaxing if it
weren't for Tim's obsessive need to push our band to great-
ness. The worst part was how easy Tim made the whole
process look. Then again, even Chris had commented on
Tim's unnerving ability to work his ass off and never be
caught sweating.

I had no idea how he consistently came up with such killer
lyrics for us. The only words I could think of were: *I'm so
screwed. I can't think of anything. My career is over. La, la, la!*

Not exactly Grammy material.

I was just starting to think that maybe I should call him

back tomorrow and admit to needing some help—just to get going—when I heard the flush.

I'm not a paranoid guy. Or at least I've never thought of myself that way. It's just that when the press hounds you and your best friends and all of your acquaintances on a regular basis, you get real good at looking over your shoulder.

It's not paranoia if someone's actually out to get you.

And knowing that we do receive death threats . . . it's more than a little unsettling. Lennon might have been killed a long time ago but that doesn't mean that the threat of crazy fans no longer exists. Half the threats in our file folder have hearts doodled in the margins. And every time something really weird happens, like a celebrity gets tackled in a mall, I can't help thinking that it could have been worse and that next time it might be me. No matter how many hundreds of thousands of cheering fans you have, it only takes one nutcase to pull a trigger.

So paranoid or not, I got out Tim's pepper spray and crept as silently as I could toward the bathroom. I felt like an idiot, standing sentinel outside my own bathroom when the noise had probably come from a neighboring suite and I had just overreacted.

But then I heard the faucet turn on and the faint squeak of the towel holder as someone dried their hands.

Holy shit. I had an intruder.

I still tried to remain calm. Maybe it was someone else from room service. They might have needed the toilet *really* badly and so they broke protocol just this once. That made sense. It wasn't like I had someone lurking in my bathroom who wanted to take photos of me while I slept . . . probably. That had only happened to Tim once before. I was still bracing myself for an attack when a hideous figure lurched out.

It was impossible to tell the gender of the creature since a blanket shrouded its slight frame. Long, stringy hair fell across a sweaty face that looked inhuman in its pallor, ashen gray from forehead to lips. There was a glaze to its eyes and its jaw dropped open as if preparing to infect me with a rabid zombie virus.

And I panicked.

"Zombie!" I yelled, jumping back and laying in on the pepper spray.

I'm not proud of myself.

Although if it really *had* been the beginning of the zombie uprising I would have kicked some serious zombie ass. And really, it wasn't like *I* was the idiot who had snuck into someone's suite looking like death warmed over. That alone warranted me being a little jumpy.

Nevertheless, I felt a twinge of guilt for overreacting a split second later when the figure dropped to the ground screeching in absolute agony. And swearing. Last time I checked, zombies didn't have that kind of extensive vocabulary.

The blanket that had shielded the figure drooped lower to reveal an all-too-familiar shirt.

Well, crap. I had probably just pepper sprayed my biggest fan.

Not that she didn't deserve it after spying on me from my bathroom. That was way past the line of acceptable fan behavior and deep into crazy stalker territory. She probably wanted to sell my boxers to the highest bidder on eBay.

Of course, it was just my luck that the one fan on the ship to recognize me had to be certifiably insane.

If it hadn't been for all the potentially embarrassing questions about my pepper spray, I'd have called the concierge and reported the break-in while she was still writhing on the floor. By all rights the little maniac should have been their problem, not mine.

But if I lodged a complaint word of my presence would get out on the ship. Then the screaming female fans might appear in droves and I'd be even worse off than before.

I still wasn't inclined to show sympathy to my mentally

unhinged fan, but it would be much easier to get her out if she walked than if I dragged her. It would also play better with the media, if word leaked. So I did my best to slip back into the role of the relaxed rock star.

I crouched down closer to her level. "Are you all right?"

"What do you think, dumbass?"

So my fan was going to be difficult, too. Great.

And while The Mess had looked like, well . . . a mess, earlier, she had now reached a whole new level of crappiness. Her eyes, which moments before had been eerily glazed in her pale face, were now violently red-rimmed and watering. She looked so pitiful that I almost felt sorry for her. Even though none of it was my fault . . . well, almost none of it.

"Sneaking into other people's rooms is illegal, you know."

"Thank you, Captain Obvious. I didn't realize that pepper spray was the penalty, though. Or is that treatment reserved for *zombies?*"

Her face reddened in anger, but I chose not to mention it. Probably best for her to get the yelling out of her system before I kicked her psychotic ass out the door.

"Zombies!" she continued raving. "Look at you, all ready for the Apocalypse and everything. Oh, wait! I can't look because *my eyes are on fire!"*

"I'd, erm, like to apologize for that part."

"That's the part you want to apologize for? Not for mistaking me for a zombie. Not for attacking me in the first place. Oh, no, you're sorry for shooting me with . . . what was that? Pepper spray?"

"Yes."

"For *pepper spraying* me in the face! *Who does that?"*

That last part didn't appear to be hypothetical: She really didn't know whose bathroom floor she was writhing on in agony. If she had, she would have mentioned it already. Which frankly was a relief. Apparently, I wasn't being targeted by a fanatical ReadySet fan, which should make extricating myself from the situation much easier. All I had to do was mutter something vaguely apologetic and send her back to her own room. Then everything would be fine.

And I'd have my suite all to myself again.

"I'm sorry you were hurt," I specified. Time to start showing her the door. "However, that's a risk you take breaking and entering. Care to explain yourself?"

She buried her head into the blanket and snuffled. "No, I'd rather not."

"Too bad." I sank down until I was sitting next to her on the bathroom floor. "I think I deserve to know why you broke into my bedroom."

"Bathroom," she corrected. "I didn't go near your bedroom. That would have been creepy."

"Breaking into my *bedroom* would be creepy but skulking in my bathroom is fair game? I don't think so." My patience was definitely nearing its limits. "How did you even find my room anyway? What did you do, follow me from dinner?"

She stared at me in confusion. "No! Why would I do something like that?"

"I don't know. Why were you staring at me?"

Well, that shut her up fast. Her eyes jumped from the pile of geek clothes I had on the floor to my chest. That's when I realized I was still only wearing my boxers. Fine for pacing in my suite and trying to figure out song lyrics. Not so fine when the semi-hysterical girl you just blasted with pepper spray is huddled on your bathroom floor.

"Since you're already so at home with my bathroom, why don't you clean up. I'll be right back." Then, without waiting for her response, I made a tactical retreat so that I could pull on some clothes, take a deep breath, and hope that by the time I came back Zombie Girl wouldn't look quite so demoralized.

But when I reentered the bathroom, not a lot had changed. She had dragged herself off the floor and she had clearly splashed water at her face, probably in an attempt to flush out any residual traces of pepper spray. Still, she looked like something the dogs of hell had chewed on before losing interest. Not that I had any intention of telling her as much. My mom drilled into me that there are some things you never say to a girl—one of which is that she looks like shit—even if it's true.

Judging by the way she clutched the sink as if she didn't trust her trembling legs to support her, she probably felt worse than she looked. I cracked open one of the water bottles that lined the sink and handed it to her.

"Here. Drink this. Water should help."

The Mess just nodded and sipped while I briefly considered letting her finish the bottle in silence. But I wanted answers. And she was going to give them to me.

"So let's start from the beginning. You were staring at me over dinner because—" I prompted.

She pressed her lips tightly together and straightened her shoulders. "I wasn't staring. My cousin pointed you out as her next fling. I was merely observing."

That part caught me off guard. "Uh . . ."

"Don't worry, I won't tell her about your pepper spray fetish."

Even drained of color she still had some spunk to her, something I might have appreciated if she wasn't making our conversation so difficult.

"So this was what, then? A reconnaissance mission so that you could report back whether I prefer boxers or briefs?"

"Boxers," she replied without hesitation. "Plaid boxers, to be more specific. And no, that has nothing to do with this." She clutched at her stomach for a minute and her shaking grew worse before she took a deep breath and steadied herself. "Believe it or not, this is not about you. At all. I just needed to use your, erm, facilities."

I should have figured it out sooner. I mean, the girl was

rubbing her stomach, clearly in pain, her face was devoid of life, and she was shaking like a leaf. Add that to the toilet flush and I was starting to get a better picture of what was going on.

She was pregnant.

Holy crap.

Who knew what that pepper spray could do to a fetus? I didn't want it to be my fault if the thing came out with webbed feet and brain issues. Maybe I should take her to the onboard doctor. Suggest a sonogram or something to make sure everything was okay in there. Maybe I should mail her a ReadySet baby onesie when I got back to LA. That might be a good *I'm sorry for endangering the wellness of your baby with pepper spray* gift.

"How far along are you?" I asked, trying not to let my panic show.

"Um, I don't know. I only just started puking." She blew out a sigh. "It's not a big deal, okay."

Maybe it was too early in the pregnancy for pepper spray to cause damage? I didn't think it worked that way, but the last thing I wanted was for her to start freaking out too. Stress had to be bad for a growing baby.

"Is there, uh . . . anything you can take for the morning sickness?"

"What are you talking about? Morning has nothing to do with . . ." Her voice dropped dangerously low. "Do you think I'm pregnant?"

"Uh—"

Crap.

"Oh, my God. You think I chose your bathroom to deliver my zombie spawn, *don't you?*"

There was a dangerous glint in her eyes and she looked ready to rip my face off.

"It's just that you, uh, don't look so good and—"

I could mentally see my mother thwacking her forehead at that one.

"For your information"—she drew herself up rigidly again, her hands turning whiter with the effort—"I happen to be *seasick*. Which is a problem since I am *stuck on a ship in the middle of nowhere with an idiot who thinks I'm a pregnant zombie!*"

Her voice cracked on the last few words and she sank back to the floor in a boneless heap. And then she began to cry.

It was the tears that had me opening my big mouth and making The Non-Pregnant Mess an offer she really should have refused.

Chapter 7

Holly

Pregnant.

The Hot Guy from dinner thought I was growing a zombie baby. After having my family critiquing my stomach for hours, that was the last straw.

I dissolved into tears.

Not that I thought Pepper Spray Guy was concerned about my eating/exercise regimen. He was way more distracted by my resemblance to a flesh-eating monster. Which, after seeing myself in the bathroom mirror, I was willing to admit he might actually have a point about—the ashen tinge to my flesh gave me a very *back from the grave* look. But still. Who thinks *zombie* and then reaches for their handy bottle of pepper spray?

A total nutcase.

One who apparently had multiple personality disorder too, judging by the way his whole *everything is going to be okay, here, let me hand you some bottled water* routine kept switching into a full-on interrogation. Plus, what was with the Hawaiian-print shirt on the floor? That didn't seem his style at all. Not that I really knew anything about him except that he had a severe case of paranoia and a jumpy trigger finger.

Oh, and that he was a royal jerk. That part was pretty obvious from the way his mouth appeared set into a permanent scowl.

But even though I wanted to place all the blame for my latest string of disasters on him, it was my own fault. *I* was the one who had gotten seasick and broken into *his* cabin. Well, *technically* it was Allison and Claire's fault for kicking me out of our cabin in the first place.

I swear I didn't mean to start crying.

It wasn't some sympathy ploy to make The Jerk feel bad for me. Technically, I suppose the tears had first started dribbling down as a defense mechanism for the pepper spray. It was only when my legs gave out from under me that I began to sob in earnest, much to The Jerk's horror.

"I'm fine," I mumbled, trying to staunch the flow in my blanket. "I'm just having a really bad . . ."

I didn't know what to say. A bad night? That was obvious. A bad day? Yeah, sitting through that dinner had pretty much been torture. A crappy week? Well, there was the whole pervy Santa disaster in the mall. . . .

". . . a really bad time lately," I finished lamely. "I'm sorry for disturbing you and, uh, taking over your bathroom."

"Don't forget the breaking and entering," he added, but when I looked up his scowl had eased into something approaching a smile.

"Yeah. Sorry about that."

"And I sprayed you with pepper spray." He shook his head in disgust, although whether that was aimed at himself or at me was hard to tell.

"Um, yeah."

"Well . . ." He shifted uneasily. Claire and Allison had a talent for flirting, but me? Oh, yeah, I've got a knack for making hot guys with dark brown hair and deep blue eyes uncomfortable. "Do you want help getting back to your room?"

"Uh, no thanks."

"You sure you can make it on your own? No offense, but you look like cra . . ." He clamped his mouth shut. "Uh, you don't look like you'll get very far."

Well, he was right about that, at least. My legs had turned completely gelatinous and the thought of even trying to reach the elevator seemed beyond me.

"I don't have a room," I mumbled.

"How is that possible?"

"Well, I do, but my cousins—"

"The ones who picked me as their fling?"

"Yeah, Claire and Allison. They're, erm, *entertaining* right now, so they sort of kicked me out."

"Define 'sort of.' "

I might as well just come clean.

"They kicked me out, okay! They're hanging out with some skeazy guys and didn't exactly want to share the room with a seasick cousin. So I can't go back there. At least not for another few hours." My head lolled against my shoulder as if my neck had decided that carrying such a dysfunctional body part was no longer worth the effort. "Look, you didn't sign up for this on your vacation. I get it. So I'm sorry I ruined your night. If we see each other again we can just pretend we didn't." I struggled into a crouched position and then stood. "Now I believe the Lido deck is calling my name."

He looked disbelievingly from my blanket to my backpack and settled on my pale but determined expression. Then he sighed.

"I can't let you do that."

"Funny, but I don't recall asking for your permission."

He ran a hand through his hair, making the ends stand up in ridiculous little spikes.

"Look, you can't sleep out on a deck, and I feel kind of responsible for your present state . . . because of the pepper spray."

He looked like a guy who badly wanted to kick me out of his suite but whose well-ingrained manners wouldn't let him do it. There was no sign of the utterly confident stranger from the dining room anymore.

"I insist," he grumbled.

Okay, so he didn't look happy about the situation, but even spending the night curled up in his bathroom would probably be a vast improvement on the deck . . . or my cabin. Plus, if I just stayed with him then I wouldn't have to move. Given the current state of my stomach and legs, that sounded pretty damn good.

"I have a foldout couch, and we can pretend we've never met starting tomorrow. Come on, what's the worst that could happen?"

"Since I've already been pepper sprayed, I'm waiting for you to pull out a Taser from a matching purse."

It probably wasn't the best idea to mock the guy offering me a pretty great setup, but Sensible Holly was long gone.

His expression turned thoughtful. "You know, I can still call security for the breaking and entering. It'd be a bit inconvenient for me, but for you . . . it would be an absolute nightmare. Or you can spend the night here so I'll know you aren't breaking into anyone else's suite."

I blinked. Well, that sounded smug.

"Hand it over and you've got a deal."

He looked confused. Perfect. "What are you talking about?"

"The pepper spray, of course. Hand it over."

He glanced at the can that was sitting right next to the sink, well within my reach. Still, if I was going to spend the night in his room, I wanted him to give me the great equalizer. He warily appraised me.

"You're not planning on using this on me, right?"

"Not unless you turn into a zombie."

"Very funny."

"Thanks. Now hand it over."

He hesitated and I nearly told him to forget it, because I wanted to stay there, with or without the pepper spray. Luckily, he didn't know that, and with a muffled curse he deliberately placed it in my hand and took a large step back.

"Happy now?"

I dropped it in the trash can and grinned. "Much better."

He shook his head and then, slinging an arm around my waist, he pulled me out of the bathroom and into the rest of the suite. Which was actually pretty nice of him since my legs still didn't appear to be functioning properly. Then he unceremoniously shoved me into a plushy armchair while he converted the couch into a bed. I should have at least offered to do *something* . . . but we both probably knew I'd be more of a hindrance than a help.

So I sat there in silence until I remembered the question I'd been meaning to ask him.

"What's your name?"

He stopped straightening a blanket mid-jerk. "Uh, that depends."

Well, that answer made no sense. Then again, things were turning fuzzy.

"Depends on what?"

"On the person. I have a lot of nicknames."

"Okay." I nodded. "What should I call you then?"

He placed another blanket down on the makeshift bed and then turned to get a good look at me. "Why do you need to call me anything? I thought we were going to pretend that none of this ever happened tomorrow."

"Well, yeah, I guess. But that's hours from now. I can't call you Hot Guy until then."

He laughed, but it still took a moment for my brain to catch up with my mouth. I was too exhausted to care so I just waved my hand and said, "You know what I mean."

"Why don't you tell me anyway?" His grin didn't make

him look nearly so unapproachable. "I think this is the first nice thing you've said to me."

"Well, I wasn't exactly inclined to be nice when you whipped out the pepper spray," I pointed out drowsily. " 'Inclined' is a funny word, isn't it? It makes me think of mountains. I like mountains. I don't get seasick on mountains."

"You can call me Nick."

"Okay. That's good. Night, Nick." I shut my eyes only to mutter darkly when he yanked me from the chair to my new bed. I would have protested except . . . the couch/bed was so much nicer. I sighed happily and snuggled deeper into the fabric only to groan again as another wave of seasickness hit me. "I hate the ocean. Someone should drain it."

Strong arms with thinly corded muscles dragged me into a sitting position, then disappeared only to return moments later holding a can of Coke.

"Here, drink this. The carbonation should help settle your stomach."

I sipped from it, willing to try anything that might help. "Thanks. For everything. Well, except the pepper spray, but everything else. I appreciate it."

He smiled, and it slowly started to sink in that I was actually having a nice interaction with Nick, even though he had seen me at my worst and knew that I obviously found him attractive. He didn't seem fazed by it anymore. Just amused.

"So, uh . . . sorry, what's your name?"

He looked at me guiltily for not asking the question earlier. "Holly Dayton."

"So, Holly Dayton, I take it you're a big ReadySet fan."

I waited for him to get to his point but he didn't say anything else, so I took another gulp of Coke and said, "Yep, me and at least five million other people."

He settled back against his headboard. "What do you think of their song lyrics?"

I scrunched up my nose as I concentrated on giving a well-thought-out response when everything kept going hazy. "Well, the lyrics are poetic but sharp. And usually there are wildly divergent ways to interpret their songs—even the love songs are ambiguous. I like that. Although I've been thinking . . ."

"Yes?" he said, encouragingly.

"I could be totally off on this, but I wonder if Timothy Goff is gay. It makes sense to me. I bet he's got a thing going on with his drummer."

Nick jerked upright. *"Timothy Goff does not have a thing going on with the drummer!"*

"Um, wow. Overreact much?"

Nick just glared at me. "He doesn't."

"Well, how do you know?"

"I just . . . you can tell."

"What does that mean? I know some people claim to have gaydar, but you can't *know* someone's sexual orientation for sure just by looking at them!"

"He is not hooking up with the drummer!"

"Fine!" I said, a little taken aback by his intensity. "He's not hooking up with the drummer." I shrugged, took another sip of Coke, and giggled. "Maybe he's with the other guitarist instead."

"What the hell is wrong with you?"

"Nothing."

"Oh, yeah? Then why are you so sure ReadySet is gay for each other?"

I tried to consider it seriously, but I couldn't help shutting my eyes and grinning exhaustedly. All I really cared about was sleep. "I don't know. Three guys on tour . . . with each other all the time. You've seriously never considered the possibility?"

"NO!"

Huh. Well, that was definite.

"I'm sure they're just close friends."

I waggled an eyebrow at that, and Nick tossed a pillow at my head, nearly jolting my drink.

"Hey!"

"Just go to sleep, Holly."

Which sounded like a fine suggestion to me. Although I could have sworn that I heard him mutter something like, "Gay for each other! Christ, of all the people to break into my suite it had to be The Mess!"

Not exactly flattering, but I was willing to believe I'd misheard him.

Chapter 8

Dominic

She thought I was gay.
More accurately, she thought that Dominic Wyatt was gay for his bandmate. She appeared to find "Nick" plenty attractive, if her exhausted ramblings were to be taken seriously. Holly Dayton might be a walking disaster, but that particular admission had still felt damn good.

Then she had announced her theory that the guys of ReadySet were probably gay for each other.

Christ. The girl was even more screwed up than I had originally thought.

And even snoring on my couch, she was messing up my plans. All I had wanted out of this vacation was some time to relax, get some space to myself. Not an option that night. I couldn't even sleep my way through this living nightmare, because the coffee I had ordered from room service now had me wired. Which left me supercaffeinated and unable to make any noise in the room, in case it woke her up.

In my own damn suite.

It would have been one thing if I liked the girl. If we had met by the pool, struck up a casual conversation, and I had invited her to hang out in my suite . . . that would change things. Instead, she had commandeered my bathroom before openly speculating on whether I was sexually involved with my two best friends. Generally speaking, I prefer sane girls to crazy ones who demand pepper spray before they'll take me up on an offer that, frankly, they don't deserve.

Oh, yeah, she was a real treat.

I found myself glaring at her sleeping figure until she let out a pained groan and tossed around under the covers. She really had it bad: Not even a superfan could fake turning *that* sickly pale to meet me. I studied her carefully and was relieved to see that she didn't look quite as deathly ill anymore—even her lips were starting to look more normal.

But while she might be looking *less* awful, the only real benefit of having Holly Disaster around was that she had effectively eliminated the deafening silence in the room. Now I just needed to tune out the moans and whimpers long enough to compose a song. Absentmindedly picking up my drumsticks, I began tapping out a beat that sounded sort of like her: a bit sharp and staccato, but with a pulsing, jagged edge to it. It sounded nothing like anything else ReadySet had produced before . . . but it wasn't bad. Switching over to guitar the instant lyrics started coming to me, I lunged for my notebook and started scribbling:

> You've got me seasick. I don't know how you do it,
> But my legs aren't steady, they just won't hold
> The deck is buckling and it's ready to fold
> And I can tell, it's my personal hell,
> It's been torture for us both
> Someone's got to stop, stop the boat.

And, okay, maybe it wasn't quite as good as Tim's stuff, but I didn't think it was terrible, either. Not once we added in Tim on vocals and Chris on guitar. I scrawled madly across the pages, desperately trying to write the chords I was seeing for each instrument. I had to be able to replicate it perfectly back in LA. Tim would kill me if he ever found out that I had forgotten *exactly* how the bridge was supposed to go.

So I kept at it, tweaking old lyrics and adding new ones until the finished product actually looked producable to me. It might not be the cutting-edge indie-rock sound ReadySet was known for, but it was solid. Definitely something to keep in mind if the movie sound track contract came through. Rumor had it that the film under discussion was loosely based on Tim's boyfriend's best friend, Mackenzie, and how her embarrassing attempt at performing CPR on a high school football player (after she had accidentally body-checked the jerk with her backpack) launched her into YouTube fame.

Mackenzie probably wouldn't be thrilled to be the center of any more speculation. I doubt there is a girl less predisposed to be part of the glitter and shine of Hollywood than Mackenzie Wellesley, geek extraordinaire. Not that there is anything wrong with her. In fact, if she hadn't been so obviously hung up on a guy from her high school, I might have asked her out myself.

Thankfully, I realized early on that anything beyond basic friendship with us would be a royal failure. A long-distance relationship was the last thing Mackenzie would agree to—especially with a rock star. She had more than enough notoriety without dating me.

But my song sounded about right for her loosely based biopic. And even if the studio hired some starlet who would be in treatment for drugs, alcohol, or anorexia in a few years, the music should at least be good. I tapped the cover of the notebook thoughtfully. I might just have something of quality to show the guys after all.

Thanks, in part, to Holly.

I glanced over at her and noted that she wasn't even slightly perturbed by the music. Once she was out, apparently nothing could rouse her. I yawned hugely as my caffeine buzz faded into oblivion and blearily eyed my watch. Four in the morning. No wonder I was exhausted. The whole reason I had insisted on taking a break was because the long days, and even longer nights, of nonstop work were wearing me down. Yet my first night of official vacation and I had been busting my ass every bit as hard, if not harder, than usual.

It had to stop.

So I flipped off the hall light I'd used so as not to disturb Goldilocks on the couch and fell asleep wondering what the guys would think of the new song.

I woke up only a few hours later to a loud thump and muttered curses from my suite guest.

I growled and pulled the blanket over my face. I didn't want to deal with Holly Dayton's latest disaster. I had played white knight long enough to make amends for the pepper spray. I didn't care what she needed; I was done.

"Nick?" she called out tentatively.

"Go away, Holly."

"Uh, do you mind if I use your bathroom first?"

Now she was asking permission? Seriously? She was only, oh, about ten hours late on that one.

"Sure. Fine. Leave me alone."

I heard her mumble something like, "Well, I guess *he's* not a morning person," and fought the urge to snarl in response.

What I wanted to say wasn't complimentary.

I tried to think of the shower as a good sign that she'd be gone soon. I'd probably only have to act semi-polite for another hour, tops, before I could luxuriate in my private suite at last. And if I could just fall back asleep before she stepped out of the bathroom, I wouldn't have to do or say anything.

A brilliant plan . . . if Holly hadn't been a shower singer. It started out quietly enough but then she must have gotten caught up in the song.

A ReadySet song.

Maybe it should have been flattering: She had our band shirt, she knew all the words to our songs . . . clearly she was a superfan. And she had no idea she was enjoying a shower in the drummer's suite.

But I wasn't smiling.

Holly couldn't sing if her life depended on it.

She could warble. She could screech. She could make sounds remarkably similar to the yowling of a cat in heat. But singing? Yeah, not so much.

She was single-handedly butchering all of our biggest hits. It was so painful, I almost yelled for her to stop, but I thought better of it. Knowing her luck, my shout would startle her into slipping in the shower. Then I'd be stuck with a concussed naked girl in my bathroom.

The naked part might not be so bad if the other factors didn't exist.

Factors such as that she was more than slightly unhinged.

I could still hear her singing brokenly as she used up all the towels I had requested for *myself* the night before. Then she strolled into the room, wearing her jeans from last night and *my* stupid Hawaiian-print shirt as if she owned it.

Well, today Goldilocks was going to get chewed out by the bear.

"What the hell are you doing?" I ground out.

She looked at me in surprise. "I was about to fold up the couch. I'm sorry, did you want to do that yourself?"

"No, I didn't."

"Okay then." She walked over to her makeshift bed and started pulling the blankets off.

"That still doesn't explain why you're wearing *my* shirt!"

She turned back to me, and while she was looking better than she had last night, that wasn't saying much. Her face was still too pale and her hair clung together in long wet strands that made her look like a rather destitute, down-on-its-luck rat.

"What's the big deal? It was lying in an ugly heap on the floor. I didn't think you'd miss it."

"You can't *steal* someone's clothes while they're sleeping!"

"I have never stolen anything in my life!" Her glare made it clear that I was irritating her almost as much as she was me. Good.

"No stealing. You just restrict yourself to breaking and entering then."

She rolled her red-rimmed eyes. "Will you let that go, already? I became seasick. Obviously, I would've been better off puking in anyone else's bathroom!"

I saw red. "Oh, really? *You* would have been better off. I bet you think someone else would applaud your screeching at this ungodly hour too! You're mental."

Her back straightened. "I don't screech!"

"Trust me, I know music. The sounds you were making? That was not music."

Holly shot me an intense glare. "I don't know what your problem is, but for the record, you're being a total jerk right now."

There was a flurry of knocking at the door and her scowl darkened even as understanding appeared to sink in. "Oh, I get it! You're mad because you invited girls over and don't want me around. You could have said as much." She shouldered her backpack. "It's been . . . *interesting*, Nick. Have a nice life."

And before I could say a word about how, yes, I wanted her out but not because I had a harem of women coming, she jerked open the door.

She wasn't even able to cross the threshold of my suite.

The hallway was crammed with girls. Dozens of them, varying in ages, shapes, and sizes—but all uninvited—crowded in the doorway. Holly froze, dumbstruck in amazement, as they blinded her with camera flashes and shrieked some version of: *"DOMINIC! I LOVE YOU! MARRY ME! OH, MY GOD, DOMINIC, I WANT TO HAVE YOUR BABIES!"*

I think one of my fans might have even fainted.

Sprinting to the door, I grabbed onto Holly's backpack, yanking her back into my room, and slammed the door shut. It locked with an audible *snick*.

Shit.

Holly stared at me for a long moment. "Who the hell are you, *Dominic?*"

And that's when I knew I was officially screwed.

Chapter 9

Holly

Okay, rewind. What on earth just happened?

I remembered waking up on the couch and feeling slightly better, with the nausea from yesterday lingering like the vague threat of exams at the beginning of the school year—unpleasant but not imminent danger. At least I no longer felt immobilized by my seasickness. That was a vast improvement, especially since waking up in a stranger's room was highly disconcerting. Although, I could think of worse ways to start my day. Especially since Nick, unarmed with pepper spray, was exceedingly fun to look at.

Something I distinctly recalled mentioning the night before.

I sat bolt upright, lurching out of the makeshift bed. Instead, all I accomplished was twisting the blankets around my feet, tripping myself up, toppling over . . . and landing ungracefully in a heap.

Well, that was one way to make an entrance.

Not that Nick seemed to notice. He just grumbled something into his pillow and then told me to get out. Real nice. Then again, considering the way I had barged into his life, I hadn't expected him to order breakfast and insist that I share it with him.

But we could at least try to depart on good terms.

And politeness dictated that I ask permission to use his shower instead of just helping myself. Not that I had any experience with morning-after etiquette. Maybe I should have just slipped out and returned to my cabin, but I hated the clammy layer of sweat that lingered on my skin. I seriously needed a shower before I turned my makeshift bed back into a couch. I even considered calling in for coffee as a thank you before leaving as a way to eliminate potential future awkwardness.

And maybe after a real conversation we'd even *want* to hang out. It would be nice to have someone to spend time with while I avoided the majority of my blood relations. So I shrugged off his growl and headed for the bathroom, determined to make a better impression than I had the night before.

The hot water felt absolutely fantastic, and for a minute I could ignore all the weirdness in the situation. But stepping out of the shower forced me to take stock of my clothing options. I hadn't thought to pack a change of clothes in my backpack the night before, which meant that all I had available were my jeans, the ReadySet shirt I now associated with nausea, pepper spray, and general disgustingness . . . and the Hawaiian-print shirt still lying in a wrinkled heap on the floor. Desperate times call for ugly shirts.

So I buttoned up his shirt, which effectively dwarfed my body, fully planning to return it to him that day—just as soon as I had changed into some fresh clothes of my own. Honestly, I would probably be doing him a favor if I kept the shirt, though. The thing was hideous. Even Nick of the broad shoulders and dark blue eyes couldn't make it look good.

But I guess he was pretty attached to it because his eyes

started shooting daggers the second I stepped out of the bathroom.

My good resolutions evaporated when he actually *accused* me of trying to steal the damn thing.

He was being such a jerk and, frankly, I didn't have to put up with it. He could simmer in his own anger for all I cared. It's one thing to put up with criticism from my family with my grandpa around, it's quite another thing to let a guy who had recently mistaken me for a zombie make *me* feel like an idiot.

That left me with exactly zero desire to linger.

Which was probably what he was aiming for anyway: to make me leave as quickly as possible. I never should have tried to be friendly in the first place. Clearly, he thought he was above common civilities like politeness and basic courtesy.

But, whatever, he wasn't going to be my problem.

And if he thought so little of me then maybe I *wouldn't* return his stupid shirt . . . but probably not. I'm not very good at holding grudges, and becoming a thief to upset a stranger was flat-out petty. I'd just have to "rise above" again.

Later.

I stomped over to the door like a cartoon with a dark, squiggly storm cloud over my head as I wrenched the door open.

And then all hell broke loose.

There was a huge crowd of teenage girls in the hallway who must have agreed to stay silent until the door opened. But when I emerged they couldn't seem to hold back their wild screaming a moment longer.

Except at first all I registered was a wave of bright lights from the flashes and total confusion. The girls must have had the wrong room because they weren't yelling for Nick. Instead, all the girls kept screeching weird stuff like marriage offers to someone named Dominic.

And all I could think was: *Who the hell is that?*

I was about to tell them that they'd made a mistake—picked the wrong suite—when an arm roughly yanked me back into the room. Swearing profusely, Nick locked the door to keep the howling girls at bay. I had expected a vapid, shallow jerk like Nick to be taking them up on their offers before telling his buddy Dominic all about it—locker-room style. The two of them had probably set this whole thing up to help Nick impress girls. Not that I expected he would need any help in that department . . . at least until he had flipped out over his butt ugly Hawaiian shirt.

Except the screaming had definitely increased when Nick sprinted into view and slammed the door.

What was it that he had said the night before about nicknames? He had a lot of them? Something along those lines. My concentration had been pretty shoddy at the time.

Now I wished I had paid closer attention.

I was staring at him, open-mouthed, when it hit me: I knew even less about The Resident of Room 329 than all the girls clamoring outside the door.

"Who the hell are you, *Dominic?*" I asked, deadly serious. I needed to know. He clearly wasn't just plain Nick the way he had claimed. Only famous people, royalty, or the exorbitantly wealthy have girls camped outside their rooms.

And it would make some sense for a member of one of the above to carry pepper spray.

So which of the three was he?

I took a step back from him. "Why do you need pepper spray, *Dominic?* Who are you?"

I don't know what I expected him to say. *I'm actually a cousin of Prince William. I rule a small country you may never have heard of, that is primarily known for its ski chalets and excellent spas.*

But whatever I could have imagined him saying it wasn't, "Look at your shirt."

I stared down at the ridiculous Hawaiian print. "What? You invested in palm fronds?" I said sarcastically. "I don't think so."

"I said, look at your shirt. Not *my* shirt. Your shirt."

Which could only mean my ReadySet shirt. I started walking backward away from him and when my knees bumped into his bed, I sat.

"Holy shit. You're Dominic Wyatt. From ReadySet."

He smiled, which I took to mean that he was back to being smugly confident again. "Yes, I am."

"Huh," I said articulately. "And you are sure you're not gay?"

That zapped the cocky look off his face pretty fast. "Positive!"

"Really? Because I could have sworn—"

"No!" He raked a hand through his dark brown hair, mussing up his just-rolled-out-of-bed tufts even more. It wasn't fair that on him, even that looked good. "Look, I had a late night, so why don't you try not to annoy me. For a few minutes. That's all I'm asking."

"Fine." I eyed him expectantly while he just stood there.

"What?"

"Nothing. I'm just waiting for you to come up with a plan, right? Because I'm a little nobody who can't handle anything."

"You've got that right," he muttered and I glared at him.

"I was being sarcastic!"

"Yeah? Well, it's a fact. You have no idea what you've just landed us in!"

I rolled my eyes and pretended like I saw crowds of screaming girls every day. "All those tween girls outside your door were *so* terrifying. I'm shaking in your Hawaiian shirt."

Nick—scratch that, *Dominic*—took a deep breath. "Okay, here's what's happening: Those girls are going to send those photos to all of their friends. Someone will post them on

Facebook. Someone will sell them to the highest bidder. Either way, they're going to be leaked. Now, someone is bound to identify you and even before that happens there is going to be lots of speculation. Are you following me so far?"

I gulped and nodded. "What kind of speculation, exactly?"

He laughed but not like he actually saw any humor in the situation. More like if he didn't laugh he would be tempted to yell or start punching pillows. It was weird, but the longer I spent around him the more I wondered how I could have ever been fooled by his relaxed persona.

The guy was stiffer than a starched shirt.

"Speculation on everything. Where and how we met. How long we've been dating. That's what I have to look forward to and for you it'll be so much worse."

"Worse?" I squeaked.

"Oh, yeah. The media always puts the girls through hell. They'll evaluate your every outfit. Then there are the death threats."

I was starting to worry that my brain couldn't process any more because it had hit maximum capacity.

"Why would I have death threats? People like me. Well, most people ignore me, but the ones who don't do that generally like me."

"People might *like* you," he explained calmly, "but they *love* me. As in, I have a fan group that feels personally insulted if anyone ever criticizes me."

"And that explains your ego," I muttered because, well, it was the truth. Then again, if I had thousands of fans I'd be feeling pretty good about myself too.

"I still don't think you're getting this. ReadySet fans don't take too kindly to us forming relationships."

I couldn't resist. "Maybe because they think you secretly belong with each other."

"Will you get off that already?" Nick snarled.

His raised voice only set off more screeching from the girls who were probably jostling each other in an attempt to place their ears against the door.

"Dump her!" seemed like their common consensus.

"Shit."

The guy really looked like he was nearing the end of his rope.

"Look, this whole thing will blow over. We'll just tell people the truth. I was seasick and you let me crash on the couch. I'll even leave out the pepper spray part. You'll look like a hero."

He looked at me like I had smacked my head in the shower. "You're kidding, right? First of all: No one will believe that we didn't have sex. No matter what we say, they're not going to believe it. But that isn't even our biggest problem."

I glared at him. "Really? Because having people implicate that I slept with you, yeah, that's problematic from where I'm sitting."

"The problem is that you look like crap."

I reeled back like I'd been slapped.

"No offense," he added as an afterthought.

"Right. Because ordinarily when someone tells me I look like crap, I take it as a huge compliment."

"It's just . . . I'm trying to be honest here. Now I'm sure ordinarily you don't look . . . like you do now. But your eyes are still red-rimmed from the pepper spray, your face is still sickly pale, and your wet hair makes it look like you just tried drowning yourself in my shower. . . . Did I leave anything out?"

I crossed my arms defensively. "No, I think you've made your point. I suppose if I looked like a model this would be so much easier to explain. Getting caught with your pants down with a girl like me, that *must* be humiliating for you."

I gave his boxers a pointed glance and he hurriedly grabbed his jeans from off the floor and pulled them on. Honestly, until that moment I hadn't noticed he was sleeping in the same boxers and plain white T-shirt from the night before. The blankets on his enormous bed had done an excellent job of obscuring him earlier, and when there are roughly fifty screaming girls snapping photos in your face, it's rather distracting.

"I don't sleep in my jeans," he growled. "Not that I need to defend my actions to you. This is *my* room, goddamnit!"

"Something you've made perfectly clear. So if that's all, I think it's time for me to go."

Nick's iPad began ringing from the other side of the bed and he scrambled for it, calling over his shoulder, "Just hold off a damn minute!" Then, ignoring me completely, he accepted the call and said without preamble, "I know, Tim. I screwed things up. I'm sorry, man."

Oh, my God, he was talking to Timothy Goff.

"You better have a real good explanation for why people are saying you're abusing a new girlfriend. I just booked my flight to Portland! Tell me this is an easily fixed misunderstanding, Dom."

"It wasn't my fault."

I glared at him. "Oh, and it was mine, I suppose!"

Nick pointed a finger at me, mouthed "breaking and entering," then pointed at himself. "Self-defense. Not the same thing."

"She's still there!" Timothy Goff yelled indignantly at Nick. "Jesus, Dom. You've got a royal ass-kicking coming your way. Put her on."

"I'm not so sure that's—"

I ignored Nick, walked into camera range, and waved to the rock star I've been crushing on for the past two years. In exactly none of my daydreams did I meet him after illegally using his drummer's bathroom.

But at that moment it really didn't matter because *I was speaking to the lead singer of ReadySet.*

Definitely time to play it cool.

"Hi, uh, Timothy Goff. Mr. Goff? I don't know what to call you, but . . . uh, hi!"

Mental head slap.

"Call me Tim," His smile faded as he took in my less-than-polished appearance. "You look—"

"Like crap," I finished for him. "Nick said as much earlier."

Tim's head whipped over so he could glare at his bandmate. "Real nice, Dom. Kick any puppies lately too?"

At least Nick had the decency to look embarrassed. "I'm working on that part. Puppies are hard to find on a ship."

Tim only ignored him and focused back on me. "Ignore my friend—I generally do. I was *actually* about to say that you look like you might need some help. Do you mind telling me what happened?"

I melted right there on Nick's bed, something he must have noted since he snorted in disgust. That was enough to get me pulling myself together again. I didn't want to play the starstruck girl for any rock star, not even Timothy Goff.

So I focused on telling him the whole story: my seasickness, Nick's attack with the pepper spray, how I woke up to find a crowd of screaming girls outside the door, with only a few interruptions from Nick. It was pretty clear from the looks that Tim kept shooting him that he was in the doghouse.

Which, strictly speaking, wasn't exactly fair.

"It was nice of him to offer me a place to crash," I admitted to Tim. "He didn't have to, and I wasn't in any shape to refuse so, uh, that was nice."

Not exactly poetry, but I thought I felt Nick relax just a little beside me.

"Right," Tim agreed. "Listen, Holly, it was great meeting you, but I need to talk to Dom alone. There's some confidential band stuff we need to discuss."

"Of course." I nodded until I probably resembled a bobble-head. "I should probably head out anyway so—"

"No!" both boys hollered.

"Uh, you should really stay right there until we get every-thing sorted out. Maybe you could order up some coffee or something?" Tim suggested.

I looked between him and Nick. Dialing in room service for some free coffee didn't sound bad to me.

"Sure."

Nick grabbed his iPad back before I could change my mind and headed straight out to the balcony, shutting it firmly behind him.

Successfully shutting me out while they discussed my fu-ture.

Well, that was comforting.

Not.

Chapter 10

Dominic

Of course, Holly would be perfectly agreeable . . . when she was talking to Tim.

Even disasters like Holly acted . . . *nice* around him, which was one of his skills that I usually admired with only a small twinge of jealousy. Then again, usually I wasn't operating solo on roughly four hours of sleep with dozens of screaming girls camped outside my room. In this case, "usually" didn't apply.

And I was getting sick and tired of telling Holly that I wasn't gay while she made moon-eyes at Tim.

The irony of which had not escaped me.

"I don't know how this happened," I admitted to Tim. "This kind of stuff happens to *you*, not me."

"Funny, I can't remember the last time I pepper sprayed someone in the face."

"I meant getting cornered by fans. And you're the one who gave it to me!"

"Yeah, and using it on a seasick girl was *exactly* what I had in mind. Dom, do you have any idea how bad this is?"

His words mirrored what I'd said to Holly only minutes earlier. I hoped it hadn't sounded so pompous coming from me. "Yes. I do. Look, I'm sorry that we're in this mess. Obviously, I never planned on any of this—I don't know how anyone found me in the first place."

"I think the answer to that is pretty obvious. Google yourself. You'll see what I mean."

I did as he suggested and was greeted by two pictures of myself in the latest news story. The first was taken over dinner and claimed that I was meeting my *rumored girlfriend's* father, Mr. Ridgley, and taking a well-deserved vacation with Famous cruises.

So at least one of the Ridgelys had to be behind it. Good to know.

The second picture was a particularly awful shot of an open-mouthed Holly with me right behind her wearing nothing but a white T-shirt, boxers, and a glare. The text beneath the photo was even more damning than the rumor that I was dating Cynthia.

Busted! ReadySet drummer Dominic Wyatt bangs (and beats) an unidentified girl while on vacation with his girlfriend?

"Holy shit," I breathed.

"It gets worse," Tim said grimly. "The press is gearing up to label you the next Hollywood Bad Boy—and not in a good way."

"Look, I've never hurt Holly. Well, except for the pepper spray and that doesn—"

"We both know the facts don't matter. Just the narrative. And right now the narrative is that you've been toying with a young girl and hurting Holly on the side."

"We could sue for defamation of character."

"Sure, but that means a long legal battle that we would probably lose since they included a question mark in the headline. Accident or not, I would seriously love to kick your ass right now."

"I'm guessing Chris feels the same way."

"Oh, yeah, we agreed to take turns. He's letting me take the first punch."

I winced. "Generous of him. How badly will this screw up the sound track negotiations?"

Tim glared at me and I almost wished I hadn't asked. "How badly do you think, genius? This whole deal hinges on our ability to maintain our family-friendly reputation. Hell, our *careers* depend on it! If we become associated with sexual misconduct . . . people are going to stop returning our calls *fast*. So guess how Chris and I will be spending our Christmas break?"

I groaned. "How?"

"Canned food drives for the poor. Then we're throwing a turkey dinner for the homeless. Oh, and we're putting on a small benefit concert for orphans. None of which would bother me if it weren't for the fact that *I planned to spend Christmas with my new boyfriend!*"

"I'll clean this up on my end, Tim. I'll arrange an online press conference with Holly today. She'll tell everyone I never hit her, and I'll fly out of Mexico tomorrow." I started searching for flights. "I can make it back by four; that should give you guys plenty of time to kick my ass before the canned food drive. I'll make it up to you both, I swear."

"You can't fly out because you are on a romantic vacation with your girlfriend, Holly. A girlfriend you treasure so much you were trying to keep her out of the media spotlight. And the press is going to take pictures of you romping together in the freaking surf until you're Hollywood's cutest couple."

"You can't be serious."

"Oh, I'm serious, all right, Dom. You wanted a vacation? Well, you got one. With Holly. Make the most of it, because when you get back we're going to have to work twice as hard as before."

Tim disconnected the call before I could complain further.

So much for my vacation.

I could handle the canned food drive, the dinner, and the orphanage gig, no problem. I've got plenty of experience being involved in charity events since we've always believed in putting our celebrity status to good use. We've done concerts to help out hurricane victims, to clean up oil spills, to support the Trevor Project . . . we're all for contributing to a worthy cause.

It's exhausting, but at least I know what to expect.

But hanging out with Holly? Yeah, that wouldn't be giving me any of those great, *I feel like I'm making such a positive contribution to the world* moments. More like *God, why am I stuck with this walking disaster?* moments. And I wouldn't just be hanging out with her as a buddy, but as a boyfriend.

Hell. Just hell.

I opened the sliding door on the balcony and saw her flipping through the pages of notes I had written the night before. Which was intrusive on a whole new level. I wanted to snatch my song attempt out of her hands, but I couldn't risk pissing her off.

So I settled for flopping onto the bed, looking at her skeptically, and saying, "Are you morally opposed to respecting people's privacy or something?"

She flushed and shut the notebook. "There were a bunch of pages ripped out but I thought you might still want them so I . . . sorry . . . It's a good song though, Nick. Did you write it last night?"

"What makes you think I wrote it at all?"

She looked at me as if the answer were obvious. "Well, it doesn't sound like anything else by ReadySet, and since I found it in *your* suite and it has *your* name on the inside flap, I used my brilliant deductive skills. How'd I do, Watson?"

"Not bad, Sherlock," I admitted. "And, yeah, I wrote it last night."

"Well, then." She grinned. "Looks like you don't hate me after all."

I stared at her. "What are you talking about?"

"Using me as your muse . . . writing about being seasick in love . . . it sounds like you're dangerously close to *liking* me. Quick, you better tell me I look like crap again!"

The girl irritated me, but I never meant to make her feel bad. I just wanted her to turn somebody else's life upside down.

Anyone but *me*.

"I didn't, uh, mean to make you feel bad, Holly."

She snorted. "You mean like when you called me a zombie? Or asked if I was pregnant? Or accused me of being a thief?"

Well, when she put it that way it sounded . . . not so good. But oddly enough she didn't look upset, more like faintly amused.

"Well, anyhow," I faltered. Damn, I felt like an idiot, but I had to get her to agree with the plan. "You're not, uh, hideous."

Holly burst out laughing. "Not hideous. That might be the nicest thing you've said to me." She paused and seemed to consider for a second before asking one of those questions that all men should instinctively fear.

"Beyond that, how would you describe me?"

"Hell if I know."

She nodded. "Fair enough. So . . . what's our plan to get me out of this?"

Now here came the tricky part.

"I need you to do me a favor, Holly. A big one."

She sat bolt upright on the bed. "I'm listening."

"I . . . well, we . . . see, the thing is . . ."

"Just spit it out already, Nick!"

"We need to do a press conference."

"Okay." Holly nodded. "I'm fine with telling everyone the truth."

"Well, I was thinking we could tweak the truth a bit."

She narrowed her eyes at me suspiciously. "There's no 'tweaking' with the truth. Either we tell them what happened or we don't. Which option are you interested in, Nick?"

From the tone of her voice, I was pretty sure she already knew the answer.

"More on the lying side of things."

She didn't so much as blink. "What do you want me to say?"

"Well, I'd really appreciate it . . . ReadySet wants you to consider . . ."

"Seriously, just tell me, Nick!"

It was the hardest thing I've ever had to say.

"I need you to be my girlfriend."

Chapter 11

Holly

"You need me to be your *what?*"
I stared at him, waiting for the words to make sense.
So far that day, Nick had seemed interested in one thing only:
getting rid of me. Which meant that his sudden announce-
ment couldn't have anything to do with actual feelings. I
rubbed my stomach as it rolled queasily. The motion of the
ship wasn't the only reason I felt like puking.

He wanted me to be his girlfriend.

Seriously?

I was the worst possible candidate for that particular role,
and we both knew it. He needed someone model thin with
lustrous chestnut hair, a dazzling smile, and clear aqua eyes.
Not someone who could naturally double as a zombie in an
Apocalypse film when seasick. I might be a California girl
but I have never been glamorous.

So why was he asking me?

Judging by the horrified expression on his face, I was a last
resort. Not that I blamed him. Dominic Wyatt's life was
probably pretty close to perfect: He could do whatever he
wanted! Party with models, drink all night in exclusive clubs,
hang out with all the A-list stars of Hollywood.

He could probably say, "I'll have my people call your people" in complete seriousness since he had agents and publicists and assistants and . . . a whole entourage.

Probably.

"So to handle this uh, *incident,* we need to control the narrative. Here's how it works: We talk to the press, say that we're dating and madly in love. Then when we're back in LA, we can pretend to drift apart. I'll have my publicist announce an amicable parting of ways and we'll put this whole mess behind us."

I nodded as if what he was saying made even the slightest bit of sense. "And why can't we just tell the truth?"

Nick started pacing the suite. "The press thinks I've been physically abusing you because the photos from this morning weren't exactly flattering. For either of us."

Now I bet that wasn't true. He probably looked all sexy in an *I just rolled out of bed, don't disturb me,* rumpled kind of way.

But at least he was no longer saying that I looked like crap. That was a minor improvement.

"So? I'll just tell them that isn't the case."

"The problem is that the truth doesn't make a good story. Even if they did believe us, they'd probably insinuate that I bought your silence."

I stared at him in disbelief. "So we can convince them that we're dating but not that I puked in your toilet and then crashed on your couch? That's crazy!"

"Look, I don't make the rules. I pay the consequences when they aren't followed. So what do you say, Holly? Are you willing to be my fake girlfriend?"

Well, that was the million-dollar question.

Literally.

I eyed him cautiously. "I have some conditions."

"Of course you do. You couldn't just say, 'I really owe you

for last night, Nick. Sure, no problem.' Oh, no, you have *conditions*."

He said the last word as if it were toxic.

I folded my arms in silence.

"Fine, let's hear it."

My mind started whirring like an old computer getting rebooted. Even with provisions, what he was offering was insane. Turn me, Holly Dayton, into the temporary fake girlfriend of a rock star?

That was ridiculous!

And yet . . . Claire and Allison would never be able to make fun of my love life again if they thought I had even briefly dated Dominic Wyatt.

"You have to be crazy about me," I blurted out. "Head over heels, romantic comedy, love at first sight, crazy about me. And when we supposedly fizzle out it's not going to be because you lost interest. We'll say that while you miss me *terribly*, I felt it was getting too serious and broke things off. You'll probably need to observe a mourning period."

He stared at me. "You can't be serious."

"You want a girlfriend? Fine. I'll be the best fake girlfriend you've ever seen, but you have to treat me like a princess."

"A princess."

"Yeah, Nick. A princess. I know that it's stupid and petty and *small* of me to use you to make my cousins jealous but . . . I'm okay with that. If it gets my family members off my back even for the rest of this stupid cruise, then it'll be worth it."

"Is that it?" he demanded tersely. "I treat you like a princess *in public* and you'll be my fake girlfriend?"

"Not so fast. I'll also be moving into your suite." I held up my hand to cut off any protests. "I'm more than happy with the couch arrangement that we used last night. And it'll only help our cover."

"I'm trying to pass you off as my girlfriend, not sneak into a Russian military compound or infiltrate al-Qaeda."

"That's good; you wouldn't last a week in the CIA. I don't think their operatives are trained exclusively with pepper spray. And they can't get so bent out of shape over ugly shirts."

I swear, he growled at me. "Why can't you sleep in your own damn cabin?"

"Because my cousins also sleep there. Allison and Claire. You should probably remember their names since we're supposedly dating. And then there are the boys, Andrew and Jacob, but they're harmless."

"The two blondes didn't look that scary to me."

I did my best not to roll my eyes. "*Allison* and *Claire.* Just because you can't see the forked tongue doesn't mean they aren't snakes."

His smile was full of smug male arrogance. "I bet I could keep their tongues preoccupied."

"First of all: gross. Second, they're like Medusa, okay? You try to cut off one viper head and it'll just grow back. They're vicious. Which is why I want to avoid them and my aunt Jessica as much as possible."

"Hence staying in my suite."

I beamed at him. "You're catching on. Now we should probably discuss my birthday."

"Of course we should."

Nick looked tempted to stalk to the balcony and jump overboard when we heard an official-sounding knock on the door and a male voice boom, "Room service!" over the female pleas for attention.

He made no move to answer the door. "Do we have a deal or not?"

My heartbeat spiked to the steady *thwap, thwap, thwap* of helicopter rotor blades.

"We've got a deal."

"Just a second!" Nick yelled to the poor, besieged room service guy as he handed me a striped shirt from his dresser. It looked masculine and professional and perfectly appropriate for a rock star at a business meeting. "Open the door wearing this and smile for the cameras. Can you handle that?"

I nodded, then raced to the bathroom to swap shirts, impulsively deciding to leave two buttons open at the collar. Sexily disheveled. Excellent.

Showtime.

I opened the door, simultaneously calling out, "Nick, you've got fans at the door. Do you want to tell them about us, or should I?" Without waiting for a response, I gave the horror-stricken young crowd my warmest, most sympathetic smile. "I'm sorry, ladies, he's taken."

Then, grinning at the room service guy, I took the coffee and said, "Thanks, I think we're going to enjoy this in bed," before I slipped back into the suite.

I handed Nick a cup and braced for his critique. "So how'd I do?"

He gave me the once-over, taking in every detail of my admittedly bedraggled appearance.

"You'll pass."

Chapter 12

Dominic

The good news: She had agreed to go along with it. The bad news: She had agreed to go along with it.

Which meant that I was officially stuck with Holly Dayton until we docked in Los Angeles again. A situation she found considerably more appealing than I did, if the triumphant grin lighting up her face was any indication.

"That was so much fun! The first time when I didn't know they were there . . . that was terrifying, actually." Holly was buzzing high on adrenaline and she hadn't even taken a sip of her coffee. "But that was seriously fun!"

She was practically rubbing her hands together in glee. "What should we do for our next outing? Something couple-y, right? Maybe you should get me an ice cream cone or something." I half expected her to start twirling around my room. "This is so much bigger than making my cousins jealous! I can't believe I didn't figure that out earlier. I'm practically going to be a celebrity when I go back to school."

I crossed my arms and waited for her to calm down. "A celebrity. Sure. We should start prepping our story for the interviews."

"I mean it!" she insisted. "You have no idea what this

could mean for me! I could actually get invited to parties now. Jen and I might even become popular!" She ran over to my iPad. "We have to call her together. She won't believe me otherwise."

"Hold up," I ordered.

She didn't seem to hear me.

"Holly!"

Her head jerked up a fraction. "Uh, yeah?" she asked distractedly. "What's up?"

I walked over and reclaimed my iPad. "You can't tell her anything, Holly. Not yet. Not until we have our cover story and then we share exactly what we're telling the press."

This time she was entirely focused. "You expect me to lie to my best friend?"

"If you don't want everyone to find out that this romance isn't real. I'm not going to trust some strange girl to keep her mouth shut."

"Jen would never do anything to hurt me. Never."

"And while I'm sure the two of you have traded friendship bracelets, that isn't good enough for me."

"So Timothy Goff and Christopher . . . something-or-other get to know exactly what's going on, but *my* friends don't?"

"Forester, but we call him Chris. And, yeah, my friends get to know because their careers are on the line if you screw this up."

She stiffened. "Considering that I'm actually enjoying myself while you're being uptight in the extreme, I'd say you're more likely to make a mistake."

I bit back my retort that if it hadn't been for her intrusion I wouldn't have been faking a relationship.

"I'm an excellent actor." And to prove my point I looked right into her eyes and said seriously, "Holly, I've been crazy about you ever since I saw you at dinner, looking all wind-blown and tousled. You stole my breath away."

"Oh," she said. "But I thought you—"

"And . . . scene." I drank more of my coffee. "The press might be a little harder to fool, but I've got it under control. Now let's prep. How long have we been dating?"

She blinked and then focused on my question. "I'd guess a week or two, tops. Otherwise Jen and the media would probably already know about it."

"Let's go with a week. I can say that we met . . . in a bookstore."

She lifted an eyebrow. "A bookstore? Seriously?"

"What's wrong with it?"

"How often do *you* hang out in bookstores?"

"I almost forgot. I'm illiterate. I only go there to flip through the kids' books because of all the pretty pictures." I glared at her. "I like to read when the band is on tour, which is a lot of the time. What about you? Ever enter a bookstore?"

"Yes."

"Glad we got that cleared up. So we met in the bookstore and started talking about . . . books."

Holly nodded. "We can say that I couldn't reach my grandpa's Christmas present so I asked for your help."

Not a bad cover story, and it sounded realistically bland. We were just two people who had happened to meet in a bookstore. People meet that way all the time.

Probably.

At least more often that way than through breaking and entering.

"Okay," I said, picking up the thread of the narrative. "Right. So I asked you out."

"And I gave you my number and you called me the next day." She sighed and hugged her knees to her chest. "We could say you brought me flowers. Tulips."

Yeah, I wasn't a fan of that genius idea.

"Or we could not."

Her eyes narrowed. "Princess, remember."

"Trust me, I haven't forgotten your demands. But I'm not saying I brought you flowers for our first date. That's way too much."

"Yeah, we wouldn't want anyone thinking you could be nice," she said sarcastically. "Where's the fun in that?"

"I let you crash on my couch, remember?"

"Reluctantly. You let me crash there *reluctantly*."

It was true, but I thought I had done a decent job of hiding my irritation.

Apparently not.

"Let's focus on our story. We met up the next day and have been seeing each other ever since. So when you mentioned that your grandfather was taking you on a cruise, I was determined to come along."

"Okay, we don't want you to sound stalkery, though. Why don't we say that I thought this would be a good way for us to celebrate my birthday together and for you to meet the family?"

"Sure. When's your birthday?"

"Day after Christmas."

I did my best not to swear. "That's six days from now."

"Yep."

"That's not exactly giving me a lot of notice."

Holly tilted her head in mocking disbelief. "It's not exactly something I can move for your convenience."

True, but I didn't want to hear it.

"I'll figure something out. Who else do I have to meet? Mom? Dad? Give me the rundown."

Holly shrugged. "Neither."

"They don't like cruises?"

"The larger obstacle is that they're dead."

I winced. Great, I had pepper sprayed an *orphan*. Yeah, I really needed to find those puppies. Maybe attack a nun while I was at it.

"Uh, Holly, that, erm, sucks," I said awkwardly.

She smiled and though it wasn't a full-wattage grin it didn't look pained. "Look, they died in a car accident when I was a baby. It's not like I haven't had time to process it. Not a big deal. I've got my grandpa, so all things considered I'm pretty lucky."

I didn't have the faintest idea what I was supposed to say to that so I just nodded and kept my mouth shut.

"What about you?' Holly asked, as if the conversation had never steered into her parentless past. "Got parents?"

"Uh, yeah, two of them. Music teacher and florist. They're great."

She nodded. "So why aren't you spending the holidays with them?"

"Well, we try not to make too big a production out of Christmas. As long as I give them a call they understand if I can't necessarily visit. Our tour schedules aren't exactly flexible. This is my first vacation in I don't even know how long."

"And now you're stuck with me." Holly grimaced. "That's got to have really screwed up your plans."

"You mean turning this into a working holiday? Yeah, I'd been hoping to actually relax. Soak up some sun, maybe enjoy some diving in Cabo." I couldn't resist seeing if my next words would rattle her. I said I could act: best to get into the character of the fearless rock star before the cameras started rolling. "Chat up girls in low-cut dresses. Now *that's* a vacation."

Holly rolled her eyes as if she had expected no less from me. Damn judgmental of her really.

"Well, that makes complete sense to me."

I stared at Holly suspiciously—no way was she going to tell me she was on the cruise for the same thing. She didn't seem the type to enjoy a one-night stand. Holly would ask to use the shower the next morning and then try to make the bed. Oh, right. She'd already done that with me.

"Sunshine. Snorkeling. Sex. What's not to like?" I smirked.

"Oh, I agree. About all three of those activities, actually."

She couldn't be hitting on me. Holly Disaster could not be offering me vacation sex. I was reading into things that weren't really there, probably because I was operating on little to no sleep. Sure, Holly was enjoying our act more than I had ever expected, but she wouldn't try to make this *real*. No way.

She leaned back on the bed and stretched. "Sounds like a great way to spend a week on the Mexican Riviera."

Holy shit.

Then her grin widened. "Unfortunately, only two of the three are available to you."

"Sunshine and sex? Deal. Snorkeling is overrated."

Holly laughed and the sound was surprisingly musical, considering the racket she made in the shower.

"Sunshine and snorkeling are the *only* options on the table." She tucked her long strands of hair behind one ear uncomfortably. "As long as we're fauxmantically involved, neither of us can be caught hitting on other people."

She didn't have to warn me about the risks: I was the one who would get plastered all over magazines with the headline: ROCKSTAR BREAKS MORE HEARTS—THE TRUTH BEHIND HIS LIES!

"Fauxmantically involved? That's how you're putting it?"

"Sure, it's a fake romance: a fauxmance."

"Please tell me you're not one of those girls who connects celebrity names every time they so much as have lunch together."

She shook her head. "I have no idea what you're talking about. You mean how ReadySet fans created Chrisonic for you and—"

"You got me. I'm gay and Chris is my secret lover. How did you know?"

Her jaw dropped. "Seriously?"

"NO!"

Apparently, Holly was way too gullible for her own good, which only made the idea of teasing her all the more appealing.

So I merely nodded. "No other girls until you fake break things off," I promised and waited for her to take the expected breath of relief.

"Well, great! I'm glad we finally agree on something, Nick."

But I wasn't finished yet.

"As for sex, well, that's up to you."

Oh, yeah, I was rattling her. Really well.

Chapter 13

Holly

He had to be messing with me.
Unless the rock star was lowering his model standards . . .
because he was desperate. Oh, yeah, that idea was doing wonders for my self-esteem.

Unless . . . maybe he meant it in a reassuring *hey, if you don't want to have sex, I won't pressure you* kind of way. The two of us were about to share a suite, after all. Maybe he was trying to eliminate any potential awkward tension.

In which case, Nick had failed completely: I felt more comfortable crawling around the mall in my elf outfit than I did sitting on his bed at that moment.

Probably because of the intimidation factor in having this conversation with the drummer of one of the hottest bands in America. When I thought of him as *Dominic Wyatt: Grammy-winning artist,* yeah, I froze. So I had to keep mentally repeating that it was Nick. Just a guy I'd recently met who, despite his off-the-charts good looks, could also be kinda . . . awkward.

Sometimes.

Especially when I mentioned my parents' death and he started tripping over his words.

When he made sexual allusions probably intended to rattle me: not so much.

That's when I became the awkward one.

Still, I didn't want Nick to see how much his words had thrown me, or that I had actually considered having a strictly physical relationship with him for the rest of the cruise. Well, considered for about a nanosecond. Part of it sounded kind of . . . fun. A brief Christmas fling before I returned to my normally scheduled life. There was still a week left for me to be as wild as I wanted without having to worry that I'd run into him in the hallways of my high school.

But making sure that I didn't develop any feelings for Nick during our fauxmance would be hard enough without adding a physical component to it.

The weird part was that when he said having sex was up to me, I wasn't really thinking of doing it with *him*. Well, okay, yes, it would be *with* him. But he would just be the available means for losing my virginity so that I wouldn't have to deal with it anymore.

It might not sound too good, but honestly, sometimes being a virgin feels really stressful. So many people make sex out to be the single most important decision of your life, as if there's only a handful of "right" ways to lose it or you're automatically a slut. You can only do it after two months of dating, only after marriage, only if you would want to raise a baby, etc. And then there were all sorts of Exceptions to the Rules, like: It's not sex unless he's inside you.

Except, what?

I'm pretty sure that gay/lesbian/transgender/queer couples have sex too.

And the whole conversation gets so intense that getting really drunk and having a one-night stand just sounds . . . easier. Especially because if you don't do it *eventually,* people won't see you as someone who happens to enjoy living with felines but as a confirmed spinster cat lady.

So, yeah, for a nanosecond I considered saying something incredibly stupid like, "If we both agree never to speak of this again . . . I'm in."

Thankfully, my brain kicked in faster than my hormones.

"Thanks, but I'll pass." I smiled to mask my discomfort. "So do you think we're ready for the interview?"

"Actually, yes. So if you just follow my lead, we should be fine." Nick scrolled through his Skype contacts and settled on Kate Hamilton, *People* magazine.

Two rings later it was showtime.

"Hi, Kate!" Nick flashed her a grin, which was clearly meant to be charming. Actually, it was pretty damn charming.

Which was straight-up unfair.

"Hey, yourself! So what's this I hear about a new girl, Dominic? I thought you were pining after me."

He laughed and pawed uncomfortably at his hair, which only made it look even more disheveled. I didn't think that was the look he was going for, though. "You'll always be the one that got away, Kate. But I'd like you to meet Holly Dayton."

He turned the iPad toward me as I snuggled in closer and waved. "Hi, Kate, it's nice to meet you!"

The woman filling up the screen looked to be in her late twenties and was polished to a glossy Hollywood sheen. Her hair was tied back in a chic chignon, which emphasized her enormous brown eyes and her bronzed skin. Kate looked effortlessly stylish while I looked like I spent the night puking and bawling my eyes out.

Great.

She swiftly studied my bedraggled appearance but she didn't comment on it. Maybe because I was wearing Nick's shirt and he had slung his arm around my shoulder to pull me against him. The two of us were obviously together.

Or at least we were obviously pretending to be together.

"So when did this happen?" Kate beamed, but there was

something feral in the look, as if she couldn't wait to post a scathing story about our torrid affair all over the Internet.

"We met in a bookstore," I replied before Nick could open his mouth. "Nick here helped me reach the novel I was interested in."

"Nick?" Kate repeated. "That's a cute nickname."

I plastered a besotted look on my face. "I wanted to have something between us that was, you know, special."

"And what does *Nick* call you?"

"Holly Disaster," he replied smoothly, taking over. "Every now and then I'll call her Holly-day."

I wasn't sure where those nicknames had come from, but I wished that he could take them back. I've had teachers cracking stupid "happy *holly-day*" jokes since *elementary school*.

They get old. Fast. Not that being called Holly Disaster was any better.

I couldn't let my annoyance show, so I just smiled sweetly for the camera . . . and discreetly pinched his side.

"How long have you two been dating?"

"Coming up on two weeks together." Nick's smile broadened. "We couldn't be happier."

"That's not long to be taking your romance abroad."

"I've been spending all my time with the band lately, so when Holly told me about this cruise we thought it would be a great way to relax and spend some time together."

"And it's my birthday soon," I added. "We wanted to celebrate that together too."

He nudged me with his knee to get me to shut up. I just ignored him.

"Are the two of you doing anything special to celebrate?"

"Nick won't tell me. He wants it to be a surprise."

I could tell that Nick wanted to glare at me from the way his smile stiffened as if he was fighting with himself to keep it in place. "Well, Holly is so full of surprises, I thought it'd be fun to turn the tables on her."

Oh, boy, I was going to be in big trouble later.

"And has your family met Dominic yet, Holly?"

"Not yet. We were hoping to delay the introductions for another day or two."

"And how do you think they are going to react to the news?"

I laughed. "Honestly? I'm not sure. My grandpa will probably worry that Nick isn't good enough for me."

Kate laughed too hard, as if I had told a *hilarious* joke by even suggesting that I could do any better than a rock star. "So, Dominic, are you good enough for her?"

He looked down at me, as if soaking in every detail, from the dusting of freckles across my nose to the exact green tint of my eyes. "I have no idea what I ever did to deserve her."

Only the two of us knew he didn't mean it as a compliment.

"Do either of you want to comment on the rumors that Dominic has also been dating"—Kate glanced down to look at some papers scattered across her desk—"Cynthia Ridgley?"

Nick shook his head. "It's a lie, Kate. She's just a kid who doesn't deserve the media making up stuff about her. Not to mention, I'm only interested in Holly."

"And, Holly, there are some, ahem, alarming photos of the two of you where Dominic looks quite angry. Can you comment on the rumors that Dominic is abusive?"

I felt the tension radiating off Nick as his muscles tightened reflexively.

"I think that whoever is spreading those rumors is a pitiful excuse for a human being. Nick is an incredible boyfriend! Do you want to know what he did last night?"

"Holly." Nick tried to cut me off. "You don't need t—"

"I was seasick," I informed Kate. "My face was sheet white and I looked like a zombie."

Kate chuckled indulgently. "I'm sure it wasn't that bad."

"No, I honestly looked like a zombie and I felt even worse. But Nick wasn't even fazed. He helped me right through the worst of it. *That's* the kind of guy he is."

I tried to do the whole googly-eyes-of-love thing, to sell the act, and found myself seeing him a little bit differently. His dark brown bangs flopped across his forehead appealingly, while tufts stuck up in back, and the beginnings of a real smile tilted his lips into a smirk. He looked the same as he had fifteen minutes ago. But while I gave him a glowing boyfriend review, I could almost forget his tendency to be arrogant and uptight. And that he was overprotective of ugly Hawaiian-print shirts.

Yeah, real Prince Charming material.

Not.

"Well, I'll leave you two lovebirds alone then."

That snapped me back to reality. We were done. And from the sound of it, I had passed muster once again. Being a celebrity was even easier than it looked!

"We appreciate that. Always good talking with you, Kate."

"It was nice meeting you," I added politely.

She smiled distractedly as her fingers appeared to fly lightly across her keyboard. The action didn't take anything away from her polished sheen.

"Nice meeting you too, Holly. And happy birthday! I can't wait to hear all about Dominic's surprise for you."

And with that she disconnected.

"A birthday surprise." Nick instantly unwrapped his arm from across my shoulder. "I can't believe you roped me into that."

"Well . . . surprise!"

He just kept glaring at me.

"Princess, Nick. Just for a week. In private you can call me a pain in the ass, although for the record, I just nailed that interview. I mean, you should be *thanking* me right now for even going along with this plan. I'm going to be the best girlfriend you've never had, and in return, for just one week, I want the rock star experience."

"So you want me to throw you some big, over-the-top party."

"I want something special, and I don't want you to skimp. But if you want, I can return whatever gift you get me when we end our fauxmance."

He looked appalled. "So I have to throw you a party *and* buy you something."

"Well . . . yeah. That's what a devoted rock star would probably do for his girlfriend, right? Something extravagant. And when we go our separate ways, I'll hand it right back. You can give it to your mom as a belated Christmas present if you want. I'm not after your money."

"No, you just want to take advantage of my fame."

The truth stung but I refused to be ashamed of it. "And you want to take advantage of my wholesome, good-girl image. We're both after something. I'm just being straightforward about it."

"A birthday party," he repeated. "I don't like it."

"Tough."

He grimaced. "I'm hungry. Let's get some food."

Then without waiting for a response, he laced his fingers through mine, unlocked the door, pulled it open, and started flat-out running with me down the long hallway toward the elevators. I ignored the way the action made my stomach churn angrily as we kept our heads down and barreled through the screaming fan girls. We sprinted down two flights and a long hallway before we risked taking an elevator up to the Lido deck.

I was out of breath and panting heavily by the time we finally slowed down. No wonder the Hollywood starlets were so thin. Being chased by fans was one hell of a workout, especially for a girl whose lingering seasickness refused to leave.

Still . . . all things considered, life was starting to look up.

Chapter 14

Dominic

Okay, so maybe she wasn't as naïve and gullible as I had originally thought.

She was devious.

The girl had somehow conned her way into throwing herself a surprise birthday party. Oh, and somehow I had agreed to picking up the tab for both the celebration and an exorbitant gift.

She wasn't just a wind-tousled mess with a weird aversion to pie like I had thought last night in the dining room. Oh, no. She was a conniving, wannabe princess, set on destroying my life. Possibly with a weird aversion to pie.

But even clutching at her stomach and gasping for breath, Holly managed to be all smiles when we slowed to a casual stroll on the deck. "That was fun! A little intense with the running, but I don't know why you rock stars make such a big deal out of it. Those fan girls were just a little excited, that's all."

"Trust me, the fun wears off." I headed straight for one of the outdoor breakfast buffets and started plating some scrambled eggs and bacon. Holly tentatively picked up a plate of her own and slid a few pieces of fruit on it. Apparently, she still hadn't gotten her sea legs yet.

"I don't believe it. Only someone who has never been a geek could get tired of being called awesome! Most people dream of becoming a celebrity for exactly that reason!"

Right on cue, a group of giggling tween girls glanced at me, then their cell phones, before gasping loudly. The news that I was on board must have already spread. Well, the sooner people got used to seeing me eating and relaxing like a normal person, the sooner they would stop screaming at me. I just had to wait for the thrill of a celebrity sighting to fade. By that time, I'd probably be back in LA.

"Oh, my God! It's totally Dominic Wyatt! You're right!" one of the girls squealed to the others. "I'm going to go talk to him."

That's when the other girls screeched that she couldn't just walk up and *talk* to a rock star. What would she say? What did she think I would say back? And *ohmigod this is the coolest thing ever to happen in the history of cruises!*

None of the girls seemed to notice that the guy in question, me, was standing right there, listening to everything they said while growing increasingly uncomfortable.

Not that Holly noticed any of it.

She dropped a piece of pineapple on my plate and whispered, "Those girls are obviously thrilled to see you. Isn't that cool?"

So she wasn't completely oblivious . . . she just had no idea what life was really like in the spotlight. I was tempted to try and shield her, but even after our fake breakup she would have to deal with it. She ought to be as prepared as possible.

Plus, I wanted to see how long this cheery, upbeat version of Holly would last. I had a feeling that pretty soon she would morph back into the snarky girl who was miffed about being mistaken for a zombie.

"I've got twenty bucks that says in under an hour you'll change your mind about life as a celebrity."

She nodded. "You're on."

The bravest girl in the tween group sauntered over and started shaking my hand formally, as if we had just finalized the details of a new contract. She didn't say a word.

"What's your name?" I asked nicely, wondering if maybe I had bet Holly a little prematurely. I was expecting the fan to be bratty, not speechless.

"L-Laura," she stuttered.

"Laura," I repeated and she blushed crimson.

"Laura Brimsyk."

"Well, it's nice to meet you, Laura. I'm Dominic."

She let out a high, keening giggle then instantly looked appalled that such a noise had come from her. I had expected it. Normal people have a tendency to do strange things when they meet a celebrity, even people who are positive that they won't be fazed. I always have to pretend like it's completely natural for girls to start tittering hysterically until they are unable to form complete sentences . . . because that's part of the job. I have to maintain the cool rock star image. No matter how much the squealing creeps me out, I'm supposed to absorb it with a complacent smile.

"This is my girlfriend, Holly."

"Hi, Laura. It's nice to meet you." Holly extended her arm for a handshake of her own, but it didn't look like Laura was interested in taking her up on the offer. Laura looked horrified.

I leaned back against the counter and started mentally counting.

One.

"But you don't . . ."

Two.

"But I thought . . ."

Three.

Laura collected herself enough to give Holly a slow once-over, before she sent me a dazzling smile. "You can do way better, Dominic."

"Hey!" Holly didn't find my young fan's attention cute anymore. "I'm standing right here!"

"So?" Laura dismissed her with a flap of her hand. "It's pretty obvious that you're not exactly a ten. You're more like a three trying to pass herself off as a four."

Holly flushed in indignation and I relaxed, waiting for the fireworks.

There was something about seeing Holly's hands fly to her hips that was distinctly appealing. Laura had definitely under-estimated her.

"I don't use *numbers* to rank people. I'll leave pettiness like that to you and your little friends." Holly hastily propelled one of my arms around her waist, so that her body was pressed against mine. It felt damn good, actually. "My *boyfriend* and I were enjoying ourselves before you came along."

Laura's face crumpled when I merely nodded and ran my hand through the ends of Holly's long, silky hair. I don't know what Laura was expecting, since insulting a rock star's girl-friend is never a smart way to promote yourself. Still, she stiffened her spine and struck a pose.

"You really can do better, Dominic. My friends and I will be right over there if you decide to start trading up."

Then she sauntered away with Holly's mouth dangling open in outraged disbelief.

"Can you believe that?" she demanded. "I mean, she just waltzed over here and told you to dump me. After I was so nice to her too!"

"Yeah, it was almost like she wanted me for herself."

Holly stabbed her fork into a slice of pineapple. "Okay, well . . . she sucks."

"She sucks or being a celebrity does?"

Holly considered that as she ate. "No. Just her."

"I have a feeling you'll change your mind when all of their unflattering photos of you hit the Internet. Especially when they start comparing you to previous girlfriends."

"Who was your last girlfriend?" Holly asked curiously.

"I went on a few dates with Taylor Swift. Nothing serious." I shrugged. "We're still good friends."

Holly choked on her omelet. "Taylor Swift! As in the Grammy winner. The CoverGirl. The *SNL* host. Seriously? She was your last girlfriend?"

I merely smiled. "That's what the press thinks."

She narrowed her eyes at me. "Was that another fauxmance? I have trouble seeing the two of you together for real."

"Because she's so nice and I'm not."

"Well . . . yeah."

"Thanks."

"You're welcome. So was it?"

If she thought I was arrogant already I might as well play the part. "It was real but not serious. No girls have ever faked anything with me."

She snorted in disbelief. "So you only pretend to be in relationships with *some* girls. Interesting."

"And you only illegally break and enter into *some* rooms. Interesting."

This time she reddened and took another bite of fruit. "Shut up."

"So you plan on admitting that you lost the bet?"

Her eyes widened and she grabbed my sleeve. "My cousins are coming. Shut up and hide!"

All of which she said while yanking on my arm as she tried dragging me across the deck, apologizing to strangers the whole time.

"Excuse me! Sorry! Coming through!" She neatly dodged a little kid only to pull up short so as not to crash into a waiter.

"Why are we running?" I demanded, putting on the brakes. She tried tugging on me harder, but I don't move unless I want to go somewhere. And I wanted to resume eating my breakfast. "I thought you wanted to make them jealous."

"Of course I do! It's just . . . who am I kidding? I can't pull this off. We'll have to tell everyone the truth. I'm so sorry, I just can't—"

Holly's cousins might scare the crap out of her, but she couldn't have a panic attack and bail on our arrangement. Not after our *People* interview. Not ever.

So while I felt confident that I could deal with her relatives once she calmed down, her timing couldn't have been worse to lose her head. We were attracting a crowd that *wasn't* made up of squealing teenagers.

The paparazzi.

Shit.

How had they had found us so quickly? We hadn't docked at a single port of call and nobody had even known about my travel plans. Nobody . . . except Mr. Ridgley and Cynthia. Which explained a lot of things, like that picture of the three of us having dinner. Except there hadn't been paparazzi outside the door this morning, only screaming girls. Maybe Mr. Ridgley had told them to lay low for a while?

I didn't have time to puzzle it out. Whether or not Holly knew it, we were surrounded and it was way too late for her to back out. The paparazzi wanted their "happy couple" shot, and it was my job to see that they got it. Any photos of Holly freaking out had the potential to bury the sound track project—and then Tim and Chris would attack me with canned soup. I had to shut her up.

So I did what any normal guy would do in my situation.

I kissed her.

Chapter 15

Holly

I had to tell everyone the truth.

Sure, when the two of us had been back in the suite, I thought I could handle it. I just kept telling myself to grab this golden opportunity to become someone popular. I even tried a few pep talks by reminding myself that Jen would look at it as a starring role. Then again, Jen is one of those LA kids who keeps hoping that she'll be "discovered" by a talent agent while eating dinner. She would be all for this ruse.

But as much as I wanted to view this as my chance to deliver Oscar-level material, the whole thing sort of . . . scared me. Especially when the fan girls were not safely on the other side of a locked door and could call me worthless to my face. I hadn't prepared my ego for that kind of a beating.

Our story was supposed to be sweet. The rock star and the average girl: That's how it was supposed to play out to the press, and I thought I could handle it. Except I didn't want to be seen as too ordinary and dull and generally uninteresting for anyone.

It was all just too much.

And that fact came into focus when I spotted Allison and

Claire sauntering toward the pool right behind us, wearing two flimsy-looking bikinis that flaunted their considerable assets. If one snot-nosed brat could make me feel crappy, then my self-esteem didn't stand a chance against my cousins. They would take one look at me wearing Nick's striped dress shirt and make some comment, like, *God, Holly! Just because your stuff is hideous doesn't mean you should beg for other people's clothes. Pathetic much?*

Dominic Wyatt might need a way to clean up his image—but I, Holly Dayton, wasn't the solution.

Something I might have been able to convince him of if he hadn't decided to become impossible to budge. Which left me babbling in the hope that something would stick and he would agree to head for the hills . . . or back to his suite. That was the only way to prevent my cousins from making it their mission to destroy me for messing up Allison's holiday fling.

But Nick didn't appear to be paying any attention to me. Instead, he was eyeing the people milling around us on deck with a mixture of horror and dread. I had no time to ask what was wrong since the Twins from Hell were aiming right for us and approaching fast.

Time had run out: We had to tell everyone the truth.

"I'm so sorry," I told Nick, meaning every word of it, "I just can't—"

I never finished that sentence because he kissed me.

He gave a quick tug on my arm so that we were smooshed against each other as he pressed his lips against mine. The guy clearly had way more experience in the kissing department than I did. Either that or he was naturally quite skilled.

But unlike in all the romance novels Jen has loaned me, my brain did not go beautifully blank as music swelled. Instead, one all-consuming thought reverberated through my mind:

What the hell?

Was he kissing me to throw my cousins off our scent?

Maybe he just wanted to shut me up. Or could he actually be lip-locked with me because his ardent passion could not be restrained a moment longer?

I had a hard time buying that last theory.

Moving my head slightly back, I opened my mouth to demand some answers.

Except this time I found his tongue in my mouth.

Which wasn't exactly an unpleasant sensation. In fact, the parts of me that were supposed to go all melty went as soft as a Hershey's chocolate bar left in a warm pocket all day. My eyes closed on their own accord, but I could have sworn I saw fireworks. I wanted to wrap my arms around him even tighter while one hand rumpled the tufts of his dark brown hair even more.

I might have even done it . . . if I hadn't heard the cheering.

"That's right, Dominic! Kiss her!"

"Turn this way!"

"Dominic! Who's the girl?"

And finally a scandalized voice I did recognize:

"Holly?"

Hearing Claire's evident disbelief was the fastest way to cool me down short of shoving me overboard. But separating from Nick to discover that we were surrounded by paparazzi busily snapping photos . . . that had me feeling downright chilly.

Dominic Wyatt had played me.

He had known about the press and started that *display* for them. It had nothing to do with me. Nick had probably been pretending the kiss was with someone else too.

But I couldn't haul off and slap him without riling up the photographers even more.

Part of it was my fault. I should have asked Nick about our public displays of affection to sell the story instead of just assuming it would be limited to hand-holding, cuddling, and a few pecks on the cheek. I should have forced myself to ask all the awkward questions. Although I doubted any conversation would have prevented me from feeling like a wad of used Kleenex afterward.

But even worse than knowing I'd been tricked into having my first major Frenching session plastered in magazines was that it had been . . . amazing.

Sure, I still wanted to haul off and slug Nick for using me, but picking up where we left off held a lot of appeal too.

Maybe boy-related recklessness and stupidity was a family trait I shared with my cousins.

Leaning in toward Nick, I whispered in his ear, *"What the hell was that?"*

He laughed as if I had made some clever inside joke, then tucked a strand of hair behind my ear. I swear the crowd watching us "aww"ed as he muttered softly, "Follow my lead, Holly. And keep your big mouth shut."

Yeah, he was romantic all right . . . as romantic as the bubonic plague.

Still, at least his plan had succeeded in making my cousins jealous. They were still staring at us in absolute shock when Nick casually strolled the few feet between us.

The guy was playing the part of the unflappable rock star to perfection.

"Allison and Claire, right?" I thought I detected something slightly wicked flash in his blue eyes. "Holly has told me so much about you."

"Uh, but, um," Allison said stupidly, before she caught herself. "That's funny, Holly has never mentioned you before." She tossed her hair back so that it cascaded beautifully over toned shoulders as she gave him her most seductive smile. "I would remember."

My stomach lurched and once again I didn't know if it was because of the stress of the situation or because of the ship. If my grandpa ever invited me on another cruise, I planned on politely but firmly refusing him. Vomiting in front of the press was the last thing I wanted to do.

"We both wanted to keep our relationship private at first."

It was a fine answer, but I awkwardly cleared my throat and was about to excuse myself, when he pulled me against him even more tightly. I could practically hear him thinking, *Just keep your mouth shut for once!*

The two of us were going to have a long conversation back in the suite.

"I'd like to join the family for dinner," Nick continued. "One of these nights."

Now that wasn't the best idea. My grandpa can be a bit . . . gruff. I wasn't kidding when I told Kate Hamilton that he probably wouldn't consider Nick good enough for me. Age hadn't done anything to diminish his mile-wide protective streak.

So joining us for dinner probably wouldn't go the way Nick anticipated, although I couldn't help admiring the bold move. Especially since he was making my cousins believe that he was absolutely crazy about me. Nick was definitely trying to live up to his end of the bargain in making me feel like a princess. Not even the prospect of lying to my grandpa could destroy my excitement at finally being chosen above my cousins.

Even if I had inadvertently rigged the competition.

"Of course we don't mind," Allison replied smoothly. "We have so many stories about Holly that you are going to *love*. Why, just last week she—"

"Why don't we save those for later? Nick and I need to finish breakfast, and you're losing prime tanning time talking to us." Somehow I managed to maintain my fakest smile as I gripped Nick's waist even more tightly.

"It was great meeting you both. I'm sure we'll be seeing each other soon."

Apparently, Dominic Wyatt was fully capable of being polite around everyone else in the known universe except me.

But at least this time he took my hand in his as we walked back to our table where he resumed eating. Sipping at a glass of orange juice was about all I thought my stomach could handle—even now that the photographers seemed willing to give us some space. I think most of them were already sending their photos, hoping that would give them an edge in securing the front page. Thinking about that kiss still made me want to smack Nick. Hard.

"We need to talk."

Nick glanced up at me, but didn't stop eating. "Why is that?"

"Because we need to set some ground rules."

He leaned in toward me. "As long as you don't have another panic attack and threaten to tell everyone the truth, we should be fine."

"I was actually referring to you sticking your tongue in my mouth."

I was sure there was a better way to phrase it, but at the moment that was all that came to mind. Well, sort of. I wasn't going to tell him just how much I had found myself liking it. Because kissing was *way* out of bounds for us. I had agreed to be his fake girlfriend, not a make-out buddy for whenever he felt like it.

I'm nobody's plaything.

"It shut you up," Nick said smugly. "So I'd say it worked."

"Way out of line."

"Just as unacceptable as what you were about to do." He shrugged. "Desperate times call for desperate measures."

"Well, it's *not* going to happen again."

Which really sucked because Nick was an excellent kisser. If it hadn't been for his complete lack of actual interest in me, I would have enjoyed making out with him for the remainder of the cruise. Too bad I'm not good at forgetting important details.

"Actually, it is going to happen frequently."

Well, that got my back up fast.

"No, it isn't."

"Holly, we're playing a role. And this particular role requires kissing and romping in the surf. No one will believe it if we don't."

"We could always tell them the truth!"

He groaned and stabbed at a bit of egg on his plate. "You keep saying that as if it were an option. We're both in too deep to tell anyone what happened last night. Even if the press did believe us, they'd skewer us for lying. And ReadySet could say good-bye to our spotless reputation. I'm not going to let that happen."

"I'm just . . . not sure I'm the right girl for this job, okay?"

"You're the *only* girl available." He eyed me contemplatively. "Would it be easier if I hired you?"

I'm pretty sure my mouth fell open. "If you *what?*"

"Hired you."

"Like a prostitute?" I asked, mentally shooting fireballs at him.

"Worse." He grinned. "Like a publicist."

That surprised a laugh out of me. "How would that help?"

"As a ReadySet employee you'd get a nice Christmas bonus if it works."

"I meant it when I said I wasn't in our fauxmance for the money."

"I still think that word sounds stupid. And I know: You were in it for the fame. But now that you realize not all of the celebrity package is glamorous, I thought you might need a bigger incentive."

"So you're trying to buy me off?"

He rolled his eyes. "It's not like I'm a mafioso trying to

throw an election here. I'd be giving you a small stipend to pretend to like me."

"Wow. That's pretty degrading for you, isn't it?"

He glared at me but didn't say anything.

"I mean, Mr. Ladies Man has to pay little ol' me for a kiss. I'd find that pretty embarrassing."

"Shut up, Holly."

"Sorry, the stipend doesn't cover that."

"Fine, I take the offer back. I was trying to make this easier on you since you are every bit as locked into this nightmare as I am. But forget it."

He had a point. I mean, my cousins knew about him now. If I told the truth they would mock me mercilessly about it for the rest of my life. Literally. I could picture them holding up their wineglasses at my wedding and saying something nasty like, "We never thought this day would come! When Holly said that she had met a wonderful man, we assumed he was forced into pretending to like her. Again. Anyhow let's raise our glass to the fake bride and her pretend husband!"

Maybe I should consider eloping.

I set down my empty glass and reached for his hand. "I'm feeling a bit queasy. Let's go back to the suite and negotiate the terms."

He seemed to take this small act of PDA as a signal of my capitulation.

Except he wasn't looking nearly so self-satisfied when I whispered, "Your publicist has all sorts of ideas for her surprise birthday party."

Score.

Chapter 16

Dominic

For a girl who only moments before had been approaching a full-blown panic attack, she had quickly adjusted to the idea of being on my payroll.

Not that I was surprised. The first rule of Hollywood is that money talks. You can have a fantastic product, but if nobody is willing to spend the big bucks, you've got nothing. In my case, the value of the product would increase if the scent of a scandal decreased. Otherwise my two best friends would happily kick my ass all the way back to Mexico.

Tim, Chris, and I weren't interested in becoming a band where people think, "Oh yeah, *them*. They were really big for, like, a minute. I wonder whatever happened after the drummer got caught roughing up some girl in his room...."

I couldn't let that happen.

So if Holly needed a monetary incentive, that was fine by me. Most of it would probably have to be spent updating her look anyway. Not that she didn't look good in my shirt with her tousled dirty-blond hair almost obscuring the collar. In fact, she looked downright hot. But slathering on the goop and the products would go a long way toward making her more acceptable to the public.

Whether she wanted it or not, I would have to supplement her wardrobe. And if the photographers happened to see me tilt a sunhat on her head for better access to her lips, well, that would just be an added bonus.

I had every intention of kissing Holly again. Repeatedly. Sure, I had done it on the deck primarily to shut her up and give the press their photo op, but I had also enjoyed it. Holly might be a walking disaster, but when her body was pressed against mine, that didn't bother me too much.

My vacation was finally looking up. A few make-out sessions on the beach, holding hands, frolicking in the waves, and then returning to the suite where I could write lyrics and Holly could . . . do whatever she wanted. All we had to do was keep things light and casual.

But judging by Holly's determined expression when she mentioned her birthday party, she wasn't going to make anything easy for me.

Still, I hadn't expected her to haul off and slug me as soon as we were alone in the suite.

"Ow! What the hell was that for?"

"That was for the uninvited oral assault."

I did a quick translation from crazy talk to normal-people speak. "For the kiss?"

"Yes!"

"Really." I settled myself lazily in one of the large sofa chairs. "Interesting. You seemed to be enjoying it. I think you might have moaned."

The glare she shot me should have been deadly. Except her hands landed on her hips again and she looked more cute than ferocious. Then again, maybe I shouldn't have smiled. The girl really did have a good left jab.

"I did not moan," she said evenly.

"No, I guess it was more of a whimper."

Her hands clenched and then after a tense moment she relaxed them. If my mother could see me right now she would have smacked me upside the head and said something about "raising me better." But I couldn't resist, especially since Holly always tried her damnedest to give as good as she got.

"There was no moaning, whimpering, or breathless sighing, and furthermore—"

"You sure about the breathless sighing?" I interrupted. "I could have sworn—"

"You were mistaken. I'm also accepting your offer to make me a publicist."

"That was taken off the table."

"Now that I've accepted, it's back on. And as your publicist I get to decide when, where, and how we turn this fauxmance of ours into media fodder. Got it?"

Maybe she would do better in Hollywood than I'd originally thought. With the exception of her cousins, she didn't let herself get bullied or settle for anything less than what she wanted. She would probably love interning with a real publicist since it would allow her to boss people around. She already enjoyed telling me what to do.

I crossed my arms. "The kissing is nonnegotiable. We need to sell the act, and there is no way that two people, in the beginning of a relationship, on a tropical vacation, wouldn't make out in public."

She seemed to consider this. "Fine. We can kiss."

Her words hit me like a shot of espresso.

"With some requirements. One: All kissing must be for the cameras only. Two: Both parties must be fully aware of the situation at all times. Three: All kissing must be—"

"Under twenty seconds in duration," I interrupted mockingly.

"No, but that's a good one. As I was *saying,* all kissing must be—"

But I didn't let her finish that time either. "This is ridiculous. We'll kiss when we need to kiss to protect our cover."

She shot me a stern gaze that had angry elementary school

teacher written all over it. "If I ever feel like you're using me I will make that punch earlier look like a love tap. I'm a publicist, not a prostitute. Are we clear?"

"Clear."

"Good. I want a signed ReadySet poster."

"And . . ." I prompted, waiting for the demands to start pouring in.

"Well, I'd really like to meet Tim, but I know our fake breakup might complicate that so . . . yeah, I really want that poster."

I grabbed one of the cruise ship pens and pulled out a band picture from my backpack—I never travel without a few just in case I need something to distract our fans—then I hastily scrawled my name across it.

"Here you go."

She took it from me but she didn't exactly look thrilled. "This isn't what I had in mind."

"You said signed." I shrugged. "It's signed."

"Yeah, but you don't really count."

I raised an eyebrow. "I'm the drummer. Since when does that not count as being part of the band? I've got a Grammy sitting on my shelf at home to prove it."

"Maybe if we had met under different circumstances you would count," she said thoughtfully. "If you hadn't pepper sprayed me and then acted like a crotchety old man, for example. But now you're not *Dominic Wyatt*, you're Nick. It's hard for me to get all excited about having it signed by a celebrity when it's you."

I leaned back against the headboard, insulted even though I should have felt relieved. I hate it when girls keep stuttering, or cooing, or gasping, or whatever noises they make, when they come within fifteen feet of the band. Tim might get the brunt of the attention but Chris and I experienced more than enough.

But here was Holly, a girl who had only been at a loss for

words once when I had mistaken her for a zombie . . . and she didn't think I counted.

It rankled me since she so obviously had a thing for my best friend. It was only a matter of time before she started asking if Tim happened to be involved with anyone. That was one question I wasn't at liberty to answer. As far as fodder for tabloids, getting caught with a girl in my room was *nothing* in comparison to coming out of the closet. It was stupid that anyone cared about Tim's relationship status . . . or would withhold a job because of it. But homosexuality wasn't part of the image that the entertainment industry wanted to promote—not when we appealed to such a large tween-age demographic. We needed to be good, clean, heterosexual, all-American boys who also happened to rock.

That, more than anything, infuriated me.

Chris and I had told Tim during at least fifteen band meetings that we would fully support him if he decided to come out. We would join him on the *Ellen DeGeneres Show* for moral support—whatever he needed: We'd be there.

Tim might prefer keeping his private life, well . . . private, but it wouldn't take much to uncover that Timothy Goff was dating Corey O'Neal, currently a student at Smith High School in Forest Grove, Oregon.

I was surprised it had remained a secret for over two weeks, actually.

But since Tim wanted to wait for the right time to come out—although he never explained when this "right time" might be—Chris and I had developed a "no comment" policy that involved wide grins, expansive shrugs, and keeping our mouths shut.

So it should have been amusing that Holly had a thing for the one member of ReadySet who plays for the other team. But I didn't exactly enjoy being told that I "didn't count" as a rock star.

Or being compared to a crotchety old man.

"I'll get Tim and Chris to sign it before I mail it to you. Now is that all?"

She nodded and then her expression turned thoughtful. "Actually, I have one last stipulation: You can't leave me alone with my family. I came way too close to stabbing my aunt with a fork last night and . . . I could just really use a friend in the trenches. So lunches, dinners, excursions—if I have to be there then so do you."

"I have no problem with that. Your cousins were very *friendly*."

"You make a move and so help me—"

It was fun watching her get riled up all over again.

"Relax. I'm not going to do anything . . . much."

She narrowed her eyes. "Let's talk about my birthday instead, shall we? I'm thinking we go all out. Diamonds. Emeralds. Sapphires. What's the going rate for a rock star's fake girlfriend?"

I hoped she was kidding.

"Yeah, that's not happening." I started walking her toward the door. "You need to get the rest of your stuff before we try to make you look, uh—"

She glowered at me. "Care to finish that thought?"

Not particularly. My life would be so much easier with Tim's ability to charm people.

"Better. More . . . polished. I'll even pick up some . . . girl products for you. While you grab your suitcase."

God, I would much rather face Tim's and Chris's punishment for screwing up their holiday plans, than spend my time shopping for Holly. But if I didn't buy the junk, I doubted Holly would. When it comes to making sure everything gets done, it's often best to handle it yourself.

She did a classic double take. "You're going to *what?*"

"I'll grab mascara and . . . stuff."

Damn, that was painful to say.

"*You* plan on buying *me* mascara?"

I raised an eyebrow skeptically. "Did you bring any with you?"

"Well . . . no."

"Okay, then. I'll do it."

Hell.

"Seriously?" She burst out laughing. "I'm sorry, you should see your face right now."

"Look, just get your suitcase, all right?"

"Sure." Her grin was out in full force again. "I wouldn't dream of keeping you from your shopping."

And with that, she left.

Damn nuisance.

Chapter 17

Holly

He was buying makeup for me.

I probably shouldn't have laughed in his face, but judging by his disgust you'd think he had just volunteered to bathe with flesh-eating snails. America's favorite rock star drummer was about to buy me *girl stuff*.

Hilarious, especially the way he scowled at the thought.

It was also really cute.

Or it would have been if his motivation hadn't been strictly work-related. Given that his exes were all glamorous singers and actresses, he needed to convince people that I was pretty enough to meet his normal standards.

Nothing cute about buying someone makeup because she's too plain without cosmetics.

Still, he was right about one thing: I did need to move my stuff into the suite.

But when I slid the key card into the lock on Allison and Claire's door, the room looked completely different—and not because I'd been so seasick last night that I couldn't remember it properly. My stuff was sprawled everywhere: clothes strewn under the bed, on the desk, even crumpled in the bathroom. If I hadn't taken my sketchpad with me in my backpack it would probably have *LOSER* carved into the cover.

With relatives like mine, who needs enemies?

They had been thoughtful enough to leave a note on my cot, right on top of some of my underwear.

> *Hey, Annie,*
> *You really shouldn't leave your crap lying*
> *around for people to trip over. And since you*
> *acted like such a bitch last night, we don't want*
> *you coming back. We've actually got social*
> *lives. Unlike you. Tell Grandpa anything about*
> *this and everyone will know about Santa's*
> *sluttiest little helper.*
> *Merry Christmas, loser.*

Okay, that was so not what I'd been expecting. Maybe I should have anticipated it. After all, Allison and Claire were probably lounging on the chairs by the pool, trying to come up with new ways to torture me while guys of all ages scoped them out.

Still, it would have been amazing to wheel away my suitcase with a casual parting remark like, "I'm staying with my rock star boyfriend. Enjoy the space, ladies."

I bet Cinderella never had to deal with this before her happily ever after. No motion sickness in her pumpkin coach, and her prince probably sent servants to retrieve her belongings from her wicked stepfamily's house. Then again, she wasn't faking the whole thing in an attempt to become popular.

Still, was it too much to ask that I feel like a princess for a little while?

Apparently.

I scooped up handfuls of clothing and crammed it all back into my suitcase, feeling as crappy as Allison and Claire had probably intended. Everything about that note was designed to make me feel as unwanted and unlovable as possible. Mission accomplished.

Part of me wanted to do something to make them back off, but . . . they had the Santa photos. They weren't afraid to release them either. That threat had been terrifying when I thought the pics would make the rounds at my school, but now . . . it was so much worse. They could sell any of those shots to *People* magazine and turn me into a national laughingstock.

I had to be careful.

Not just of Allison and Claire, although they were the two people I had the most reason to fear, but anyone and everyone who had photos of me that weren't particularly flattering. Most of which were safe with Jen. Then again, maybe that wasn't such a good thing. Of course Jen would never *intentionally* humiliate me, but we don't always share the same idea of what constitutes embarrassing. Whenever she posts photos of us on Facebook I have to untag myself in at least half of them.

I definitely had to contact Jen. She was the one person I trusted to help me out, even though she would probably think of Nick as the sweetest, kindest, most gallant man on earth once she saw photos of us together. She would probably see me as Cinderella no matter what I told her to the contrary. But that's Jen: determined to see the good in everything and everyone.

That's partly why we work so well as friends: She encourages me to be daring while I double-check that she stays safe. Somehow it balances out. Well . . . usually. When it goes wrong, I end up slapping Santa and getting blackmailed by my cousins with the photographic proof.

Still, whether Dominic Wyatt liked it or not, I wasn't about to keep something of this magnitude from Jen. Or a secret of any size, for that matter.

Zipping up my suitcase, I decided it was about time that I refigured my plans. Since Nick was putting his best interests first, then I should be doing the same thing.

It didn't matter that Nick was probably hating every minute of shopping. We weren't friends—we were acquaintances who had been saddled with each other.

I couldn't lose sight of that little detail.

It was business.

This was my one shot to experience life as a Somebody, and I didn't want to miss out on anything because I had failed to brainstorm with Jen.

I started back to the suite, wheeling my suitcase behind me, and trying to gauge how much time I had before Nick would be back. Hard to know how seriously he took this makeup stuff. Most likely he would take it as seriously as he seemed to take everything else. Odd how I always noticed Nick's inability to relax and yet Jen constantly reminds me to loosen up and have fun.

Well, whatever. I should have enough time to Skype Jen without him ever finding out.

Who says an ordinary girl can't be devious?

I swiped his key card for entrance and considered the best way to go about, ahem, *borrowing* an expensive electronic device from Nick. One thing I didn't own was a laptop, which meant that if Nick had taken his iPad with him, I was screwed.

So much for my deviousness.

I wheeled my suitcase into a corner and began systematically searching the desk drawers in the hope that he had forgotten it there. No such luck. The iPad had left the building . . . or at least the suite. I eyed Nick's leather messenger bag suspiciously, feeling guilty even considering digging through it. Somehow logging into Skype didn't seem quite so intrusive if he'd left the necessary technology out in the open, more or less. But rummaging through his bag would undeniably be an invasion of privacy.

But talking to Jen would be worth it.

I hit pay dirt the instant I flipped back the leather flap and unzipped. A MacBook Pro. The guy clearly had a thing for Apple technology. Not that I blamed him, but, really? An iPad *and* a MacBook Pro? Because heaven forbid he was out of range for so much as a minute.

Then again, considering my willingness to paw through his belongings for Internet access, I was in no position to judge.

Especially since his controlling nature was now providing me with exactly what I wanted.

I logged into my email only to find thirty messages waiting in my inbox, fourteen of them from Jen. The subject lines said it all:

How's the cruise? I miss you! Good luck with your cousins!

Dominic Wyatt's new girlfriend looks EXACTLY like you. I mean it!

You're not secretly dating Dominic Wyatt, RIGHT?

Kidding.

OH MY GOD, YOU ARE DATING DOMINIC WYATT! WHY DIDN'T YOU TELL ME?

People magazine is saying you've been dating for TWO WEEKS!?

HOW could YOU keep this a secret from ME!?

You're not still mad about the Santa thing, are you? I'M SORRY, OKAY!

So I'm NOT your best friend, is that it? FINE BY ME!

Sorry. I take it back.

Email me already!

My inbox is still empty.

I CAN'T BELIEVE YOU'RE DATING A ROCK STAR!

Oh, yeah, Jen had definitely seen the article.

I quickly logged onto Skype and called her. Every year, Jen loves to redecorate the Christmas tree by herself accompanied by loud carols blaring from her computer. Well, it used to be her mom's computer, but then Mrs. Lawley got a new one and it officially became Jen's. Still, with all this media excitement surrounding me there was no way she would be able to go more than fifteen minutes without checking to see if I had responded to one of her billion messages. I was afraid to check Facebook and see how many posts she had left for me there.

She answered on the second ring.

"Oh, my God! Okay, tell me everything! When did the two of you start dating? Was it love at first sight? He's so dreamy . . . I bet it was love at first sight. HOW COULD YOU KEEP THIS FROM ME?"

"It's complicated," I muttered lamely.

"Complicated. COMPLICATED! What kind of an answer is that?"

"Look, we met on the cruise, but we don't want the media making a big deal out of how quickly we got together, so just . . . play along, okay?"

She let out a big breath. "Okay. So you weren't keeping this from me, then?"

"Of course not! You're the first and only person I'm going to tell. And this can't go any farther than us."

She nodded. "I won't say a word!" Then her smile turned mushy and I knew her common sense had probably just melted. "So you met on a cruise to the Mexican Riviera. Wow, that's just so *romantic!* So how did it happen? You saw each other from afar?"

"Uh, yeah, sort of."

Well, he had spotted me staring at him in the dining room.

"And then what?"

"I . . . well, I—"

Jen clapped her hands together in excitement. "Yes?"

"I puked in his bathroom."

It's amazing how quickly a smile can disappear from the face of a hopeless romantic.

"You did *what?*"

"It was an accident!" I said defensively.

"I should hope so!"

"It was just . . . one of those things."

Jen stared at me as if her video wasn't working properly and I had suddenly spouted an extra head. "Oh, yeah, one of *those things*. Because people barf around *rock stars* all the time."

"Sarcasm doesn't suit you, Jen."

She ignored that entirely. "Okay, so he saw you in distress and chivalrously offered to help, right?" Jen sighed wistfully. "I guess that's romantic after all."

"Well, first he mistook me for a zombie and nailed me right in the face with pepper spray."

"Be serious, Holly! I want to know what actually happened!"

Apparently, the truth was too far-fetched for even my best friend to believe.

I rolled my eyes. "Yes, he was very gallant. A regular knight in shining armor."

It was the only answer she'd accept without protesting.

"That's what I thought," Jen replied smugly. "I could tell that just by looking at him."

"Tell what?"

"That he'd make a great boyfriend, of course! He's so easygoing. I think the only time he's ever been caught scowling at *anyone* was in that photo with you."

Well, that made me feel *wonderful*.

"I'm sure that had nothing to do with *you*," Jen added quickly. "He probably just didn't appreciate the interruption."

No, he definitely hadn't appreciated it. Primarily because it had forced him into a fake relationship with me.

"Uh huh," I said, for lack of anything smarter. I couldn't confirm any of that nonsense, but I didn't want to correct her either.

"God, Dominic Wyatt." She laughed. "*Dominic Wyatt is dating my best friend!* I never thought I'd say that."

"Me neither."

Jen brushed her long auburn bangs away from her eyes. "So . . . is he a relaxed kisser?"

"What does *that* mean?"

"You know," she said, even though clearly I *didn't*. "Slow, smoldering kisses that are casual but really, really hot?"

"I'm confused," I admitted. "Words are coming out of your mouth, but all I hear is the back jacket of a romance novel."

"Is he a *good* kisser, then?"

I didn't want to answer that question. So I secretly hoped that her brothers might light something on fire, like they'd done last Christmas, and she would have to evacuate the building.

But no fire alarms went off. Jen was staring at me so intently there was no way I could even distract her with cute puppy videos on YouTube—and she *loves* watching anything that involves small dogs leaping into large bodies of water.

"Uh, well . . . he's . . . erm—"

"Spill it, Holly!"

"Oh, yes." An all-too-familiar voice said coolly from the other side of the room. Nick stood in the doorway, clutching a shopping bag and looking like he was trying very hard to remain calm. I watched the navy color of his eyes turn darker—more gunmetal gray than blue. "Don't hold back now, Holly."

I was so incredibly dead.

Chapter 18

Dominic

I was an idiot.

And not just for leaving Holly alone in my suite, but because I had stupidly thought I could handle picking up some girl stuff. I figured it would be easy. A quick in-and-out job.

Except I became overwhelmed within minutes. There were spinning racks full of lipstick and at least thirty different kinds of mascara all claiming to do different things: Thickening, lengthening, plumping, and on top of that there was black, midnight black, and ultra-black mascara to either add volume or supervolume.

How was anyone supposed to know the difference between the tubes?

Clearly, I was way out of my league.

Which is why I pulled out my iPad and called Tim's boyfriend, Corey. He was the only person I knew, male or female, who enjoyed makeover projects.

"Hey, Dom," Corey answered smoothly on the third ring. "Mackenzie and I were just about to check in with Tim, see if he had any sound track updates. Have you heard anything?"

"Uh, no news," I muttered softly, so as not to annoy my fellow shoppers. "But . . . I could use some help."

They both sat up straighter while I tried not to let my discomfort show. They had never heard me ask for anything before, probably because asking for help isn't something I did . . . until Holly made it absolutely necessary.

"I, uh, need to go shopping for a girl," I mumbled.

"Is this for your new girlfriend?" Corey demanded. "You know, the one you should have mentioned to us *weeks* ago!"

Apparently, Tim hadn't filled Corey in on the real story behind the Holly situation. It struck me as a little paranoid. I mean, all of us trust Corey and Mackenzie to keep their mouths shut. Still . . . if that was the way he wanted to play it, I could stick to the script.

"Uh, yeah. Holly. The two of us just went public and she could use a makeover, I guess."

"You guess?" Corey smirked. "You've seen the photos of her on the Web, right? The girl needed a stylist yesterday. Possibly *years* ago."

"That's a bit harsh," Mackenzie pointed out, elbowing Corey in the stomach as a not-so-discreet signal for him to shut up. "She just looked really, uh, tired."

Mackenzie might be an Internet sensation but she wasn't a hypocrite. She couldn't ream Holly's look while wearing basic jeans and a sweatshirt with a stain that looked distinctly like mustard.

"Right. So what do I buy to fix that?" I aimed the camera at the display racks. "Seriously, Corey. Help."

He laughed and then rubbed his hands together in excitement. "Mascara, eyeliner, lip gloss, concealer, blush, and eyeshadow. At least." He turned to Mackenzie. "Am I forgetting anything?"

"I don't think so."

I tried to push down my panic. "So . . . volume mascara? Supervolume? Clump-free or plumping wand? *What the hell do I get her, Corey?*"

"Wow, man. Breathe. Okay, so what kind of lashes does she have?"

I stared at him on the screen. "What do you mean? Normal ones. Is this a trick question?"

Mackenzie laughed. "Are they light colored? Long? Short and bushy? Or—"

"How should I know? It's not like I've been examining her eyelashes!"

Corey decided it was time to take over. "Okay, we get it. You don't know. Grab a few and move on, okay? Get dark brown and dark black. Can you do that?"

"Sure."

"Good. Now some black eyeliner."

"Okay," I mumbled, feeling even more foolish with the tubes clenched in my free hand.

"Almost halfway done already. Now, what color are her eyes?"

"Uh . . ." I drew a complete blank. "You know . . . normal eye color."

Mackenzie shook her head in amused disbelief. "You know that tells us absolutely nothing, right?"

I tried to think back to the first time I had seen Holly up close: Her face deathly pale, her mouth hanging open, and her red-rimmed eyes . . . that was all the detail I could recall.

"I think they might be brown. Sort of. Maybe."

"Wow. You're not very good at this boyfriend thing, are you?" Corey drawled. "And to be clear, by 'not very good,' I mean you suck."

Mackenzie elbowed him with enough strength to make him wince.

"That's just mean, Corey!"

Corey shrugged. "It's the truth. You seriously need to step up your game, Dom."

At that point I was ready to agree with anything to get me out of the shop.

"Fair enough. I guess I should probably start thinking about her birthday present soon too."

Mackenzie raised an eyebrow. "When's that?"

"Day after Christmas."

Both of them jerked in their seats, as Mackenzie demanded, "And you're only getting to it *now?* That's, what? Five days away?"

"Something like that."

She swiveled to face Corey. "You're right. He does suck at this."

"I've got plenty of time," I protested.

Mackenzie remained skeptical. "Plenty of time to find something thoughtful and personal yet beautiful? Right. Good luck with that, buddy."

Well, crap.

"I'll deal with it later. Now, what else should I buy?"

I slowly panned the shelves with my iPad.

"Okay, stop! That eyeshadow. Yeah, okay. Now grab a range of lip gloss. Yep, some blush and you should be good to go. On the makeup front anyway."

I bobbled the cosmetics as the pile spiraled out of control.

"Thanks, guys, I appreciate the help."

"No problem. Don't forget the makeup remover!" Mackenzie blurted before I disconnected.

All I wanted was to return to the suite and kick back with my music. Snag a beer from the fully stocked minibar, sit out on the balcony, and make the most of my vacation. But I would have Holly waiting for me.

Which reminded me . . . I began loading my arms up with every drug they stocked that claimed to combat seasickness. Given the unpredictable way color flooded or fled from her face, I had a feeling she might be visiting my bathroom again in the not-so-distant future.

Corey and Mackenzie were wrong about me: I could be a good boyfriend. I'd even figure out the color of her eyes. If knowing that junk was important to selling the role, I'd pay closer attention.

The woman at the counter gave me a funny look as I handed her my credit card. I wondered how quickly rumors would start spreading that I had a raspberry lip gloss fetish and a major case of seasickness.

Tim and Chris would mock me mercilessly if that actually caught on.

Which is why after making one quick stop to pick up a second key card for my suite at the concierge desk, I headed back to the room . . . and to the privacy of the balcony.

It was about time I enjoyed the view and kicked back.

So when I opened the door I expected to see Holly unpacking her suitcase or watching TV or generally making herself at home in the suite that used to be mine. *Our* suite now.

I hadn't anticipated finding her sitting cross-legged on the bed, using *my* laptop to discuss my kissing prowess with a girl I could only assume was Jen.

The girl was an absolute nuisance, but I found myself wondering just how she would describe our kiss to her best friend. Something she didn't look inclined to share, considering the way her lips were pressed tightly together and her face had flushed.

I decided to enjoy making her squirm.

Which was easily accomplished by moving into the sight line of the laptop and draping an arm across Holly's shoulder.

"You were saying, Holly?" I prompted.

Her back straightened in indignation. "Just that I don't kiss and tell."

"Since when?" the cute redhead on screen demanded. "Don't tell me you've been holding back on me all these years! After I told you *everything* about Jason too!"

"Jason Treadwick never even learned your name, Jen. And

believe me, I wish you had kept more about him to yourself. I really didn't need to know every detail about the one time he asked to borrow a pencil."

I quickly turned my laugh into a cough.

"We had a moment!" Jen insisted. "There was an undeniable connection!"

"I'm pretty sure he would deny it. As would his current *boyfriend.*"

"Shut up!" Jen mock-scowled at a now grinning Holly. The easy back-and-forth made it pretty clear that they probably knew each other better than anybody else ever could. In fact, their exchange reminded me of some of the long bus rides with Tim and Chris. Especially late at night when we're buzzed off performance adrenaline and heading for a new crowd in another city.

"I, uh, don't think we've actually been formally introduced, Dominic. I'm Jen. Jennifer Lawley, Holly's best friend."

Jen shot me an adoring look at the same time that Holly stiffened up. It was almost as if Holly were *jealous.*

But that couldn't be right. The girl could hardly stand being in the same room with me.

"Nice to meet you, Jen. Call me Dom," I replied easily.

"Dom?" Holly repeated. "Since when have you used *that* name?"

I raised an eyebrow. Her voice certainly had a brittle edge to it, as if she didn't like what she was hearing. "It's what most people call me."

"And I'm not most people?"

"Nope, you're not." I turned back to Jen, who didn't appear to have any idea how to handle having her best friend cutting her out of a conversation with a rock star. "Don't you agree, Jen?"

"Uh . . ." she said uncertainly. "Yes?"

"I bet the two of you go way back too."

Jen bobbed her head enthusiastically in the affirmative. "Way back."

"So I'm guessing you know all of Holly's embarrassing stories."

"Sure! Not too long ago, actually—"

"*Jen!*" Holly interrupted. "Zip it!"

"Oh, but Jen would never share something too personal. Isn't that what you told me earlier, Holly?"

She looked fully prepared to take that statement back, but I didn't give her the chance. "You should hear the way she talks about you, Jen. She considers you safer than Fort Knox."

"And we've got to go." Holly was clearly desperate to end the conversation. "Important stuff to discuss. I'll talk to you later, Jen."

"Right. Later." Jen paid her almost no attention. " 'Bye, *Dom.*"

A silly smile crossed her face as she tried out the truncated version of my name as if it were an expensive wine she was sampling for the first time.

I winked back. "Take care, Jen."

Holly instantly shut the computer, disconnecting the call.

Making it feel very private with the two of us sitting on the bed together with my arm still draped over her shoulder. She adjusted her position but her face remained close enough to mine that kissing would have been the simplest task imaginable. I could feel the warmth of her breath on my ear when she finally spoke.

"So . . . what girl stuff did you get me?"

Yeah, that was one way to kill the mood.

Chapter 19

Holly

I didn't know how to feel.

Okay, technically, I did. I was *supposed* to feel very cool and important. Regal. Princess-like.

What I *wasn't* supposed to feel was miffed that he had told Jen to use a nickname that I thought had been reserved for his ReadySet buddies. Apparently, it was just set aside for people that he genuinely liked.

I also wasn't supposed to feel jealous that he had gotten along so well with *my* best friend. Or nervous that he might, rightly, blast me for using his laptop without permission. Or jittery because for a second there I thought he might be interested in, erm, *practicing our chemistry* again.

Nick's scowl made it clear that not only was he completely disinterested in me *that* way, he loathed my choice of conversation topics.

"I'm never buying girl stuff again," he growled. "Never. I don't care if that makes me a bad fake boyfriend. From here on out, if you need something you buy it yourself."

"Okay."

His glare didn't soften. "See, you act all agreeable now,

but in about ten minutes you're going to be doing something to annoy me."

Apparently, the very mention of shopping was bringing back all sorts of bad memories, like he was having post-traumatic stress disorder from selecting mascara. Best to tread carefully.

"Probably true."

"Great. Just . . . great. Well, here you go. All yours."

He dumped out the contents of his bag on the bed and stepped back as if the cosmetics might be harboring some kind of terrible infection.

"What is all this?" I demanded, fighting back horror at the massive pile that tumbled across the bedspread.

He shrugged. "Girl stuff."

I scrambled for an excuse not to touch anything.

"But . . . I can't afford all of this!"

"Sure, you can. You're getting paid to be my publicist, remember?"

"But . . . I don't know how to use most of this!"

Nick didn't look surprised by that confession. "Well, don't look at me. I don't even know your eye color."

I widened them intentionally. "They're green. Jen swears I've got flecks of chestnut brown too, but I've never spotted them."

Nick's intense look might have been romantic if it hadn't creased his brow like he was trying to figure out an SAT math question.

"I don't see the brown either. Just green."

"And your eyes are blue. Then again, I suspect you know that already."

He grinned and it was the first time I had seen him look even remotely relaxed since I had turned the topic to the shopping bags.

"Now that we've got that sorted out . . ." I held up a medieval torture device that was masquerading as a beauty device. "What do you expect me to do with this?"

"Use it," he said simply.

I glared at him. "Easy for you to say!"

"Definitely." His smirk spread and I knew he was inwardly laughing at my expense. "But it can't be that hard," Nick said at last. "You brush some stuff on your face. Simple."

I glared at him. "This from the guy who nearly had a panic attack at the mere mention of shopping."

"Believe it or not, this is one particular area where male rock stars generally don't have to venture. Unless that's their thing, obviously."

"Great!" I threw my hands up in disgust. "That's just fan-freaking-tastic!"

"Now *that* screams maturity."

Which actually reminded me of something I'd been meaning to ask him. "Just how old are you, Nick?"

"Twenty-one."

Well, I felt foolish. Why hadn't I thought to look up that information online? Then I wouldn't have been gaping at him like a particularly dim-witted fish.

"Really?"

"No, I'm lying. I'm actually twelve."

"Now *that* I might believe," I quipped, trying to play it off as no big deal. Except even a few years in high school . . . it matters. That's why college guys showing an interest in high school girls often comes across as being supersketchy . . . and why I've never been a fan of vampire stories. Anyone over one hundred years old panting after an angsty high school kid—that's not sexy. It's gross. Don't even get me started on the desire to suck blood. I'm sorry, but any guy longing to chomp into someone else's neck is just asking to get his butt kicked.

And while there might not be a vampire age difference between us, the gap still made me uneasy. It felt like yet another advantage for Nick, and considering that he's the rock star, I'd say he already had more than enough going in his favor. So to find out that he was more talented and ridiculously successful and older . . . yeah, I felt a little inferior.

In the way that a stray, flea-ridden cat might feel inferior to a lion.

"I never considered your age," I admitted. It was true—I had gotten hung up on his looks first, then on his zombie fixation, and then on his fame, never on the years between us. "It isn't *terrible*. I guess."

He stepped away from me. "What kind of a difference are we talking about, Holly?"

The tension vibrating off him was practically palpable. The guy was probably wishing that he had thought to ask my age before enmeshing me further into his life. Making out with a fifteen-year-old girl in front of the paparazzi . . . that would definitely be a solid blow to his all-important reputation. Especially since the abuse rumors were probably still swirling around us.

"Well, it's *almost* my birthday. So that helps things."

"How old, Holly?"

"Almost eighteen."

He released an enormous sigh of relief. "That's not a problem, especially now that you've taken a couple years off my life expectancy."

"Worried about corrupting a minor, Nick?" I laughed, making sure it sounded like I had trouble believing that he could possibly corrupt me. If my cousins couldn't tempt me over to the dark side, I doubted Nick could fundamentally alter me either.

"How old did you think I was?"

He frowned, probably because age is so difficult to determine with zombies, given the whole dead factor. Not that he would say as much, of course.

"I thought you were legal. Not jailbait."

"Oh, yeah. Jailbait, that's me. Because I love seducing older men. I've already sent a dozen guys to the slammer."

"I'm guessing you sent them to a mental ward first."

I wasn't sure if he meant that as a comment on my ability to drive people crazy or that someone would have to be unhinged to be attracted to me in the first place. Either way: not exactly complimentary.

I held up my hands. "Let's call a truce, okay? It's a beautiful day and I only sort of feel like puking. So I'm going to make my excuses to my grandpa and then I'm going to go relax on the balcony. If you want to hang out: great. If not: That's fine by me too. But I fully plan on holing up here tonight."

The crease between Nick's eyebrows returned. "You should probably practice with that, uh, girl stuff now while you've got a chance."

"Probably," I agreed. "But it's not going to happen. I'm on vacation and there's an ocean view calling my name."

I didn't give him time to respond. Instead, I scooped up my backpack, which still held all my drawing supplies, and began sketching outside. I heard Nick making some noise from inside the suite but I resolutely refused to look. If, perhaps, I listened a little too intently, waiting for the telltale squeak of the glass sliding door in case he followed me outside, that was nobody's business but my own.

But when the door protested its use five minutes later, I jumped about a foot and a half. Nearly sending the high-quality artist pencils in my lap to a watery grave.

So much for playing it cool.

Still, Nick didn't let on that he had noticed a thing. He just sank into the other chair and began plucking away on his guitar.

It actually sounded really good. Which surprised the hell out of me since I hadn't heard of Dominic Wyatt playing anything beyond the drums. Then again, I also had no idea he enjoyed songwriting either.

I was starting to wonder whether anyone really knew what Dominic Wyatt was capable of . . . including himself.

Kind of strange, considering the way every move ReadySet makes is diligently followed by *People's* Star Tracks.

Not that I had any intention of commenting on it . . . even if I couldn't resist changing my drawing from the expanse of blue before me to the rock star sitting about two feet away.

I thought I might call it *Rock Star in Repose.*

And for a brief moment everything was simple. My cousins, his fans, our fauxmance—none of it could touch me on the balcony.

Too bad I couldn't stay out there for the duration of the cruise. Because all of those complications I wanted so desperately to ignore?

Yeah, I had no idea just how complicated they could get.

Chapter 20

Dominic

I had nearly given up on ever getting a real vacation, and yet there I was on the balcony . . . *relaxing*.

With Holly.

I was almost afraid to classify it as unwinding in case that would somehow tempt fate to smack me upside the head again. But the source of most of my latest aggravation looked utterly absorbed. She wrinkled her brow in concentration as she erased something before starting again. Holly's single-minded focus on her art, the amount of satisfaction she took in getting it the way she wanted, it made me try to remember the last time I had played music without some specific end goal in mind.

I kept drawing a blank.

Even when I was toying with a work in progress with the guys, the pressure of a deadline was always looming right outside the tour bus. The very air felt electrified—as if even the oxygen particles knew we were fighting for a career that couldn't last.

And that scared all three of us shitless.

I had no backup plan and I wasn't qualified for anything else. . . . Even worse: I didn't *want* to do anything else.

So it felt good to fool around on the guitar. Especially since if it sounded crappy there was no one besides Holly, who apparently thought yowling and singing were the same thing, around to judge.

No deadlines. No pressure to nail it the first time around. Just music.

So I kept plucking and strumming until the pads of my fingers couldn't take it anymore. Then I swapped out the guitar for my drumsticks and began tapping on the railing, the small outdoor table, and the glass sliding door. Anything I wanted to use was fair game. Best of all, Holly never complained that I was messing with her concentration or passive-aggressively glared to shut me up.

Instead, Holly's gaze kept flickering between me and her sketch pad. Anyone else I would've suspected of flirting . . . but this was Holly Disaster. No game of sneaking sidelong glances from her.

She was drawing me. Normally, I would ask her to stop. I'm just not a big fan of being artistically rendered. Photo shoots are hard enough to get through—mainly because I'm powdered to "reduce shine" and then yelled at to look "more relaxed." It's not easy trying to appear laid-back under lights that literally scorch.

Still, I doubted anyone was going to see whatever Holly created so I just enjoyed my music. I didn't even notice how late it was becoming until Holly stood up, stretched, and disappeared inside the room. Moments later I heard her talking on the phone.

"Yeah, I'm just not feeling up to a big family dinner." Long pause. "No, Grandpa, this has nothing to do with last night. Of course, Aunt Jessica didn't mean anything by it. I just haven't found my sea legs yet."

That was the understatement of the century.

"I'm going to call it a night. Have fun at bingo and I'll see you tomorrow. I'll be fine! Allison and Claire are taking great care of me. Go enjoy yourself!"

Apparently, her grandpa wasn't thrilled with her little disappearing act. Then again, I didn't relish the idea of going out in public and slipping into the rock star façade tonight any more than she did.

"It's *your* birthday trip, Grandpa." She winced. "You see me enough as it is. We dock in Cabo tomorrow; I'm sure I'll be up for dinner then. Yeah, I love you too."

A quick good-bye later and she was calling up room service to order two cheeseburgers, fries, and sodas. So much for not having an appetite while seasick. Either that or she had noticed the veritable pharmacy of anti-seasickness pills I had purchased for her.

Holly handed me one of the plates, settled back into her chair, and the two of us enjoyed the meal in companionable silence. Neither one of us wanted to mess up the good thing we had going so we kept things casual as we ate our food and began preparing for bed.

Maybe it was lame for me to be exhausted at nine at night. Elementary school kids stay up later than that on a regular basis. Then again, they don't have to launch fake relationships with total strangers either.

For once, I had no interest in pushing myself just a little bit harder for a little bit longer. I crashed hard . . . waking up early again to the sound of running water in the shower the next morning. Sharing my space with a girl was going to take some getting used to, but at least she had curbed her desire to sing under the spray.

For now.

She hardly made any noise at all, which was a vast improvement on the day before.

Maybe having a temporary female roommate wouldn't be so bad after all.

Since Holly clearly thought I was asleep, I saw no reason

to disabuse her of the notion. Which is why I heard her rustling through yesterday's purchases before she murmured, "Hello, drugs! Good to see you again!" Then she started popping seasickness pills.

As far as a dependence on medications go, it could have been significantly worse.

"I am *not* going to vomit," Holly promised herself. "Not again. Not for me."

I fervently hoped she was right.

More shuffling followed and then silence except for the quiet scratching of a pencil on paper. Considering the amount of time she spent drawing, either it was her passion or I was so irritating she had turned to her one stress release outlet for constant emotional support. It had me wondering whether she was any good at it. Plenty of people want to be rock stars or artists but the lifestyle demands more than talent: It takes persistence, dedication, and a small amount of luck. Since most people *talk* about how they are in the process of creating their grand something-or-other without producing a thing, I tend to doubt ability until it's been substantiated.

Holly definitely committed a lot of time to it and I found myself wondering if I could check out the final product. That only seemed fair since she was drawing *me*. And if she had talent then I might be able to hook her up as an intern with some people in Hollywood.

It would be a nice way to show the public that our brief romance had ended on amiable terms.

Sitting up in bed, I squinted at her. "You're not drawing my good side."

"That's because you don't have one."

I grinned. "According to *People* I have a 'charming boyishness' that girls can't resist."

"So do five-year-olds," Holly pointed out. "Then again, they also enjoy banging on things and have an aversion to sharing." She cocked her head to the side and pretended to study me. "Hm . . . I see the makings of a made-for-TV-movie here: Rock star swaps bodies with a kindergartener. Think Timothy Goff would be willing to play the lead?"

It was the reminder of a potential movie deal that brought the seriousness of our situation crashing back. I hadn't heard anything about the blowback of our fake relationship hitting the press. Hopefully, our excessive PDA session on the Lido deck the day before had put to rest the rumors that I was an abusive scumbag. Then again, the gossip sites aren't exactly known for being overly concerned with the rumors that they spread.

Especially during a slow news week.

Maybe, if I was lucky, a starlet would be photographed crawling into her car without underwear. That might distract people from discussing my nonstory. Although, given my luck, it would probably take the split of one of Hollywood's most stable couples or maybe another major political sex scandal.

"We're going to be in Cabo today," I reminded her as I headed straight for the shower. Not that Holly seemed to care. When I emerged, she was sitting out on the balcony, nodding along to the music piping through her headphones and adding some extra shading to her sketch.

Her art was good. *Really* good, actually. I could definitely see a band using it for their album cover. It had a neat mix of realism and hyperrealism that fused into a sea of curlicues and swirls that exploded on the edges. I would've shown it to Tim and Chris if it hadn't been for one very important detail:

I looked awful.

Okay, maybe *awful* was an exaggeration. She hadn't made me bald or added a beer-gut or a handlebar mustache. But Holly had me fingering the guitar with a fierce scowl on my face, as if I expected it to mutiny at any moment.

Not exactly the laid-back image I presented to the public.

"I wasn't glaring yesterday."

Holly jumped in her seat, knocking the headphones off her ears. "What the—oh, you scared me." She whacked me in the chest with her sketch pad. "Stop creeping up on me!"

"What is this?" I was determined to stay on subject. "Why'd you draw me like . . . *that?*"

She laughed. "Aw, does the rock star feel self-conscious without his 'charming boyish' smile. Poor baby."

Damn, she was annoying.

I gritted my teeth. "I didn't look like that yesterday."

Holly shrugged. "Not most of the time. Every now and then . . . let's just say, I nailed it."

"Well, find someone else to draw."

She made a big show of looking around her. "You know, I would except . . . oh, wait. We're all alone. In hiding."

I couldn't wait to get off the damn ship . . . in LA.

Chapter 21

Holly

I probably should have gone easier on the guy.

But it was difficult being nice when you felt like a prisoner. Sure, my cell was awfully plush, but I couldn't move freely outside of the suite . . . and I didn't have too much freedom inside the room either.

There was nothing for me to do.

At least, for the next few hours until we could disembark.

I wondered what all the die-hard ReadySet fans would think if I leaked the truth that spending time with one of America's most sought-after musicians made homework look interesting. Considering that I'm a straight-B student with a tendency to copy down my math answers from the back of the textbook, that said a lot.

Still, it wasn't fair for me to take out my frustrations on my fellow captive. My parents would probably find that rude. Sometimes it seemed like my life would be a lot easier if I didn't imagine them floating around, commenting on my every move. It's sort of hard to tell your imaginary dead parents to shut up.

But I was really wishing I had kept things polite when

Nick pulled up Jen's Skype contact information on his laptop.

I hadn't realized that by inputting it earlier Nick could contact *my* best friend whenever he wanted. Mainly because I didn't think he would catch me talking to her in the first place.

No such luck.

Nick's finger lingered over the phone icon. "I wonder what Jen will think of your drawing. She seemed to find my smile boyishly irresistible yesterday."

Oh, yeah, I had noticed that too. Jen might be a total sweetheart who sees the good in everyone, but subtlety is not her specialty. I personally enjoy her frankness since she never keeps me guessing. If she wants to finish a romance novel at our sleepover, I know it. And if Jen has even the slightest interest in a guy, *everyone within a fifty-mile radius finds out about it too.*

Most of the time I consider her inability to keep her own secrets just one of her many quirks.

Then again, Jen had never swooned over the rock star I was pretending to date either.

Not that I thought she would ever betray me by making a play for Nick. Well, not intentionally. But she *could* make a fool of herself by gazing longingly at him. And accidentally flirting with him.

Jen could also be convinced to share my embarrassing secrets with Nick.

Probably.

I wasn't willing to take that chance.

"Jen's busy!" I blurted.

He raised an eyebrow skeptically. "How would you know?"

"She, uh, told me. Yesterday. She has . . . jujitsu."

Nick didn't look fazed by this information in the slightest. "That's all right. I can call her later."

"It's a meet, actually. She's competing," I invented wildly. "Jen wants to become a . . . pink belt."

Nick's smug look made it clear he didn't believe a word of it. Either I was a really bad liar, or he was excellent at discerning the truth.

I had a feeling that my lying skills were sorely lacking.

"Then we have to wish her luck."

"Oh, no! That might throw her off her game. Best to let her focus."

A knock at the door and the standard call of "Room service" provided a well-timed distraction.

"I'll get it!"

Not even giving Nick a chance to offer, I sprinted to the door. Except the room service tray wasn't the only thing waiting outside the door. There were also notes littering the doorway. Some of them were cut out in the shape of hearts—and they all had the name *Dominic Wyatt* scrawled across the front in looping handwriting. The notes addressed to me weren't quite as pretty.

Most of them included thoughtful phrases like *Back off slut, he's mine.*

That wasn't creepy or anything.

In fact, the notes more than anything else made it real to me that people were paying attention to my love life. And that while our fake relationship might help Nick's reputation . . . it might also put me in danger.

Among all the fans who would do almost anything to date a member of ReadySet, there were probably a couple who wouldn't mind physically removing me from the picture if necessary.

That was one terrifying mental image.

I dropped the lot of cards into Nick's lap and he picked up a red heart-shaped one.

"You didn't have to go to all this trouble, Holly. I know you find me irresistible."

Joking around was all fine and good . . . usually. But since I had seen those cards I had some questions for Nick and I needed straight answers.

"How did you get used to all of this?" I demanded bluntly. "The fawning, the ass-kissing, the *stalking,* how did you adjust when it first happened to you?"

He shrugged. "I haven't. I just don't let my discomfort show."

"Okay." I nodded, trying to wrap my head around all of it. "That might work for you, but what happens to me after the cruise? Do we pretend to stay together in LA? Do we 'break up' before New Year's? After New Year's? Holy crap, you don't need me to go to any big parties with you, right?"

Great, I was babbling.

"What am I thinking? Of course it's not going to last that long. Right, Nick?"

He rubbed his forehead and fingered another heart-shaped note in the pile. "It shouldn't take that long. Then again, there's only one way to find out."

He clicked on to Google and typed *ReadySet drummer, Dominic Wyatt* into the search engine. Then he selected one of the first news articles to appear.

Drummer Denies Domestic Violence: ReadySet Tries to Repair Their Image

ReadySet drummer Dominic Wyatt stunned fans by revealing that he was in a secret relationship hours after reports leaked that he was dating fourteen-year-old Cynthia Ridgley. However, it was the picture of proclaimed "girlfriend" Holly Dayton being yanked away from the door by an aggressive Mr. Wyatt that has really shaken up his fans. While Mr. Wyatt claims never to have hurt Ms. Dayton, the photographs paint a very different picture. According to relationship expert Dr. Harris Van Bueller, "It's highly unlikely that Ms. Dayton hasn't recently been in extreme distress. Her red-rimmed eyes indicate prolonged weeping and her ashen discoloration suggests panic and potential trauma. Mr. Wyatt's furious facial expression combined with his forceful removal of Ms. Dayton makes a persuasive case that she isn't with him willingly."

How have the other members of ReadySet reacted to their drummer's recent scandal? Charity work. At a last-minute benefit to raise money for orphanages, lead singer Timothy Goff stated, "Dom is a great guy. He and his girlfriend, Holly, should be able to go on vacation in peace." Bass player Christopher Forester added, "They are very much in love. These rumors of abuse are just that: rumors."

According to other travelers on board the high-profile couple's cruise, the pair have been ordering in for every meal since their first (and only) major moment of PDA.

The real question is: What are they doing inside the suite?

My mouth had fallen open somewhere in the first paragraph and I stared at Nick in horror.

"Let me guess," I said at last, struggling to pass it off as no big deal, "this isn't the news you were hoping for."

"No. It's not."

That was all he appeared willing to say. I didn't know if I should be relieved that he wasn't glaring at the screen . . . or concerned by how calmly he was handling it.

Truthfully, I was freaking out. The press was making me out to be a victim of domestic abuse, which twisted my stomach into tiny ringlets. The worst part was that if I denied the claim, I would look like I was in denial.

And my supposed willingness to stay in an unhealthy relationship made me feel like an absolutely terrible role model for other girls. I didn't want anyone to think sticking around with an overly possessive jerk was okay because, hey, the girl dating rock star Dominic Wyatt did it.

But while the media was practically sending me directions to the nearest rape crisis center, the notes outside the door had been utterly vicious.

Some of the comments beneath the article were even worse:

I LOVE READYSET! Dominic rules! I bet the slut deserved it.

I read somewhere that she made him really mad and kept bitching and complaining until he snapped.

Dominic Wyatt can lock me in a room with him anytime.

It hurt.

Not just the slut part, although that didn't exactly make me feel good. But the idea that I was somehow responsible for any cruel treatment Nick had dished out . . . it hit me harder than Dominic Wyatt's alleged blow.

Because nobody deserves abuse.

I didn't want to leave the room anymore. Going out in public and having people scrutinize me for any signs of assault scared me. What if Nick rested his hand on my shoulder, but because I didn't expect it he startled me a little? Would I see: *Rock star's girlfriend avoids all physical contact* the next day online?

I sure hoped not.

"Here's the good news," Nick said slowly. "A few photos

on the beach and we should still be able to break up on schedule."

"And the bad news?" Something had to be coming.

"Lots of PDA. Hand-holding. Dancing. Kissing."

Well, when he put it that way . . . maybe that part of the situation wasn't *terrible*.

I just wouldn't share that opinion with Nick.

Chapter 22

Dominic

Cabo San Lucas in real life looks like a page from a
brochure.

White sandy beaches, clear blue skies, palm trees, and
street vendors who are ready to sell tourists cheap souvenirs,
like the plastic hula girl I planned to bring back for Chris and
Tim. Maybe I'd get them each a shark tooth necklace,too.

However, since they were stuck doing charity work during
our vacation, joke gifts might not elicit the right reaction from
them. Especially if it was another reminder that I was enjoying
beach life while they were dishing out heaps of steaming
mashed potatoes at a homeless shelter.

Not that going out with Holly was easy. She had agreed to
use a few of the makeup products before we left the suite . . .
and whined about it the whole time.

But when she emerged from the bathroom she definitely
looked . . . better. It helped that she was back to wearing her
own clothes: a plain white shirt and a pair of denim shorts
that emphasized her long legs. In fact, she looked almost . . .
hot. Definitely not a thought I wanted to have about Holly
Disaster.

I needed to focus on the mission: playing tourists.

"So what do you want to do today?"

The two of us were standing on the beach in a postcard-perfect setting, but Holly barely stopped craning her neck behind her long enough to answer my question.

"Um, what have you got in mind?"

Something fast and exciting that would get my heart rate up. "What about parasailing?"

"Well, see, I would . . . except I don't have a death wish."

I pointed at a speedboat racing across the horizon well beyond the hulking cruise ship. "That's not going to kill you. It's perfectly safe."

Holly shook her head. "Even if getting dragged across the ocean didn't kill me, my stress-induced heart attack would land me in the morgue."

I grinned. "So I'm guessing that's a no to parachuting too."

She shuddered. "Definitely."

Well, we couldn't just stand around on the beach looking like indecisive idiots all day.

"What about scuba diving?"

Holly nervously scooped her hair into an unruly ponytail so that it would stay out of her face. "I'm not sure. I've never done it before."

So maybe I would be able to go diving in Mexico after all.

"It's one of my favorite things, actually. When you're underwater, it's . . . spectacular."

If my enthusiasm surprised her, Holly didn't let on. "So how long have you been diving?"

"A few years now. You know, we should go together!"

She laughed. "Real subtle, Nick."

"You'd love it."

"Since I'm still literally sick of the ocean, I'm going to pass for today."

I wasn't about to give up now that I had sensed some curiosity on her part. "Our next port then. Trust me, you won't want to miss this."

"We'll see. In the meantime . . ." She glanced over her shoulder again and pasted on a wide smile when she spotted a photographer behind us. "Why don't we start with a walk?"

Yeah, that sounded thrilling. Nothing like a nice walk for excitement after being confined to a room for the majority of the past two days.

"That's what we're supposed to do, right?" Holly whispered. "Holding hands at Lover's Beach? Stuff like that?"

She was right. Maybe it was less exciting, but a stroll would look sexier in a celebrity magazine than the two of us wearing enormous wetsuits.

But the idea of showing Holly what she was missing appealed to me. Given the amount of chaos I had inadvertently added to her life, it seemed only right for me to add a bit of calm too. And something happens when you're defying the natural rules of human capability by breathing underwater that's . . . magic.

Still, I looped my arm into hers as we moved down the shore until we were skirting the water.

"Land!" she crowed happily, kicking sand into the water with a satisfying plop. "God, it feels good to be off the ship!"

"I can't imagine why you would feel that way. I've enjoyed the ship immensely."

She nearly stuck her tongue out at me—I'm almost sure of it—but she spotted the photographers lining the beach, documenting our every move, and decided against it.

"*You* are not going to annoy me. Because today I get to be a princess."

Then she threw herself at me, her arms wrapping around my neck as if we were advertising a honeymoon getaway.

"Can't. Breathe," I wheezed, straining not to dump her ass in the sand. That wouldn't look too romantic.

She released her death grip and sort of slithered down my chest until her feet connected with the beach again. Judging by the persistent clicking of the photographers, Holly's impulsive display of affection was definitely going to be plastered all over the ReadySet fan site soon.

"Loosen up," she muttered. "We're supposed to be having fun. In fact . . . I'll race you down the beach!"

And with that, Holly shoved me back and took off running.

To think that I'd been worrying that she'd be unable to play the part of the carefree girlfriend on vacation.

Holly might have had a head start on me, but she made the critical mistake of looking back to see if I was gaining on her . . . and nearly crashed into a happy couple in her rush.

Even on land, Holly Disaster was still a mess.

And since it was up to me to slow the maniac down—I tackled her.

Sort of.

I scooped one arm around her torso and pulled her down with me, dumping her in the sand. It felt great. The heat of the Mexican sun beat down on the pair of us as we simultaneously laughed and rolled around in the sand like a pair of lovesick fools.

Holly's legs tangled with mine as she grinned, then slowly shook her head in disbelief. "I knew you were competitive, but this is ridiculous."

I looked Holly straight in the eyes and lied. "I have no idea what you're talking about."

She rolled her eyes and then stood up, shaking off some of the sand from her shirt. "Sure, you don't."

"Not a clue."

Standing up myself, I lazily tossed an arm over her shoulder, just in case she wanted a rematch. I didn't mind the idea of chasing her across the sand again, but I didn't want to be caught at a disadvantage. Holly examined me thoughtfully. "I bet you cheat at cards when you're losing. Am I right?"

Only sometimes.

"Chris and Tim can't play poker worth a damn. Cheating would make it too easy."

She nodded as we made our way down the beach. "Still, I can't picture you ever settling for second best in anything."

"That's true for most people in Hollywood. If you want to make it in the business then you keep auditioning until you get the part. Settling means you're never going to get anywhere."

Holly paused, nearly running into a mother-daughter pair who were holding hands and appeared to be searching for shells. "Maybe that's my problem. When I don't think I can change things . . . I settle."

Well, so much for lighthearted fooling around.

"Yeah? What would you want to change?"

"Time," Holly replied simply. "I'll never get enough of that with my grandpa."

Considering that she didn't have parents, I could see why the old man would mean the world to her. My grandparents had died when I was young so it never occurred to me that I might have missed out on an important bond there. I had my parents. But for Holly . . . it sounded like he was all the family she had.

Unless she also counted her cousins, but I seriously doubted she did.

I didn't want her to dwell on it, though. Judging from her worried expression I was willing to bet she spent too much time trying to calculate the number of good years they might have left together. Definitely time to change the subject.

"Everybody wants more time." I made a big show of rolling my eyes. "What else?"

"I'd love to have that . . ." Words appeared to fail her and she gestured with her hands. "You know, *spark*."

"Spark?"

"*You* walk into a room and everyone knows it. I walk into a room and get mistaken for a zombie."

"That only happened once." I couldn't contain my grin.

"It's never happened to you!"

"Well, no. But I don't usually break into other people's suites either."

She squinted at me. "I don't think that's it. No matter what you do, it'll be cool. Guys will want to be you, girls will want to date you, and *People* magazine will want to feature you. Even when you're suspected of being an abusive boyfriend, people flock to you. And I just don't . . . get it."

That last part didn't sound flattering.

"People want to hang out with me because they think I'm living the dream," I explained carefully. "And sometimes I am. I mean, here I am strolling along a beach in Cabo with a girl on my arm and a suite booked under my name. People are going to wonder what it would be like to be us, even if it was just for a day. And a lot of them will say that they would use their fame wisely and volunteer all the time and donate all their old clothes to charities and stuff like that. Who knows? Maybe some of them would. But that's not the point."

"Really? You have a point? Here I thought you just liked the sound of your own voice."

Smart-ass.

"My point is that they aren't interested in me. Not really. What they want to know is what *their* lives would be like if they were in my shoes. People notice me when I walk into a room because they wonder if I will be anything like the image of me that they invented."

"My cousins didn't notice your celebrity status in the dining room. They noticed your body."

"Well, uh, that's different."

Her grin widened. "Are you uncomfortable with girls checking you out, *Dominic?*"

My full name rolled off her tongue suggestively. Considering that's what my parents have always called me, I shouldn't have picked up on anything even slightly sexy about it.

"How would you like guys checking you out and then *discussing* it with you?"

Holly's arm wrapped around my waist as we continued our stroll. "Are you kidding? That'd be great!"

"You would want some guy to walk up and say what, exactly?" I deepened my voice. "Nice shorts, Holly. Damn, you got legs, girl."

"Well, no. But you sound like an eighty-year-old thug on his deathbed so . . . that's disturbing."

I tugged lightly on her ponytail so that even the most observant photographer would think I was merely pulling out her hair-tie.

"Hair-pulling? Wow, so much for an age gap. Are you going to scream that I have cooties next?"

"Too much effort." With Holly tucked against me it wasn't exactly a hardship to relax and enjoy a leisurely stroll. "I've got a better idea. We'll check out the rock arch, pick up some souvenirs, get a bite to eat, and just . . . pretend to be crazy about each other."

Holly rose up on her toes and pressed a quick kiss to my cheek. Then she whispered, "Deal."

Except I had a feeling I was in for more than I had bargained.

Chapter 23

Holly

I played my role to perfection.

I ooh-ed and ahh-ed at all the right moments when we reached the spiky crags of rock that appeared to jut out of nowhere forming one stunning arch. Then again, I wasn't faking anything. It was a gorgeous day and the gray rock face only made the transition of the water from sea green to royal blue even more spectacular. The whole view was breathtaking.

Then I went into tourist mode when Nick pulled out a camera and started snapping photos of me. Not that he needed to bring a camera, considering the number of photographers trailing behind us.

But it was surprisingly fun having Nick standing next to me, trying to take a picture of the two of us without cutting off half a face. Had we been a real couple, one of those photos, probably the one where I pretended to kiss his cheek, would have ended up as a Facebook profile. Then our friends would have posted comments like *Aww, cute! Love this! Adorable!* while wishing there was a way to secretly delete the image and return our dignity.

Still, I had fun with it. And even knowing that our every souvenir purchase would be reported didn't make it any less enjoyable. I had a feeling that Jen would love her "My friend went to Mexico and all I got was this stupid shirt" T-shirt . . . especially since it would be signed by Dominic Wyatt.

He paid for it too, but I didn't plan on mentioning that part of the story when I gave it to her.

Between the shopping, the sightseeing, and the endless little displays of affection, including Nick's not-so-brilliant idea of sliding his hand into the back pocket of my jeans, which surprised me into jostling a grouchy Mexican woman, I found myself looking forward to collapsing in our suite.

I had spent the past two days longing for dry land, only to find myself missing the privacy of the ship after one day in Cabo San Lucas. For the first time I could see why celebrities would go to great lengths to hide their identities: When you know the cameras are on you, even hanging out becomes a job.

So when we finally did return to the suite, the first thing I did was toss my shopping bag in the general direction of the dresser and sprawl out on the bed.

"Now this is more like it."

Nick only looked pointedly at the clock. "Aren't we having dinner with your grandpa soon?"

I had completely forgotten about that, which wasn't like me at all. Ordinarily, I have each one of his doctor visits memorized and I know exactly what each medication does and how often he has to take it. Something my grandpa enjoys complaining about on a regular basis.

I buried my head in a pillow for a moment. "Nick, you need to be on your best behavior, all right? Because if you do anything to upset my grandpa, I *will* call you Mr. Sugarpie Honey-poo in public."

He looked appropriately disgusted by my threat. "Unnecessary. I'll be fine."

"Promise?"

"Sure."

But I wasn't feeling confident when we entered the dining room together—and I should have been reveling in it! Last time I had looked like death nuked in a microwave and now Hot Guy was escorting me to the table.

I should have been thrilled instead of nervous. After all, the main reason I had agreed to our charade was to mess with my relatives. Make them stop counting the calories on my plate. Time to see if my plan would work.

"Hey, Gramps," I said casually, as if everyone wasn't staring at me. To be fair, Allison and Claire only had eyes for Nick. I really hoped they hadn't already told my grandpa about him . . . or our new rooming situation. "I'd like you to meet someone."

He eyed the two of us suspiciously as if he expected to see *debauched* written on my forehead and *vile seducer* on Nick's. "What *exactly* have we here?"

Nick didn't so much as flinch. "I'm Dominic Wyatt. It's nice to meet you, sir."

Grandpa looked him up and down, then grunted.

"I hope you don't mind if I join you for dinner."

"Well, it doesn't look like I have much say in the matter, now does it."

Oh, yeah. This was going really well. I always wanted to put on a show for everyone in the dining room. There's nothing like having a grumpy grandfather glaring at your new rock star boyfriend to set the mood for dinner.

"Uh, everyone. This is Ni . . . Dominic," I belatedly remembered to say. "Dominic, my uncle Matt, aunt Jessica, and my cousins Andrew and Jacob. You've already met Allison and Claire."

Nick nodded in greeting and pulled a chair over from a nearby table. But apparently that didn't sit too well with my grandpa.

"Just what the hell is going on here?" he blustered. "You tell me that right now!"

"Grandpa—"

But Nick cut me off as if I had never attempted to intercede.

"I'm dating Holly. And I have a number of intentions toward your granddaughter, most of which are honorable."

"Nick!" I wanted to punch him. That was his idea of getting along with my grandpa? Seriously?

Apparently, rock stars don't have to use common sense, unlike the rest of us mere mortals.

Then again, my grandpa seemed to be taking Nick's statement in stride.

"*Nick,* eh?" He let out a mild *humph.*

"Yes, sir."

"You hurt my girl and I'll be on top of you like a ton of bricks. We clear?"

"Yes, sir."

Well, that was kind of sweet.

My grandpa turned back to me. "How long did you say this," he flapped his hand vaguely at Nick, "has been going on?"

"I didn't."

"Holly Rachel Dayton—"

It's never a good sign when he uses my middle name.

"Uh, not real long, Grandpa. But it feels like it's been forever."

"And what is it you do, *Nick?*"

"I'm in the music business."

"So you're not in school." It was less a question than a hard-edged accusation.

"No, I got my high school diploma and stopped there."

My grandpa scowled. "Didn't think you had anything left to learn?"

"Grandpa, you're being snide," I told him, hoping that would put an end to the interrogation. The rest of my family seemed too stunned to do anything more than watch the verbal ping-pong match. Yet Allison and Claire still managed to smirk.

But that might just be their default facial expression. Hard to tell.

"I'm merely trying to get to know the boy," Grandpa growled.

"I've got a steady career that I didn't want to jeopardize by taking time off for college. I can always go back later." Nick shrugged. "Or not."

Grandpa gave him another steely-eyed once-over. "Just how old are you?"

"Twenty-one."

"*Twenty-one,*" Grandpa blustered. "What are you doing with my granddaughter then? Couldn't convince anyone your own age to go out with you? Had to prey on young girls!"

"Hey! I'm right here!" I pointed out. "It's not like I can't hear you."

But Nick just ignored my protest. "Holly isn't like most eighteen-year-olds."

Only the two of us knew that he probably didn't mean that as a compliment.

My grandpa stiffened. "She's *seventeen!*"

Nick nodded agreeably. "I rounded up a few days. Speaking of which, do you have any plans for her birthday? Because I was thinking—"

"Nick has a surprise for me," I cut him off. Okay, so I had sort of coerced him into doing something special for me . . . I still wanted it to be a secret. And I wanted to get the dinner back on track instead of continuing the full-on Spanish Inquisition.

"I can guess what surprise he's looking for," my grandpa snarled. "Listen, here—"

"*Nick is my boyfriend, Grandpa.*"

The whole table lapsed into silence, not that the rest of my family had made noise to begin with . . . unless you count the clink of the ice cubes in my aunt's glass as she downed her water.

I felt like crap.

I don't lie to my grandpa. Okay, I might fib on occasion, like when I say I've finished my homework and I've only doodled in the margins.

But when it comes to the big stuff . . . never.

And claiming that a rock star is my boyfriend: That counts as big stuff.

Luckily, Allison diverted everyone's attention from me by leaning *way* over the table and shooting *my* boyfriend a dazzling smile. "Well, I can't wait to get to know you better, Dominic."

Okay, maybe that wasn't luck after all.

Just typical.

Not that Nick seemed to mind. He merely smiled, leaned back in his chair, and ordered the risotto as if he met his fake girlfriend's relatives on a regular basis.

Well, I could play it cool too.

I was just handing my menu to the waiter when my aunt hissed, "You can't get the clam chowder bread bowl! That's at least five hundred calories, Holly! Are you *trying* to gain weight?"

Oh, yeah, nothing but good times ahead.

Chapter 24

Dominic

Okay, I could see how Holly had become an unhinged mess.

Apparently, it ran in the family.

Her aunt kept calculating calories while her grandpa glared and her cousins flirted with me. The guys seemed relatively sane, but since they only spoke to each other that remained unconfirmed.

The closest the conversation got to even a semblance of normality was when Holly's aunt began describing the girls' activities in Cabo, including their bikini shopping excursion. Either Allison or Claire—I could never keep them straight—chose that moment to examine me beneath half-mast eyelashes and said, "We'll have to give you a private fashion show later, *Nick*."

Holly stabbed her spoon into her soup, slopping some chowder over the side.

But before I could reply, Mr. Ridgley and Cynthia rushed over to our table.

"Dominic, I was just informed of the breach of your privacy. I'm so sorry!"

Mr. Ridgley certainly seemed concerned but . . . surprised?

I didn't believe it for a second. Those photos of our dinner meeting weren't accidental. Mr. Ridgley was lucky that my need to make a good impression on Holly's grandfather trumped the urge to pull him aside for a private chat.

But Cynthia's fingers were already clutching at my shirt collar. "Are you okay, Dominic? Do you need to talk about it?"

They were making it sound like I'd gotten caught in a drive-by shooting.

Sure, I wasn't *happy* about my current situation, but I wasn't injured.

As firmly as I could, without hurting her feelings, I removed Cynthia's arms from my neck. Holly chose that moment to stake her claim by mussing up my hair.

"Nick looks just fine to me. No gaping wounds to report."

"Hang on a second!" one of the twins blurted out, a devilish glint in her eyes. "You're that girl with the free drinks from the b—lounge," she quickly caught herself. "The one who claimed to be dating a rock star!"

The other girl (Allison, maybe?) smirked nastily. "I guess he wasn't interested in you after all."

So that was my leak: A fourteen-year-old, starstruck girl was the reason Holly hadn't been able to silently disappear from my life.

Well, Cynthia was paying for it now. The kid looked absolutely humiliated. Her eyes darted from Allison and Claire to her father and then finally . . . to me.

"I don't know what you're talking about. You must be confusing me with someone else."

"Not likely. Unless, of course, you've got an identical twin who also claims to have a rock star boyfriend and a daddy who owns cruise ships."

Cynthia turned another shade of crimson.

"I'd . . . uh, like to offer my deepest apologies," Mr. Ridgley said at last. "Please let me know if there is any way we can make this up to you, Mr. Wyatt."

At the moment, I just wanted him gone. "I'll be sure to do that. Thank you."

My tone was an obvious dismissal.

"Well, I'll, uh, look forward to hearing from you then. Come, Cynthia. Let's not monopolize any more of Mr. Wyatt's time."

Cynthia tossed me one last desperate look over her shoulder, as if she expected me to save her as she was led out of the dining room. Like I have some kind of rock star power that could get her out of trouble and make everything perfect.

Unfortunately, I don't.

But that didn't stop me from feeling like shit for being unable to help the kid.

"I see how it is!" Holly's grandfather proclaimed, breaking the tense silence that had settled over the table. "You've got girls throwing themselves at you. Well, you listen here, boy, you—"

"I am only interested in Holly."

My interjection seemed to pacify her grandpa, but I could tell the twins didn't believe a word of it. The looks they shot me were three parts seduction and one part sympathy. As if they knew I'd been roped into this charade with Holly and could happily make my vacation more . . . relaxing.

Time to get out of there.

"Well, this was fun. We should do it again sometime."

Her grandpa smiled, which should have made him seem more approachable but instead he resembled a shark. "Holly will be having dinner with her family every night. Starting now. You're free to join us, of course."

He probably thought that just the threat of another family function would send me fleeing the dining room.

But I could tough it out.

I made a deal and I always live up to my end of a bargain.

So I leaned back in the chair and pretended that I had all

the time in the world to make small talk. "I'm looking forward to it. So tell me, how—"

But I never got to finish my question because Holly yanked on my sleeve and blurted, "Nick, we need to get out of here!"

The paparazzi weren't storming the formal dining room but everyone around us had pulled out their cell phones, hoping to snap photos of the rock star and his new girlfriend.

Apparently, Holly didn't feel like putting on another show. Neither did I.

Definitely time to hide out in the suite.

"Well, nice meeting everyone. See you tomorrow," I managed before Holly and I made a speedy exit. Not exactly the best way to leave an overprotective grandfather. So much for making a good impression.

"I think your grandpa hates me."

Holly surprised me by slipping her hand into mine and giving it a reassuring squeeze. After a day full of romping around on a beach and pretending to be madly in love, the gesture should have felt insignificant.

Except I didn't think she was playing it up for a camera this time.

"You're the first guy I've ever introduced as my boyfriend. I think he just needs some time to adjust to the idea."

That made two of us.

"So," Holly continued brightly. "I was thinking we could go horseback riding in Puerto Vallarta tomorrow. That's a tourist thing, right?"

I had no idea, but I had no intention of doing it. Horses . . . make me nervous.

Not that I had any intention of admitting that to Holly.

"I've got a better idea: scuba diving."

She sighed. "You're not going to let that drop, are you?"

"No, I'm not. The real question is whether you're going to wimp out."

I had a feeling the two of us were equally competitive people. Whether it was against her cousins or the paparazzi . . .
or me, she usually put up one hell of a fight. So daring her
into scuba diving seemed like the best way to rope her in.

"I'm not going to jump into the ocean just because you
think it's fun, Nick."

Once again, she had gotten way ahead of herself.

"I'm not *letting* you jump into the ocean with me. Ever."

Her eyes narrowed. "Nick, you don't *let* me do anything."

Crap. I had a feeling I'd just messed up one of those girl
things where you don't know what you said wrong but it still
offended her.

"I'm not diving offshore with you. Until you're certified,
you have no business leaving a swimming pool."

"Then why do you want to go scuba diving so badly if we
never leave the pool?"

Uh, yeah, she definitely wasn't following my train of thought.

"You can get a scuba lesson while I do a reef dive. Then we
can meet up for lunch."

Her look was one of complete disgust. "We're supposed to
be a *couple,* Nick. You know what that means, right? Together. Not just hanging out until it's inconvenient for you.
You can't just drop me off at a lesson like I'm in *kinder-
garten*. That's *not* how it works."

"But that's what real couples do," I argued. "Compromise. Figure out what works best for both people and then
do it. What's the problem here?"

"The problem is that we're not a real couple!" Holly
fought to keep her exasperation hidden from people walking
down the hallway with us. She lowered her voice to a muted
hiss. "Look, have you ever noticed that when something isn't
real it has to seem even more realistic than the truth?"

Um, no. I hadn't. Mainly because I had no idea what she
was talking about.

"Take our relationship, for example," Holly said, since I

clearly wasn't following her skewed line of logic. "Now I could tell people that we got together after you mistook me for a zombie and pepper sprayed me in the face but . . . no one would believe it. My *best friend* didn't even believe it. And yet, both of us know that's exactly how it happened."

"So what does that have to do with scuba diving?"

"Same principle applies. If we want people to believe that we're crazy in love then we have to act more like a couple than, you know, actual couples."

She was making my head hurt. "So you're saying you won't go scuba diving then."

"Oh, I'll go. As long as you take the class with me."

"But I'm certified."

"So you'll be the smartest kid in class. Considering how competitive you are, I bet you'll love it."

It was either resort scuba lessons or horseback riding—not that I saw climbing onto the back of a large creature with enormous teeth as an option.

"Fine."

Holly beamed. "Excellent." Using one hand to stifle a yawn she slid her key card into the door and let us into the suite. "Oh, and for the record, Nick, I get to pick our activity when we reach Puerto Vallarta. After all, that's what you said people in real relationships do: compromise."

As long as it didn't involve horses, I doubted letting Holly pick something out would be a hardship.

But having her referencing people in real relationships in the same sentence as us, that might keep me awake for a while.

Not because I didn't like hearing it but because it sounded sort of . . . nice.

Which meant that something had to be very wrong with me.

Chapter 25

Holly

This was yet another huge mistake.

Not surprising, considering that I'd been doing a real bang-up job even before I agreed to this fauxmance and started lying to my grandpa. What was one more act of stupidity to add to the list?

"It's not going to attack you," Nick pointed out calmly as I stared nervously at the hulking mass of underwater equipment. "Relax. Breathe."

"How am I supposed to breathe when that thing is going to be my only air supply?"

Nick looked bored. "We're in a swimming pool. In the shallow end. If you get uncomfortable, all you have to do is stand up."

"Oh, will you look at that? I'm uncomfortable. Let's leave. Now."

"Shut up, already. The instructor is going over hand signals."

I flipped him the middle finger. "I think I've got that one covered."

Nick ignored me.

Which is how, thirty minutes later, I knew that the scary

breathing thingie was called a regulator. And that if I put too much air in my buoyancy control device underwater, I'd go skyrocketing up to the surface—which could cause air bubbles inside me to rupture and kill me. Yeah, that was comforting.

Not.

Of course, the perky dive assistant assured me that I wasn't at risk since the pool at its deepest only reached ten feet.

Something Nick could have told me himself if he wasn't so busy smirking and discussing nearby reefs with yet another dive assistant. I thought I heard him mention something about a night dive but I chose to ignore it.

Instead I focused on remaining calm while I was strapped into the equipment by reminding myself that he couldn't let me die—no matter how badly he might want to get rid of me. If *anything* happened the press would annihilate Nick with endless speculation.

So, it had to be okay if Nick was willing to stake his career on it.

And even though I was nervous, I didn't honestly want to chicken out. Scuba diving with a rock star in Puerto Vallarta? Yeah, that story would go over well at the parties that Jen and I would doubtless be invited to now. Then again, I wondered whether that girl from last night had been thinking something similar when she tried to pass off Nick as her boyfriend.

The way my cousins had humiliated her was *nothing* compared to the way they'd go after me if they found an opening. They were probably still plotting ways of getting me into trouble without revealing that they had stumbled into the room with drunken strangers and kicked their seasick cousin out. Even Aunt Jessica would have a hard time spinning that in favor of her precious little girls.

But the time to worry about the Twins from Hell wasn't right before I tried breathing underwater.

Preparing myself for a panicked struggle for oxygen, I submerged my head completely underwater.

Except . . . well, it was amazing.

I had expected it to be exciting and different, but it took me actually pressing the air out of my buoyancy control device and sinking to the bottom of the pool to understand why Nick had been so insistent.

There was a sense of rightness that reminded me of seeing an eye doctor and knowing absolutely that the letters on the wall were easier to see with option number one. Everything came into focus. Even my Darth Vader breathing struck me as soothing rather than creepy. And for a moment I could almost believe that if I just stayed underwater long enough the life I left on the surface would fix itself without me.

I lay on my back and watched the air bubbles from each exhale make their way up to the surface.

It was so peaceful.

Or at least it was until Nick swam over to me and flashed the "Are you okay?" hand gestures with the ease of long practice.

I was tempted to send him the middle finger again, just for fun. But it seemed ungrateful since I would never have tried scuba diving if he hadn't pushed me . . . and scuba lessons don't come cheap. One glance at the price in the brochure and I knew that my publicist salary was now utterly depleted.

Completely worth it.

The last time I felt *this* relaxed . . . I came up empty. I always have a great time with Jen (exempting our Santa crisis, of course), but she's not exactly a calm person. She tends to get excited over *everything,* whether that's spotting a new guy to crush on or wearing a shirt she had forgotten she owned. Jen floats through life while I sometimes feel like a young child dragged around by an enormous helium balloon into oncoming traffic.

Now *this* was the vacation I'd been hoping for.

Minus the rock star and the rumors and the paparazzi.

But a girl can't have everything.

So when Nick flashed me the "Are you okay?" signal, looking completely comfortable underwater (no real surprise there: The guy could stroll into a ballet studio in a stretchy pink leotard and remain unfazed), I didn't even try to hide my enjoyment. Although, I did struggle to contain my grin in case the mouthpiece thingie wouldn't work as well if water seeped in.

I signaled back that I was fine and waited for him to nod and leave since I wasn't panicking or hyperventilating or anything. But instead, he took my hand and led me around the pool. Which was completely unnecessary. I might be new to scuba diving but I still knew how to *swim*.

Still, linking my fingers into his and enjoying my new-found sense of weightlessness . . . not exactly a hardship.

In fact, the scuba lesson ended too soon to my way of thinking. Although I probably should have just been grateful that I hadn't spotted any photographers, since my one-piece bathing suit isn't exactly sexy. Not something I wanted plastered in tabloids so that America could vote on whether I should call Jenny Craig or join a twenty-four-hour fitness club. I didn't want to deal with any of it.

A mentality I was determined to maintain even when we surfaced.

"Okay. You were right, Nick. That was incredible."

Nick tilted his head and hit his ear as if he thought there must be water in it. "I'm sorry, can you repeat that?"

I rolled my eyes. "You were right. Thanks for taking me diving."

For a second I thought he might keep playing it up and pretend I had shocked him into a heart attack or something. Instead, he just grinned. "Glad you liked it."

And with one easy movement, he helped me hoist my equipment onto the rim of the pool.

"It was just so . . . quiet."

As soon as the words were out of my mouth I felt stupid. There were a billion ways to enjoy silence that were significantly less expensive if that was all I wanted. But somehow underwater the silence had become something *more*. I just didn't know how to express it.

Nick only nodded. "It's even better out in the ocean." He gestured at the pool behind us. "Not much to see in here."

"I can only imagine." Which was true. Although that was definitely something I would have to check out for myself . . . someday.

"Well, what do you want to do now?" Nick hauled himself out of the water and began toweling off. It wasn't the first time I had seen his naked chest, and since his boxers covered about as much of him as his swim trunks, I should have been able to ignore it entirely. No big deal. Just a really hot guy drying himself after a scuba diving lesson.

"Uh." I struggled to string words into a complete sentence. "You know. Whatever."

"Skydiving it is, then."

I rolled my eyes, but when he slipped his hand back into mine and we dripped off to the resort changing rooms, it felt good to have an inside joke.

It meant that I wasn't the target, for a change.

And in that moment, having our every move photographed didn't intimidate me quite as much. Keeping secrets from Jen didn't appear so terrible either. And continuing this fake relationship to make my cousins jealous didn't bother me in the slightest.

Even the prospect of facing all my relatives at dinner that night didn't faze me.

But it really should have.

Chapter 26

Dominic

Nothing was going the way I expected . . . and not just because I had talked a high school girl into pretending to be my girlfriend.

Sure, I was stuck with The Mess, but that didn't mean I should be enjoying her company. Especially if it came at the price of my freedom—and my ability to scuba wherever and whenever I wanted. Still, seeing her grin widen when we surfaced . . . it almost made up for being on the losing end of our compromise.

Maybe I just wasn't thinking clearly because she hadn't looked like The Mess with her hair fanning out into a puffy cloud underwater. For a moment, I almost forgot the girl was a walking disaster who enjoyed massacring songs in the shower and annoying me. Especially when we began strolling around the marketplace together.

She studied the caricatures of a street artist briefly before tugging me down onto his stool and perching herself on my lap. I tried to remove her but she held on tight, smiled widely for the artist while she muttered, "I tried scuba diving. Payback."

"But you at least enjoyed it," I grumbled, forcing a pained smile for the man sketching furiously at his easel.

"You're not supposed to talk."

I wrapped my arms around her waist and tugged her more fully against me. Since her whole posture went rigid I had a feeling my move startled her.

Good.

"Now just me." Holly sprang up the moment the artist set down his charcoal. "For my grandpa. I still need a birthday present."

I eyed the drawing. My hair was shaggy to the point of making me look like a sheepdog, and Holly's nose resembled a map of Argentina. "What's wrong with giving him this one?"

I turned it to her and she laughed. "That's great!" Then she sobered. "Except my grandpa will want to hang it on the wall. And since we're not really . . . I mean, it's just . . . he won't take it down, and since we're not *actually* . . . it needs to be of me. Alone."

Right. Of course, that made sense. No one would want their grandpa to have a picture of their fake rock star ex-boyfriend immortalized on their living room wall.

"What should we do with this then?"

She shrugged and then forced herself to remain still while the street artist finished her solo portrait. "You can keep it. I have plenty of sketches of you already."

Not exactly comforting.

Holly glanced back at her watch. "We should probably head back to the ship. We've got a wonderful family dinner, after all."

Her tone made it clear that the two of us were equally un-enthused at the prospect of eating with her closest relatives. But she shrugged off her unease as we made our way to the ship and changed for dinner. Holly didn't even act concerned about it as she sat applying some of the midnight-black mascara I had purchased. Instead, she cracked up as I had related my shopping difficulties. Which made it somehow harder to watch. Her aunt started in on her again the second we joined everyone at the dinner table. Except this time instead of focusing on calories, she pointed out that Holly had applied the *wrong* kind of makeup in the *wrong* way, making everything "just wrong!"

I didn't even know what Holly's aunt was yammering on about, since I hadn't seen her try anything beyond the mascara. Considering that she hadn't given herself racoon eyes, I figured it worked just fine. Then again, I had been a little distracted when she stepped out of the bathroom wearing a skirt.

Not that I had let on.

Still, Holly listened to her aunt's critique in silence. Then she turned to her grandpa, the one member of her family who didn't treat her like a charity case.

Of course, he also had to be the one person in her family who hated me.

"I went scuba diving today," Holly informed the old man triumphantly.

Maybe not the smoothest topic change, but it worked.

"You *what?*" Holly's grandfather didn't look pleased—instead he looked absolutely furious, and it wasn't difficult to guess who he held responsible. "*He* took you scuba diving! Without any regard to *safety* or—"

"It was entirely safe," I interrupted, not wanting to hear him rattle off the billion reasons why Holly never should have agreed to it. "She took a lesson. In a pool. No fatalities either."

"*Hmph.*" The old man didn't look appeased. "I guess it was foolish of me to think that my granddaughter might want to spend some time with *her own family* on vacation."

Holly's smile vanished.

"If you want to do something with me then I'll be there. You know that, Grandpa. Always."

I didn't need Tim's skill with girls to understand she was talking about much more than a vacation. I'd even bet my share of profits from ReadySet's debut album that if her grandpa ever became ill, Holly would drop out of college, fly home, and put her life on hold indefinitely.

Something that I had never been forced to consider before.

Damn, I was glad I wasn't in that situation. I wouldn't have the faintest idea how to cope with it.

Then again, Holly didn't seem to know how to handle it either since her grandpa was able to maneuver her into agreeing to go on a Christmas horseback riding excursion on the beaches of Puerto Vallarta with her entire family the next day. In the space of three sentences.

The man might hate me but he was undeniably brilliant.

Although Holly hadn't exactly wanted to evade the outing.

"We haven't done that together in years!" She gestured excitedly with her hands, nearly knocking over her water glass. "Are you sure, Grandpa?"

He let out another one of his *hmph*s. "I wouldn't have suggested it if I weren't!"

Holly turned to me. "Doesn't that sound great, Nick!"

In a word: no.

"Uh, yeah. I'm going to have to sit that one out."

Her eyes narrowed. "Why?"

"I'm just not big on horseback riding. And I don't want to prevent you from having quality time with your grandpa."

I was willing to use whatever excuse I needed.

"I'll spend time with Dominic," one of the twins volunteered instantly. "Claire and I can keep him entertained."

Holly kicked me under the table. Hard.

"I, uh, I have to work."

Not the smoothest of excuses. But at least it was the truth.

I needed to check in with the guys and find out how the non-stop good publicity campaign was going.

"I wonder what your publicist will have to say about that," Holly commented.

"I'm sure she'll be glad to hear that I'm making business my top priority."

"I wouldn't bet on it."

I shrugged. "She's overcontrolling, if you ask me. I'll probably fire her soon anyway. Damn nuisance, really."

Holly forced a strained smile and shot a pointed glance in her aunt's direction. "I really think you should join us for horseback riding, Nick."

Her message came through loud and clear: She wanted me to go as her buffer.

Too bad.

"Holly, I don't want to impose on your family."

Which was the wrong thing to say because a strange glint appeared in her grandpa's eyes. "You already impose at dinner—"

"Grandpa!"

"You're welcome to join us," he continued smugly. "I think it's time for us to get to know each other."

Crap.

"Well, if *everyone* is going horseback riding then we're in too!" Claire (or was it Allison?) announced.

Holly's uncle cleared his throat. "I'm taking the boys out on ATVs."

That sounded great to me. Four wheels, I can do. Four legs, I avoid.

I was about to suggest that I spend the day with her uncle and cousins instead, when Holly sent me a pained look. One hour with the other women and she'd probably lose it for good.

And she might let it slip that our relationship wasn't real.

"Horseback riding it is."

It could have been worse. Not for me, maybe, but Hollywood does love it when a knight rides in on his trusty steed.

Unless the knight happens to get trampled by his own horse and left in a pile of mangled flesh right in front of the princess.

But, really, what could possibly go wrong?

Chapter 27

Holly

Nick looked genuinely terrified.

In the past three days I had seen him disgusted, annoyed, nervous, cynical, and snarky . . . but never with this look of full-blown panic crossed his face.

Unless I counted the time he mistook me for a zombie. But considering that a millisecond later I was blasted with pepper spray, it was hard to gauge the accuracy of that particular memory.

Performing in front of millions of screaming teenagers didn't seem to faze him, but apparently horses were an entirely different story.

Dominic Wyatt was practically quaking with nerves.

Hilarious.

"Come on, they don't bite," I told him as I slowly stroked my horse's neck. "They're very sweet."

"They have huge teeth."

"And?" I waited for him to make a point.

"I don't want to give him any reason to sharpen them on me."

Apparently, there were a lot of things I still didn't know about Nick, including where he had gone after dinner the night before. As soon as we left the dining room together he went cryptic on me and disappeared.

I probably shouldn't have cared. He didn't owe me any explanations. If he wanted to drink and gamble in the casino all night there was nothing stopping him. He was a twenty-one-year-old rock star; he could do whatever he wanted.

It just struck me as strange since we hadn't had anything even bordering on a serious dispute in . . . days? I thought we were becoming . . . friends.

I must have misread the situation. And even though I knew it wasn't worth obsessing over, I kept trying to identify what had triggered his need to ditch me. Plus the air of secrecy around it had definitely piqued my curiosity.

Especially since he wouldn't say a word about it in the morning.

Of course, one glimpse at a horse and he looked ready to tell me almost anything if it got him out of horseback riding.

"Hurry up, Nick."

He glared at me, then the horse, then back at me. "I'm not sure which of you is a bigger nag."

"Very funny."

"Not really. I fail to see any humor in this situation."

I dismounted from my horse, handed the reins to one of our guides, and walked over to Nick. "It's simple. You put your feet in the stirrups and you sit. No buttons or hand signals or oxygen pumps or . . . whatever required."

"I'll stick with scuba diving, thanks."

"I was nervous but I gave that a shot." I gestured toward the horse. "Your turn."

"*Or* we could try trekking together. Or rent off-road vehicles. What do you say?"

"I say, get on the horse already."

But because I knew the press was probably lurking around somewhere, I leaned in to him and ruffled his hair in a very proprietary girlfriend kind of way. "You don't want America thinking that a few little horses scare you, right?"

He glared at me again, but this time the look was more out of determination.

"I'm not scared. Merely cautious."

I grinned and gave him a quick kiss on the cheek. It felt warm and a little scratchy and . . . nice. Definitely time for me to get some space. Clear my head. "Saddle up, rock star."

He began to slowly approach his horse, flinching when it flicked its tail. "You know, 'rock star' doesn't sound like a compliment when you put it that way."

I was about to tell him that it wasn't meant to be a compliment when Allison and Claire nudged their horses over to us.

Well, over to Nick anyway. They ignored me entirely.

"Hey, Dominic. So Claire and I were just thinking—"

Never a good sign.

Nick just let out a quiet *"Mhm?"* as he took a few more halting steps toward his horse.

"Well, we heard that Heidi Klum always throws this outrageous New Year's party. Masks. Costumes. The works."

"Uh, okay."

Nick gripped onto the saddle for dear life and managed to get one foot in a stirrup before sliding into the seat. His every muscle remained perfectly tense as if he expected to be tossed and trampled at any minute. The poor guy looked downright miserable.

Allison continued right on anyway.

"So Claire and I were hoping you could get us in." She laughed softly. "We thought you might have some friends we could meet, you know, if you're still unavailable."

Wow. Talk about obvious. I was a little appalled by just how transparent they were being. And for the life of me I couldn't figure it out. Normally, the twins are so good at toying with people, it's scary. But Nick's celebrity status seemed to have them off their game. Either that or they felt supremely confident that they hadn't overplayed their hand.

"Uh, I can't make any promises right now."

Probably because he didn't think he'd return to the ship in one piece. The guy was really terrified of horses.

I probably shouldn't have found that cute, but I did.

"Oh, sure. We understand." For the first time that day, Claire turned to me and I saw something nasty glitter in her eyes. "Holly, we need to talk."

I could have insisted that anything they had to say in front of me they could say in front of Nick . . . but the last thing he needed was to be caught playing interference with my cousins. So, I mounted my horse again and followed Allison and Claire down the beach for a bit more privacy.

Although I instantly regretted it when Allison hissed, "We haven't mentioned that you're screwing Dominic to Grandpa . . . yet. But if you expect us to keep quiet, you better get us invited to that party."

As if I had any control over the guest list. Not so much. Plus, it felt skeezier somehow to be using Nick for his famous contacts. I didn't know why that seemed worse than wanting a rock star–related popularity bump at school, but it did.

Maybe because we had agreed to those terms. And Victoria's Secret parties had not been part of our deal.

"You wouldn't want Grandpa finding out that his innocent little girl has been deflowered, do you?" Claire added nastily. "He'd be so disappointed."

I tried to play it off with a shrug. "He already knows we're dating. It's not like it'd come as a complete surprise to him. Besides, who says we're having sex?"

Allison snorted. "Of course you are. Why else would a guy like Dominic Wyatt waste his time with a girl like *you?*"

Ah, cousinly love. So sweet.

"Well, I'm not worried about Grandpa," I lied. "You'll have to do better than that to scare me."

"We still have those photos, don't we, Allie?"

Crap. I had forgotten all about the Santa debacle.

'Tis the season, all right . . . for blackmail.

"There are some tabloids that'll pay good money for those shots. Especially the ones where Holly's skirt is around her waist and she's straddling—"

"Fine! I'll ask him!"

Claire smirked at me. "You do that. And remember: Say anything we don't like, and we'll destroy you."

This is why I don't understand the appeal of "quality family time." It never ends well. Then again, maybe most people aren't engaged in a Cold War–type situation where only the threat of mutually assured destruction keeps even the semblance of peace.

There was no childhood grievance at the root of it either. The girls had just taken a dislike to me, and years later . . . nothing had changed. And my grandpa probably thought it was normal "girl stuff" that would pass with time. Yeah, and the Israelis and Palestinians had a few "issues" that some therapy could fix.

Not likely.

I was still scowling at the Twins from Hell when my grandpa waved me over.

"Ride with me, Holly. I want to hear more about this *Nick* fellow of yours."

Which was pretty funny considering that if he actually wanted to get to know Nick he could have steered his horse over to where the rock star sat tightly clutching his reins. I felt guilty for insisting he join us. I would have backed off if I had known he legitimately feared horses. Then again, he wasn't actually there for me: He was playing it up for the press. Horseback riding on the beach with his new girlfriend and her family . . . girls like Jen would be swooning for sure.

Not that it usually required effort on his part to make that happen.

Still, he was a rock star and nothing mattered to him more than staying on top. Although I had a feeling that staying on top of his horse was his current number-one priority.

Oh, yeah, this was going to be one really long beach ride . . . for him.

Chapter 28

Dominic

Someone must have gotten the number of horses in the Apocalypse messed up, because there was no mistaking it: It was Christmas and I was officially in hell.

Or I was foretelling the final destruction of the world. Either way, I wasn't exactly enjoying myself.

It only got worse when Holly's grandfather decided to bond with me on the ride back along the beach. His "friendly chat" was focused entirely on what I would do if my career suddenly tanked. I wanted to tell him he could take his concern and shove it, but I thought that Holly might pepper spray me for revenge.

So I kept my mouth shut while he lectured me on the importance of a good education and suggested that I stop sniffing around girls like his granddaughter. He also speculated that dating her probably wasn't helping my career any.

On that point he was definitely wrong.

While Holly had relaxed in the suite last night, I had found an empty corner in one of the lounges and used it as an opportunity to Skype the guys. I didn't want to watch her mooning over my best friends—both of whom looked absolutely exhausted.

"I was serving mashed potatoes for *two hours,* Dom! *Two freaking hours in an itchy hairnet!*"

"That was, uh, very generous of you. Don't you feel like a great person?"

"I had to cancel my date!" Chris snarled, as if I hadn't spoken. "It took me ages to get penciled into her schedule and then *you had to screw everything up!*"

"I know. I owe you both. I get it. How's the sound track project looking?"

Tim's scowl softened. "We should be finding out any day now. The most recent photos of you and Holly are definitely helping the cause. You're ranked as one of the cutest couples in Hollywood. Congrats."

I nodded. "Good. I'm ready to put this act behind me."

It was the truth. I had nothing against Holly, sometimes I even enjoyed being with her, but I'm a private guy. I don't want my love life splashed all over the front page.

Chris rolled his eyes. "Oh, yeah, you look like you're really suffering. Making out with a beautiful blonde on a cruise ship—that must be so hard for you."

I couldn't help staring at Chris. "*You* think she's beautiful? We're talking about the same girl, right? Holly Disaster?"

"She won't land on any Most Beautiful lists, but she's got definite appeal. It's not exactly a hardship to picture her wearing your striped shirt . . . and nothing else."

"Okay, shut up. You're done."

Tim and Chris traded looks. "You like her. *Romantically.* For real."

I groaned. "Are we seriously going to do this right now, guys?"

"Aw, little Dom has a crush on Holly! Isn't that *sweet!*"

Shit.

"You're reading way too much into this," I told them. "She's all right. That's it."

Chris smirked. "Then I can ask her out once you're done with her."

I wanted to punch my best friend in the mouth.

"No, you can't. Holly couldn't handle a rock star like you on the make."

"Oh, and you're so different?"

I glared at him. "It's not the same."

"Well, you should make a move soon then. You put her on the map, man. Can't be pissed if another guy tries to score."

I disconnected the call.

Juvenile, maybe, but I wanted to discuss other guys hitting on my fake girlfriend about as much as I wanted Chris to chat her up.

Which was probably why I spent the rest of the night making the arrangements for her birthday party. And then, since I still felt restless, I sent my parents a Merry Christmas email, bought a double shot of Scotch, and took over the piano in the almost deserted lounge. It had been way too long since I had last played on a high-quality baby grand. Keyboards are great but they've got a completely different feel. So it was late by the time I returned to the suite, something that would've been fine if I'd been able to sleep in and then relax.

But now that I had to deal with an overprotective grandpa, wheedling cousins, and a horse who was acting about as moody as my fake girlfriend, I was really wishing I had gotten a few more hours of sleep the night before.

Christmas had already proved itself to be a full-blown disaster for me.

If I had to choose between running a food kitchen for the homeless and being interrogated by an old man on horseback, I'd wear the hairnet without complaint.

Still, it was impossible to deny the beauty of the scene. The beach stretched out ahead while a myriad of blues in the ocean glimmered in the sun. I didn't have much time to admire the scenery because I was preoccupied with my horse, but I wasn't immune to Puerto Vallarta either.

I had originally thought that Holly and I could rent motorbikes and explore more than just the touristy parts of Puerto Vallarta. And if Holly felt more comfortable riding behind me with her arms wrapped around my waist, I was fine with that too. We could have ditched her family and our paparazzi tail, leaving them all in our dust.

But we had been roped into horseback riding instead, which successfully killed any interest I might have had in straddling anything for a long time.

I was damn sore and my every muscle ached. Staying civil during the lecture Holly's grandpa gave me was almost more than I could handle. So I excused myself from the family lunch, boarded the ship alone, and headed for the onboard hot tub.

Heaven.

Then I returned to the suite only to find Holly talking to Jen on my computer. Again. She didn't even look remotely guilty about getting caught. She merely waved and then tried to end the call without hurting her best friend's feelings.

Not an easy feat, since Jen kept craning her neck and stalling on the good-byes.

"Is he there, yet? Holly, you have to let me know! Because I do *not* want Dominic Wyatt hearing that I think h—"

"He's here."

Jen's mouth snapped shut. Then she whispered, "Maybe I could talk to him for a little bit? I think we got along well last time."

The girl clearly had a celebrity crush on me but she was harmless. Especially over the Internet.

So I walked right behind Holly and winked at her. "Hey, Jen."

Her mouth bobbed open and shut a few times before words emerged. "You're ... oh, my ... uh, hi!" Then she turned to

Holly and hissed. "You didn't warn me he was in *swim trunks!*"

Holly shrugged. "He likes flaunting his chest. You get used to it after a while."

"I doubt I could ever get used to that view." Jen sighed. Seriously. She *sighed*.

And girls claim that guys have no self-control when it comes to their hormones.

"I just got out of the hot tub."

Jen sighed again. Jesus.

"I'll leave you two alone to talk. Merry Christmas, Jen."

"You're the best present of all," she replied dreamily. Then she shook her head, as if forcing herself out of a fantasy that probably featured me shirtless with a Santa cap. "I mean, uh, Merry Christmas, Dominic!"

"Smooth," Holly commented. "Real smooth, Jen."

I headed for the bathroom, but I couldn't help overhearing Jen say, "You didn't do those abs justice in your description, Holly. The guy's a *freaking* Adonis!"

Holly rested her head in her hand and then methodically began hitting her forehead against her palm.

"The things I would do if we were sharing a suite together," Jen continued, apparently oblivious to Holly's head thumping. "I mean, if the rest of him looks even *half* as good . . ."

"I have to go now." Holly's voice sounded strangled. "Merry Christmas, Jen."

"Thanks. Erm, happy belated Chanukah?"

Holly laughed. "Unnecessary, but thanks."

"Well, happy early birthday. I've got a present waiting for you here!"

"Can't wait! I'll see you soon, Jen."

"Sure. And in the meantime, I vote you start celebrating early by grabbing Dominic and—"

Holly disconnected.

Interesting. Very interesting.

It didn't look like I was the only one getting advice about our relationship from friends. Which made me wonder whether she would actually take any of it. I didn't exactly mind where Jen seemed to be going with that last comment. Something about grabbing me and . . . well, it had a lot of possibilities.

But Holly just turned to me and said, "As much as you love flaunting your body, we should get ready for my grandpa's birthday/Christmas dinner."

I narrowed my eyes. "I don't flaunt."

"Yeah, you just keep telling yourself that, rock star."

Once again, I didn't think she meant that nickname as a compliment. Then again, half of the time I wasn't sure if "Holly Disaster" was intended to be one either.

I smirked at her. "It's not my fault you can't take your eyes off my body. Out of curiosity, just how did you describe my abs to Jen?"

That shut her up. It also had her cheeks turning a bright red that I rather enjoyed.

On that note, I walked straight into the bathroom and intentionally left the door unlocked behind me.

Chapter 29

Holly

I love my grandpa, but I just wanted his stupid dinner to be over.

Once again, Allison and Claire had me in their pocket and that meant they could flirt harder with Nick than usual . . . if that was even possible. Meanwhile, their younger brothers, Andrew and Jacob, kept begging their dad to consider buying an all-terrain vehicle. For LA.

My cousins, combined with the nonstop Christmas music piping over the ship's speakers, made me want dinner to be over fifteen minutes after it started. I understood why my grandpa had scheduled his birthday party for December twenty-fifth: He didn't want his Jewish family to feel excluded from the general celebratory mood. It was sweet . . . but I really didn't want to be there. Correction, actually. *I* wanted to be there. I just didn't want the rest of our family to be there with us.

Especially now that Nick's rock star novelty had worn off, providing my relatives with absolutely no incentive to check themselves around him.

Not that they had ever tried much in the first place.

Still, I thought I was going to lose it when my aunt calculated the number of pounds I had to lose if I wanted to look "presentable" on the red carpet: fifteen. At least.

Luckily, Nick spoke up before I could blast her.

"Holly doesn't need to lose a pound. She's beautiful just the way she is, inside and out." He looked so sincere I almost believed that he meant it . . . until I remembered his very impressive acting skills. Nick could probably transition from music to television and film whenever he wanted. Hot musician with a killer body and a great smile . . . yep, all he needed was a fresh-faced starlet on his arm and he'd be the next big tween craze.

Definitely something to mention later to Nick . . . and not just because that might entitle me to a small share of the profits. I indulged in a brief fantasy of showing up to school in designer clothes, tossing back my hair, and saying, "Oh, my Gucci bag? My work in the film business paid for that. Dominic Wyatt? Yes, we're still friends. We're very close. I'm sorry, I just don't have time to answer all of your questions," then I'd let out a strategically placed chuckle. "I suppose I'm in demand now."

End scene.

I bit my lip. The only problem with my otherwise glorious fantasy was that the girl who could get anything with a look or a snap of her perfectly manicured fingers . . . I couldn't picture her as me.

Although I could definitely get used to designer purses.

Still, no amount of fantasizing could make dinner go any faster. I had to watch my grandpa painstakingly open each present, mindful of the wrapping paper, and do the obligatory "ooh" and "ahh" routine. Nothing had changed and yet everything was different. Legally, it was my last night as a kid and that felt momentous somehow.

Which probably sounds stupid.

It wasn't as if I expected to receive the secrets of grown-up-ness and be magically transformed in the space of a single day. If birthdays actually worked that way then most adults (cough, Aunt Jessica) wouldn't be so screwed up.

Still, I couldn't help becoming nostalgic over past birthdays with my grandpa . . . or wondering how long it might be before we stopped celebrating them together.

Not exactly the kind of upbeat, happy thoughts I could share.

So I was relieved when dinner ended and I could pretend that it made sense for me to snuggle against Nick's side as we headed back to our suite. I probably shouldn't have acted so girlfriend-y in case it gave one of us the wrong idea. Especially since the way he came to my defense with Aunt Jessica made him seem safe. Steady. Reliable. I hadn't had much of those things in my life.

And I craved it more than I cared to admit.

Which is why even in the photographer-free elevator we played the happy yet exhausted couple. At least that's why I kept my arm loosely wrapped around his waist. Not that he seemed to mind the gesture. Which should have been weird since both of us were faking our attraction. But the only thing that felt strange for me was stepping back into our suite and realizing that I didn't want to act any differently. I wanted to stay pressed against Nick all night, actually.

Of course, Jen would probably say that lacking interest in *Dominic Wyatt* was grounds for rushing me to the emergency room to have my head examined. When a guy looks that good, severe head trauma was the only justification for pushing him away.

It's a good thing Jen had no idea that our romance was way more complicated than *People* magazine was reporting. She was already a nuisance who demanded the physical play-by-play for my entire vacation. If she knew that everything wasn't copacetic emotionally with Nick, she'd be a royal terror.

As it was she had me confessing that yes, I had seen him with his shirt off.

Then she made me give her my (abridged) description of it.

Although I needn't have bothered, since she got quite an eyeful for herself when he had come strolling into the room, dripping wet in his board shorts. I had a feeling that Jen would go glassy-eyed over that for years to come. She'd probably mention it at inopportune moments too . . . for the rest of my life.

There are definitely times when I want to get my best friend a muzzle.

But Jen was the last thing on my mind when Nick propelled me toward the king-sized bed. My feelings were all muddled in the wake of his standing up for me over dinner . . . and I thought, *Well, that's forward* but not necessarily in a bad way. More of in a *if his kisses are every bit as good as I remember this will work out fine* kind of way.

I was even looking forward to it.

But he didn't kiss me. In fact, the only part of me he touched were my shoulders when he casually pushed me back onto the bed.

"All yours."

I stared at him in confusion, certain there was something I wasn't picking up on. Sure, he had claimed from day one that any physical relationship between us would depend on me, but saying *I'm all yours. . . .*

Then again, he hadn't said that *exactly.*

"Uh, sorry. What?"

Brilliant. Nothing like a short string of one-syllable words to make a girl appear unflustered.

"The bed," Nick replied as if it was obvious. "It's all yours. For tonight."

"But . . . why?"

Oh, yeah, nothing gets by me.

He shrugged. "Consider it an early birthday present."

Which had to be the nicest thing he had ever done for me. Okay, besides telling my aunt that I was beautiful already . . .

and letting me spend the night even when I could have been a burglar or a psychotic fan.

But this was . . . sweet.

Best of all, it was just for me. Nick's offer had nothing to do with press or publicity. Nobody would hear about it. Nobody would use it as an example of what a great guy he is just to prove a point. Not to mention, it wasn't even officially my birthday yet!

I couldn't come up with anything to say so I wisely kept my mouth shut.

"You also might want to take some more of those seasickness pills. It's nonstop sailing from here to LA."

He was right, but I didn't want to hear it. The idea of spending three days on board didn't sit too well with my stomach. Then again, ever since I began taking the seasickness pills Nick had picked up for me I hadn't felt nearly as nauseous. Which was great news for my body and terrible news for my pride since I felt like an idiot for not thinking of it on my own.

I still didn't know what to say to him. Sarcastic rock star Dominic Wyatt, I could handle. Serious *all-that-matters-is-my-career* Dominic, not a problem. Even outraged *why-the-hell-are-you-wearing-my-Hawaiian-shirt* Nick probably wouldn't faze me anymore.

But I had no idea what to say to him now that he was relinquishing his king-sized bed of luxury for . . . me.

I had gotten so used to him acting like an impatient rock star that this sudden Prince Charming maneuver sent me reeling.

"Seriously?"

Nick grinned. "Well, I don't want you puking in my bathroom again. So, yeah, you should definitely take the pills."

Not the answer I wanted to hear, but what could I say? *Why are you being so nice to me, Nick? Is this just to make sure I'll keep playing the role of fake girlfriend?*

Because that was the only reason that made sense to me.

Unless he was actually interested in me . . . but that was even less likely than Allison and Claire agreeing to delete all of my elf photos.

Still, I couldn't hold back an answering grin. "Well, thanks for the bed, Nick. Does this mean I might get the Hawaiian shirt for good behavior?"

He laughed. "You don't know how to be on good behavior."

And maybe he was right.

Chapter 30

Dominic

I had it planned out to perfection: a whole itinerary that left nothing to chance.

The guys had already given me enough shit about my lack of relationship skills that I was determined not to prove them right. And since Holly had lived up to her end of the bargain, I had to follow through on her "princess treatment" like we had agreed. Although it certainly helped that Mr. Ridgley owed me several large favors and I had no trouble cashing them in.

This was going to be one birthday she would never forget.

And it all started with a knock on the door first thing in the morning.

Too damn early to my way of thinking. I had just started berating myself for stupidly offering to take the couch when Holly rushed over to answer the door. She was practically skipping with excitement.

Freaking morning person.

I blearily watched Holly accept the breakfast tray I had prearranged the night before that featured blueberry pancakes with *Happy Birthday, Holly!* written in whipped cream on top. Nestled in the free area available on the tray were two steaming cups of coffee and a single red rose.

Not bad for a guy who generally avoids big romantic gestures.

"Nick!" The rattle of the dishes on the tray didn't bode well for me. If I was going to be on my best behavior then I definitely needed a strong cup to start me off.

"This is incredible!"

"*Mmm,*" I mumbled. "Sleep first. Coffee later."

Holly tried to tug away the blanket that I was once again using as a barrier between myself and the light pouring in through the sliding door, but it refused to budge.

"Lemme sleep!"

I might have lost some romantic points for growling.

"Nick, this is just . . . it's amazing!"

"Great. Glad you like it. Now let me sleep."

The warm scent of fresh coffee grew even more potent, and I cracked one eye open to see her blowing the steam at me. Her mischievous grin only widened when I muttered a quiet string of curses, sat up, and accepted the mug.

I wondered if I could make her smile like that again before the day was over.

"I, uh, didn't *actually* expect you to do anything," Holly admitted around her first bite of pancake.

"So you announced to the American public that I had something planned, fully expecting me to come up short?"

Holly shook her head emphatically. "It wasn't like that, okay? I just . . . didn't think anyone would take what I said seriously, least of all you."

I didn't know what to think of that, so I chose to give it some more thought later.

"Well, you're completely booked for the day, so it's too late to back out on me."

Holly set down her fork. "What do you have in mind?"

I stretched. "Yoga at ten, followed by a couples massage,

and then you have a full spa day. Manicure, pedicure, facial, the works. It's supposed to be very relaxing."

"*Couples massage!*" she croaked. "Uh, how does that work *exactly*."

Her expression was priceless, caught somewhere between disbelief, interest, and concern. "It's a normal massage."

She breathed out a huge sigh of relief.

"Except we'll both be naked in the same room."

Just as I expected, she nearly shot up off the couch. "Uh, see . . . yeah, no."

I cocked a brow. "Sorry, was that a yes or a no?"

"It was a . . . no. Definitely no."

Her long pause suggested that she had to talk herself out of agreeing to it.

Interesting.

"Did I forget to mention that it's underwear optional beneath separate sheets? And that everything else was already booked?"

Holly stabbed at her pancake in indecision. "Fine. But underwear is no longer optional. And if I catch you peeking . . . only one of us will live to celebrate another birthday. Got it?"

I grinned. "Sure. Then you've got a facial and a professional makeover before a personal shopper from the onboard boutique will help you find . . . something."

"Except for the makeover, which we should cancel . . . that sounds great."

"All of it stays," I replied firmly. "I should have planned this three days ago. Then I wouldn't have needed to buy you girl stuff."

"*I didn't ask you to do that!*"

Maybe I did suck at this boyfriend thing. If I continued our conversation I'd probably end up buying her apology roses by lunch.

"I know you didn't. But it's still useful to have when you're in the spotlight."

She nodded begrudgingly. "Maybe. But I'm not about to be groomed like a poodle before a dog show."

"You wanted the rock star treatment, right? Well, this is it: in or out."

"It's just . . . okay, you're right. I guess I was curious to see how point one percent of the population lives. But you have to admit, it's pretty insane."

I shrugged. "You should see what Tim goes through for his magazine close-ups."

"They don't do the same for you?" Holly asked in disbelief.

"Yeah, but Tim tends to be the focus. Chris and I prefer it that way, actually."

"You know"—Holly's smile widened—"if you hadn't panicked with the pepper spray, I would've bought your laid-back rock star image just like everyone else. So I get all dressed up and then what?"

"It's a surprise." I glanced down at my watch before she could protest. "And our yoga class starts in ten minutes."

Okay, more like twenty minutes, but I wanted to keep the rest of my plans a secret. I decided that if Holly was preoccupied getting ready she might be too distracted to ask any more questions. A great plan in theory. I just hadn't anticipated that Holly would be ready in half that time and kicking me out of the suite before I managed more than a hasty gulp of coffee.

Note to self: Not all girls take forever in the morning.

But getting there on time appeared to be the only aspect of yoga where Holly naturally excelled. I half expected her to mutter something about still being sore from horseback riding or being off balance because of the ship . . . but she didn't. Instead she wobbled throughout the session, nearly knocking down an elderly lady, as she tried to find her center of balance. Which left me struggling to hide my laughter as well as my appreciation for her stretchy sweatpants when she lurched into downward-facing dog.

Holly's casual attitude lasted all the way through yoga only to disintegrate the instant we reached our massage room and were instructed to remove our clothes.

"Uh, hold please," Holly replied like an automated call-waiting voice. "Nick. A word."

She grabbed the front of my shirt and hissed, "I'm *not* getting naked with you."

"Well, damn. That's really going to mess up my plans for later tonight."

"Not funny!"

I turned to the professionals who were busily moving around the room, placing towels on tables and lighting candles. "You wouldn't happen to have privacy screens you could set up, do you?"

One of the masseuses nodded. "Absolutely. Just one moment."

Holly didn't look reassured.

"Once they get going, trust me, it won't be an issue."

She rolled her eyes. "You just want the massage, don't you?"

I didn't even try to deny it. "Horseback riding yesterday really hurt!"

"That's why you were supposed to relax into the motion."

"Thanks. I'll be sure to keep that in mind for the next time an old man interrogates me on horseback."

Holly grinned. "You're just lucky I didn't start a race. No way you would've been able to keep up with me."

I felt like I had enough trouble keeping up with her without the horses.

But I decided to keep that bit of information to myself.

Chapter 31

Holly

I was naked with one of America's hottest rock stars.
Okay, slight exaggeration, since I had refused to take off my underwear and the privacy screen had been wheeled in . . . but still. We were both wearing next to nothing in a small room that smelled of vanilla and lavender candles.

Now *this* was how to celebrate a birthday.

Jen would be so proud of me for sticking with Nick's plans, especially since I had nearly bailed several times on yoga. I'm sorry, but balancing on one foot isn't exactly easy when you happen to be *on a moving ship*. I have no idea how everyone else managed what was absolutely *not* beginner yoga. It should have been called an advanced course on the art of Twister instead.

But even though I felt foolish staring at the floor mat with my butt up in the air, I toughed it out. I told myself that the ridiculous stretches would probably make my very first massage feel even better . . . only to panic when I was told to get naked. I'm not even sure what about it scared me. I'd been sharing a suite with the guy for the past five nights and he hadn't made a move. So it wasn't like I thought one glimpse at my underwear-clad figure would turn him into an unstoppable pervert. Not that most girls wouldn't *love* to have that effect on him. Hot, young musician with a competitive edge and a snarky sense of humor . . . plenty of girls would swoon if he so much as gave them a second glance.

And yet I had frozen with my aunt's advice playing in an endless loop. Suck in your stomach. Avoid carbs. Stand up straight. No desserts. You need to join a gym. Definitely not a bikini body.

How exactly was I supposed to relax on a table if I knew that Nick would have an excellent view of my less than toned stomach? The guy was used to hanging out with *actresses* and *supermodels;* talk about unrealistic standards of beauty. Even with the privacy screen in place, it took a few minutes for me to relax enough to enjoy the massage . . . but then it's quite possible I turned boneless. Timothy Goff could have strolled into the room with scorecards rating my various body parts and I wouldn't have flinched. My every muscle was letting me know that it had never felt *this* good before.

I think the massage put me in a trance-like state, because even after I was clothed my manicure, pedicure, and facial just felt like an extension of the pampering.

Then again, I think that was the point.

This must be what life was like for those women in Beverly Hills who could afford the boutiques on Rodeo Drive without so much as batting their perfectly mascara-coated eyelashes. And even though I had specifically *asked* Nick for this, I was more than a little worried about the bill he was racking up at my expense. Manicures, pedicures, massages, makeovers, shopping expeditions; all of it must have serious price tags attached that I couldn't afford to repay. Which left me with two choices: I could either obsess over the obscene amount of money Nick was dropping and whether or not I deserved it (answer: not. Definitely not) *or* I could enjoy it.

I knew which option Jen would support . . . and I found myself in agreement with her. I was cruising the Mexican

Riviera with a rock star on my eighteenth birthday—time to indulge and enjoy.

So I chose a deep reddish-purple called Plum Lovely for my nails and imagined making a grand entrance. I wanted to shimmer under the chandelier lighting while my grandpa kissed my cheek and said something impossibly sweet like: I'm so proud of the woman you've become. Then Aunt Jessica's water would go down the wrong pipe while her daughters scrambled for an insult that never emerged.

Not bad for a fantasy.

And now that I was surrounded by a swarm of women (technicians and clients) who kept admiring my choice in nail polish and complimenting my various features . . . the fantasy didn't seem ridiculous. I thought it was almost *plausible*. Then again, I was also munching on complimentary cookies with a pair of elderly ladies who declared they wanted to adopt me—my perspective might have been slightly off. I just didn't care. And when it was time for my private consultation session in the boutique, Hannah Bronstein, a high-spirited woman in her seventies, and her best friend, Deborah McLean, invited themselves along.

I didn't have the heart to tell them that private was supposed to mean . . . private. Especially since I thought the boutique ladies might be insect-thin fashionistas like my aunt. I'd much rather go shopping with Hannah and Deborah and hear, "Lovely girl like you should be showing off those gams while you've got 'em!"

Best of all: I knew they didn't count cookie calories.

The three of us were in the process of waddling carefully into the boutique, to preserve our pedicures, when I spotted the bratty girl who had informed me that I was just a three trying to pass as a four in front of Nick. I couldn't resist giving her a little finger wave. Maybe Jen's right about my trouble connecting with people my own age, but I don't have patience when it comes to unwarranted nastiness. Plus, I'd much rather hang out with an eccentric pair of ladies who reminded me of Betty White than a stuck-up brat. Not that the girlfriend of a rock star had to justify herself to anyone—except perhaps to the personal shopper who suddenly found her workload tripled.

Thankfully, Lindsay, a glamorous woman in her early forties, had no trouble finding items for everyone and was able to steer Deborah away from a stretchy sequin top that made her look like an aging hooker.

And when I found *the* dress, the other women started crowing, "That's *it! That's the one!*" before squabbling over credit for finding it.

I kept twisting in front of the mirror to make sure that the delicate one-shouldered black creation really did look good on me from all angles.

But if there was a problem, I couldn't find it.

The dress fit me to perfection.

For the first time I wasn't afraid to face the spotlight. I didn't worry that Nick would realize his mistake in asking me to be his fake girlfriend. Apparently, I'd been selling myself short. The silky material hugged my upper body then tapered downward until it swirled and stopped mid-thigh. I actually looked like one of those LA starlets who can get into any club before sliding into a limo and heading to an even more exclusive party.

Nobody was going to say that Dominic Wyatt could do better than me after tonight.

I hoped.

Chapter 32

Dominic

I had the suite to myself and I planned on taking full advantage of the privacy.

My first instinct was to Skype the guys, but I knew they would give me crap for waking up early for yoga. Chris would definitely tell me to grow a pair and ask Holly out, already. I could probably shut them up, or at least distract them, if I mentioned that it had only taken a simple phone call and everything had been booked and paid for on the house. There were times when having a cruise ship owner owe you a favor comes in handy.

Although the *I'm sorry my daughter screwed up your reputation* benefit package didn't cover the boutique.

Or what I had planned on giving her later.

I definitely didn't want to tell the guys about *that,* so I decided to simply not make the call. Still, I wasn't enjoying the suite as much as I expected. I kept pacing the room before I decided to drum on the coffee table and try to compose another song instead.

As far as lyrics go, *I don't know if she likes me back. I feel like an idiot. La la la. I'm pathetic* were less than inspired. They were insipid.

I was supposed to be writing incredible music, not mooning over a girl who broke into my room, screeched in my
shower, and, oh yeah, *kept asking if I was gay.*

And I shouldn't have enjoyed any of it.

Leave it to Holly Disaster to complicate my brilliant plan
by making me think that maybe we were . . . something. Not
the sickeningly adorable couple the press had photographed,
but *something,* nonetheless.

And now she was eighteen.

Sure, our age gap had been weird at first, but it wasn't like
I'd *planned* on getting stuck with an underage felon-in-training.
Just like there was no way I could spend the night on the sofa
without imagining what it would be like to join Holly in bed.
Not the first time my mind had wandered in that direction ei-
ther.

But I didn't want guys like Chris paying attention to her
that way. Dealing with intense family tragedy might have
made Holly more mature for her age, but it hadn't made her
any less susceptible to flattery. It had probably had the oppo-
site effect, actually. One red rose on her breakfast tray and
she was practically twirling around the suite. Something that
an unscrupulous someone could use to his advantage.

Someone, in this case, being me.

But even though I had everything planned out, I wasn't
prepared for Holly to stroll into the dining room . . . with a
little old lady on each arm.

Well, that was one way to make an entrance.

Holly's wide grin tipped me off that she had some ridiculous scheme in mind. I just hoped that I wasn't the target this
time. I was confused enough without adding any more
women into the equation.

I had nothing to worry about, because *somehow* in the
confusion of setting two more places at the table, Holly's new
friends ended up sandwiching her grandpa.

One of them winked, stuck out her hand, and said, "Hi, there, handsome. I'm Deborah."

It was almost enough to make me pity the man.

Then again, after all the interrogations Holly's grandpa had put me through I wasn't going to step in for him now. He could deal with the women on his own. Although he certainly seemed to be struggling when the women launched into how much they liked Holly, how hard it must have been for him to raise her on his own, how sorry they were to hear about his wife's passing, etc.

If I wasn't mistaken, a gleam of panic entered his eyes.

Poor devil.

Still, I couldn't focus on him when Holly scooted her chair closer to mine. She looked . . . incredible. Completely unlike a pigeon amid peacocks now, although her cousins did still look pretty hot. One of them (Allison, maybe?) was in a short strapless number that left very little to the imagination.

Holly's little black dress, on the other hand, left me imagining plenty. But she packed one hell of a punch in it.

"So I take it you made some new friends today."

Holly smiled up at me. "Absolutely. In fact, they helped me pick out this dress."

Apparently, the old ladies had a sense of style.

"It's, uh, nice." I used the pretense of surveying the dress as an excuse for yet another slow once-over.

Holly narrowed her eyes. "Gee, thanks."

Hoping to throw her off guard, I leaned in and whispered, "You look stunning, Holly."

She seemed momentarily frozen but recovered quickly, sliding her arm around my neck. "Thanks. Hannah and Deborah want to thank you for their outfits too."

"Uh, what?"

"I made sure they charged everything to the suite, of course."

"*What?*"

"Kidding." She didn't remove her arm, though. In fact, she leaned in even closer.

Excellent.

"Nice harem you set up for your grandpa."

Deborah chose that moment to giggle uproariously. "Oh, David! You're hy-sterical!"

The man looked positively terrified.

"Aren't they great?" Holly released me to focus on her menu instead. "I think he needs to get out more often. Meet women his age. Socialize."

"So this is your attempt at forcing him into speed-dating."

She tucked a strand of hair behind her ear self-consciously. "Is it that obvious?"

"Sandwiching him between them wasn't exactly subtle."

Holly lifted her chin defiantly. "Subtlety doesn't matter if it makes him happy."

"Yeah, he's obviously important to you."

Her voice lowered, turning gravelly and rough. "He took me in when I had *nobody. Important* is an understatement."

Well, damn. I really hoped he liked me, then.

Holly cleared her throat. "Uh, so on a lighter note: What else do you have planned for tonight?"

"You'll see."

"When?"

"Later."

Any further questions were postponed when one of the twins sauntered over, gripped Holly's shoulder, and announced, "Allie and I want to give you a little present. Now. In private."

Holly pointed to her menu. "That sounds great, but as you can see I'm a bit busy right now, so if you—"

"It's really more of a belated Christmas present. *Santa*-approved."

I don't know why that would rattle Holly's cool composure, but she glanced from me to her grandpa to me then back to the twins.

"Of course." Holly's smile was every bit as fake as her cousins'. "How . . . sweet."

"Well, we know how much it means to you." Claire (or was it Allison?) flipped her hair back obnoxiously.

"Right." Holly turned to me. "I have to settle something, but it shouldn't take long."

Flanked by her cousins, Holly strode out of the dining room, completely oblivious to the way Mr. Ridgley and his daughter sat gawking from a nearby table. Mr. Ridgley probably wanted to use Holly's makeover for the cruise ship brochure while his daughter envied the way she effortlessly commanded the attention of the room.

And I was so stupidly distracted watching her move in that killer dress that I failed to notice the paparazzi snapping pictures from the hallway.

I should have expected it. I'm a rock star: Sharing private moments with the public comes with the territory and definitely should have factored into my plans.

But I hadn't anticipated just how badly they could screw everything up.

Chapter 33

Holly

The girls had picked the wrong time to mess with me.
Normally, they would have perfected their blackmail technique over a longer period of time, but with the New Year's party approaching, they needed to act fast.

Except I no longer cared if those photos were released.

Okay, I cared. I mean, nobody in their right mind *wants* photos passed around school of themselves tackling Santa in a ridiculously short skirt. But the kids most likely to mock me for it would probably be too busy sucking up to the fake girlfriend of a rock star. Which just so happened to be me.

I refused to waste any more time or energy obsessing over my cousins' next evil plan.

So I turned on them the instant we reached the bathroom. "You know what? I'm going to make this really simple. You've got two options: Either you email those photos in a pathetic attempt to embarrass me *or you get over yourselves.*"

The twins glared at me, and I knew I was wasting my breath. The pair of them would probably continue treating others like crap long after they graduated from college. I doubted that they would ever change. That's what bitchy people do before they spawn and raise smaller bitchy people.

"The choice is yours," I continued. "But family or not: I will go for the jugular if you ever mess with me again."

Then I turned on my heels and marched out of the bathroom before they could test my newfound resolve. I didn't want to give them an opening to put me down, especially since I had a boy waiting who was trying to make me feel special. One who just might like *me*, the girl he had originally mistaken for a pregnant zombie.

I thought Nick was enjoying my birthday dinner too . . . even though Aunt Jessica detailed her "hot" diet (only consume things at a tongue-scalding temperature) and suggested that he share it with his actress friends. He just nodded noncommittally and changed the subject with only the hint of an amused smirk on his face.

Meanwhile, I ignored the majority of my family, choosing instead to concentrate on the people who made me feel good.

A tactic I probably should have started years ago, but better late than never.

So my aunt's present of a one-year subscription to a local gym didn't faze me. I thanked her politely and then moved on to my grandpa's gifts. That's where I hit pay dirt. He had picked up on all the not-so-subtle hints I'd been dropping about needing new art supplies. A new set of the high-quality graphite pencils, acrylic paints, a brand-new sketchbook, and an X-Acto knife made me want to put it all to good use right away. It was a struggle for me not to bail on the rest of my own dinner.

As excited as I was about the art supplies, I couldn't stop wondering whether Nick had a present for me too. Which was completely selfish since Nick had already gone way above the boyfriend call of duty. The guy didn't owe me a thing. If anything, I felt like I ought to be writing a glowing commendation to *People* about him or something.

And for the first time, I didn't want to go right back to the suite after dinner. I wanted to linger in the make-believe instead. Just for a little while longer. Which might explain why I felt my heart picking up speed as Nick and I separated from the group at the end of the meal. His hand pressing firmly against the small of my back, Nick steered me into one of the lounges. There was a woman in a sparkly dress belting out classic jazz standards, and I felt like we had somehow slipped back in time.

Nick set my bag of presents down on a chair and tugged me onto the dance floor even though I hissed, "I don't know how to dance to this!"

The only people who *did* know what they were doing were couples my grandpa's age who had probably been waltzing together for the past fifty years.

"You know, I actually guessed that," Nick whispered back. "Luckily, this is one of those dances where all you have to do is look pretty and follow my lead."

"But I'm not good at taking directions!"

"No kidding."

I intentionally stepped on his foot and smiled sweetly up at him. "Sorry. Tripped."

Nick spun me around in a quick move that had me plastered against him, clinging desperately so that I wouldn't land on my face. Which was probably the result he had been looking for all along, since he didn't release me. Although I couldn't help thinking that my new high heels should have come with a warning label attached.

Still, I managed to stay upright and we bungled our way through the rest of the song. We were probably the worst couple on the floor but it didn't matter. Nick kept spinning me until I was clutching his shirt and laughing so hard I didn't care if we looked like complete idiots. Not that any of the surrounding couples paid us much attention, beyond glancing over and mumbling about young love.

Not that we were in love. We were in . . . like?

That was probably allowed in a fake romance. Not that anyone had ever written down a set of rules for pretending to date a celebrity. Still, it made sense to me. You can *like* the other person, but get any closer than that and your heart will be pulverized with the carnage displayed on the glossy covers of magazines across America.

But when Nick pulled me into a secluded corner of the room and reached into his suit jacket everything else faded.

"I have something for you." Nick handed me a small black box. "Happy birthday, Holly."

All I could think was: That's the kind of box rings come in. Rings with diamonds. Rings that have strings attached with words like *love, commitment, forever,* and *promise.* All words that I wasn't prepared to say.

Whatever was in that box, I wasn't ready for it.

Right?

An engagement was off the table, but if this was Nick's attempt at turning our relationship into something real . . . that had my racing heart tripping all over itself.

I was already a complete mess.

"Come on, Holly," he said awkwardly, probably because I was staring at his present as if it might explode. "It's not pepper spray, I swear."

I managed a weak smile and, repeating my mantra of the trip (I will *not* throw up. I will *not* throw up), I cracked open the velvet lid.

It wasn't a ring.

Instead it was a necklace with a single dark gray pearl glowing inside.

"It's . . . it's, uh, beautiful," I croaked. Which was one hell of an understatement. Jewelry wasn't exactly my thing, mainly because it took time and energy to match it with an outfit. But I doubted this necklace would clash with anything, including my everyday jeans and T-shirts . . . and if Nick helped me with the clasp I might never take it off.

"I'm glad you like it."

"Uh . . . yeah. It's really . . . well, thanks." Damn, his gift had reduced me to incoherence. "I . . . uh—"

He shut me up by kissing me.

And it should have been perfect . . . but when the bright flash of the paparazzi cameras caught us mid-kiss, I knew it was a lie. He had set up the whole damn thing for the photographers.

Dominic Wyatt just wanted to sell the act.

And in that moment, I honestly hated him. It was one thing to pretend that we were in a relationship, but to make it seem *this* real . . . that was low.

I felt stupid for falling for his act in the first place. It's not like he hadn't been up front about caring more about his image than anything else. That was why we had started our fake relationship in the first place. I should have known better. Which only made me more determined to disembark in LA with my pride intact.

"Well," I said coolly. "Thanks for the necklace. It really helps sell the act, don't you think? I'll be sure to give it back to you after our amicable media split."

Nick looked simultaneously confused, wary, and hurt. Oh, yeah, he could definitely make a career in acting. "What are you talking about?"

"I get it, Nick," I assured him. "We've both been using each other and . . . you more than lived up to your end of the deal." I pasted on a fake smile and told myself to hold it together. "Now it's time for me to move on."

He leaned against the wall with an inscrutable look on his face, and I realized that I didn't know the first thing about him. Because the guy I thought was Dominic Wyatt would never sell out such a personal moment to the press.

And he wouldn't look at me with that mixture of disdain and contempt.

"So that's it. You've had enough."

"Well." I pretended to consider the situation even though I didn't have any options. The sooner I ended this farce the better. "I think it's in everyone's best interest to keep this short." I stepped back and wobbled on my heels.

Keep it together just a little longer.

"It's been great, Nick. And if it weren't for you, I'd still be a high school nobody instead of the girl who briefly dated a rock star." I laughed because the alternative would make me look like a heartbroken idiot. Not going to happen. "Let me know if any of your famous friends ever need a fake relationship. I think I'm getting the hang of it."

Then I gave a small finger wave to the paparazzi . . . and left.

I was officially an adult and yet I had never felt so young and clueless.

Ironic, I guess, but I still didn't feel like laughing.

Chapter 34

Dominic

I had dodged a bullet with that one.

That's what I told myself as I pretended to lounge in my chair. I was damn lucky she had shot me down before I had gotten around to asking her out. Which was a damn good thing because Holly probably would have laughed in my face.

She had straight up *told* me that she was using me.

Then again, it shouldn't have come as a surprise. She had been up front about wanting fame from the very beginning. Well, now she had it . . . and the girl who had sauntered out of the lounge didn't need me anymore. Especially if she aspired to rule her high school, something that would be more easily accomplished if she could twist the male contingent around her little finger. A rock star boyfriend would just be a liability with the potential to screw up her plans. Too great a risk. She probably had a whole strategy that included over-throwing her cousins as part of her popularity campaign.

Making me the idiot who hadn't seen it coming.

And the whole time she had been playing me like a cheap guitar, the public had been convinced I was trying to take advantage of some sweet, innocent teenager.

If only they knew the real story.

Not that they would ever get it from me. I fully intended to keep my mouth shut . . . at least until she returned to the suite. Then I planned on saying a few choice sentences.

Except she never showed.

It almost made sense. She had illegally entered my room before she knew me, which meant now that I was accustomed to having her around she was nowhere to be seen.

Typical Holly Disaster move.

Except she was no longer that girl . . . and I couldn't tell if it was my fault. I was the one who had convinced her to fake a highly publicized romance in the first place. Maybe I should've realized that for Holly and Cynthia Ridgley social status was worth any price.

The only thing I felt even relatively certain about was that eventually she had to get her stuff. Something Holly must have anticipated, since she tried to sneak past me first thing the next morning. Get in and get out was practically her motto, after all.

Except this time instead of puking in my bathroom she crept over to her suitcase, still wearing the same black dress from the night before, and began stuffing all her belongings into it. I didn't want to think about where she had spent the night or how quickly she had gotten another room. Especially if the reason she wanted this breakup was so that she could officially start seeing someone else. Maybe this whole time she was actually hiding another relationship.

After last night, a lot of things seemed possible. Especially when I watched her freeze with my Hawaiian-print shirt clutched in a tight fist before shoving it in with the rest of her stuff.

"I knew you would steal it eventually."

My weak joke was the closest to civility I was going to get talking to my . . . fake ex on a few hours of sleep.

Holly gaped at me as if she hadn't considered the possibility that I might be prepared for her attempt at early morning treachery.

"Uh . . . you're awake."

"Rather obvious."

Her mouth snapped shut. "Right. Sorry. I'll be out of your way in just a minute."

Making no attempt to be quiet she continued tossing stuff into her suitcase.

"Where were you last night?"

I realized I sounded like a jealous boyfriend only after the question was already floating there between us. Which was ridiculous because I wasn't jealous of anybody. The last thing I needed was a girlfriend primarily interested in my fame and my wallet.

The last thing I wanted was her.

"Don't worry about it."

Not an answer, but I wasn't going to press her for the truth. If Holly didn't want to stay in my suite anymore that was her decision. It didn't concern me.

Holly nervously tucked a strand of hair behind her ear. "So . . . today is the last full day of the cruise."

"Thanks for stating the obvious. Again."

She winced and I felt like a jerk.

"Right. I was just thinking that . . . I should be spending more time with my family. And you wanted to write songs, right? So I should just . . . leave."

I pointed at her suitcase. "Looks like you've already done that."

"Yeah." She zipped up the bag. "Well, my . . . *our* birthday photos should clear up your PR nightmare. And as your publicist"—she walked over to the bed and held out her hand—"I'd like to congratulate you."

I ignored it. "Have a nice life, Holly. Now get out."

She blinked as if taken by surprise by my abrupt dismissal. Then she straightened her spine and nodded. "Take care, Dominic."

Strange, but I had gotten used to hearing her call me Nick.

I think it was knowing that she had already slotted me into her past like a bad haircut that made me snap at her.

"It's over, Holly. You realize that, right? I'm not faking anything from this point on."

"Now *you're* stating the obvious." She smiled, but it didn't reach her eyes. "The only time you fake anything is when you have an audience. And since this won't land you on any *People*'s Most Wonderful lists or whatever . . ." She trailed off. "Forget it. Speaking of which, I forgot to give this back to you last night. Sorry. I'm sure your mom will love it. Thanks for the . . . loan."

I watched in silence as she carefully set the velvet box down on the smooth marble counter before she left without a backward glance. Again.

Good riddance.

Now I could concentrate on my music like I had planned.

I reached for my guitar and began strumming it while I mentally searched for anything that rhymed with "fame whore."

Chapter 35

Holly

My grandpa let me stay in his room with *almost* no questions asked.

Then again, that's what I had expected when I knocked on his door on the brink of tears the night before. Although I didn't think he would use the peephole first and then anxiously scan the hallways as if he were being stalked.

"Those crazy women aren't with you, are they?"

I had never seen my grandpa look so panicked. "Deborah and Hannah?"

He instantly shushed me. "Don't say their names! They might *appear*."

So maybe insanity runs in my family. That would explain a lot of things, actually. Although I wasn't feeling equipped to deal with anyone else's crazy when my grandpa dragged me inside.

"Grandpa, could you do me a huge favor?"

He nodded warily, probably so he wouldn't be locked into giving permission for skydiving with Nick or something. Not a chance.

"Could I spend the night in your room? And could you not ask any questions about it? Please?"

He nodded and then pulled me into his arms. "Of course, Holly."

Which went a long way toward making me feel like I wasn't the world's biggest loser for getting my heart stomped on by a rock star.

But when he inevitably demanded if Nick had done anything to hurt me, I lied.

Just like I lied to Nick the next morning when I claimed to have forgotten to return the necklace. I spent most of the night twisting the pearl around my fingers as I tossed and turned in the bed. The necklace was the most beautiful thing anyone had ever given to me, and returning it . . . leaving it in the suite while Nick scowled at me . . . it hurt even more than I had imagined.

I felt nauseous and for the first time I *hoped* I was seasick because then having my feet on dry land would solve everything. But if it was only the motion of the ocean messing with me then I shouldn't have wanted to vomit every time I glimpsed an ugly Hawaiian shirt. Or every time my iPod shuffled to a ReadySet song.

Docking in LA wasn't going to improve anything.

I tried to distract myself by toying with my new art supplies, but when I showed up alone for dinner, Allison and Claire exchanged a knowing smirk.

"Where's your *boyfriend,* Holly?" Claire rolled her eyes to make it clear she didn't think the term had ever really applied to *Dominic Wyatt.* Not if it was also associated with me.

"He's working."

Probably.

Allison flipped her hair so that it cascaded beautifully over her shoulders. "Oh, by the way, Holly, we sent those photos like you suggested. They're a big hit."

Great.

So I was officially the laughingstock of my high school.

That's exactly what I needed to hear to lift my spirits. Maybe if I got *really* lucky the photos would hit the newsstands at the same time word of our breakup spread. That would cement my reputation as a loser quite nicely.

I didn't say a word in response . . . and it was an odd kind of relief. There was no reason for me to come up with any retorts. Why waste the energy? So I kept my mouth shut for the rest of the night. And since that left me feeling neither better nor worse, I decided to continue with it as a kind of social experiment. The only member of my family who noticed was my grandpa and he completely overreacted and called Jen as soon as we docked in LA.

As much as my grandpa loves me, there are a few things he refuses to discuss—like my menstrual cycle. The first time *that* happened he had panicked and pawned me off on Jen. Then again, I had wanted to discuss my "changing body" with *my grandpa* about as much as he wanted to hear about it. Still, this time he definitely should have given me some advance warning before he called for backup.

Although it was nice to come home to find Jen sitting on my doorstep, reading one of her romance novels.

I needed my best friend . . . even if she couldn't stop swooning over the ex-boyfriend I had technically never dated.

Jen took one look at me and closed her book. "Tell me everything!"

"Holly, I'm going to go meet . . . uh, Mitch for coffee. I'll be back later." Grandpa made a hasty exit, pausing only to dump his suitcase in the hallway. His absence did make it a lot easier for me to tell Jen the *real* story about my fake relationship. At least I didn't have to worry about him "accidentally" overhearing anything.

"Well, you guys *looked* like a couple." Jen pouted, clearly annoyed that she had believed our act like the rest of America.

"That was the point, Jen."

"But you *really* looked like a couple. Have you actually seen the photos? You were always holding hands and—"

"Jen!" I interrupted. The last thing I wanted to hear described were our convincing public displays of affection. "It wasn't *real!* Don't you get it? Dominic Wyatt does *not* care about me, just about his stupid reputation!"

"But maybe—"

I cut her off before she could finish detailing some pathetic rationale that would explain away *everything*. "But nothing! I'm not doing this. I refuse to feel sorry for myself because it turns out that some shallow rock star is—brace yourself—a *shallow rock star!*"

"But, Holly—"

"We are *not* throwing a pity party. It happened. Now I'm over it."

Jen eyed me warily. "So . . . what do you want to talk about instead?"

"Art school."

"Uh . . . art school?"

"Yeah, I'm going to start looking into the admissions process. I'm not sure yet where I want to go as long as it's nearby so I can regularly check up on Grandpa. Plus in-state tuition is cheaper."

I half expected Jen to urge me to slow down but instead she nodded. "All right. We've got a lot of research ahead of us." Then she started laying out the potential benefits of attending a smaller, specialized school instead of a larger university . . . and I couldn't help wondering what Nick was doing now that he was back in the public's good graces.

Probably arranging dates with movie stars . . . and having the time of his freaking life.

Chapter 36

Dominic

"**I**f you don't step away from the drums, I'm going to destroy them."

Tim and Chris both looked ready to call security and have me forcibly removed from the recording studio.

"Drums are expensive, Tim," I pointed out.

"It'll be worth it!"

Chris nodded in agreement. "For the past four days you've been acting like someone shoved a drumstick up your ass. It ends now."

What total bullshit.

"You guys wanted me to be more focused on work. Well, I'm focused. Now let's take it from the second verse."

Chris glared at me. "Not all of us just returned from a cruise where we spent most of our time frolicking in the goddamn surf like you did!"

"Right, it was just one long walk on the beach for me," I scoffed. "Now let's take it from the top. Unless that's too much for you to handle."

Tim broke the tense silence that followed, his voice deadly quiet. "Dom, you've been itching for a fight ever since you got back. What the hell is wrong with you?"

"Nothing."

"Yeah? Then why haven't you once mentioned Holly?"

Crossing my arms, I pretended hearing her name didn't bother me in the least. "She hasn't come up."

"So you don't care about those photos of her tackling Santa? It never even occurred to you to mention it?"

I shrugged. "Those photos don't concern us."

"Of course they concern us! We're the ones who put her in the spotlight!"

"No," I corrected. "*I'm* the one who did that. And you told me yesterday that we landed our sound track deal. Plus the press is already speculating that we broke up, so none of those photos will hurt the band."

Chris nodded. "So you haven't called her then? To see how she's handling all of the media attention?"

"No." I gritted my teeth. "I haven't."

"Well, that's great." Chris grinned. "Now I can ask her out without looking like a jerk. I'll just give her a call . . . you know, to apologize for your behavior, and see where it goes from there."

My hands balled into fists and I almost took a swing at my best friend.

"Shut up, Chris," Tim snapped. "Don't kick him while he's down."

"He's *moping*. And I'm done with it."

I glared at them both. "I'm not moping!"

"Sure, you are. Poor, sad drummer boy. Well, it's getting old, so either talk to the girl or get over yourself."

"I've got nothing to say to Holly . . . and both of you should leave her alone!"

"Oh, yeah?" Chris challenged. "Why would I want to do that?"

"Because she only cares about the fame!"

There was yet another long silence while the guys soaked this in.

"Really? That wasn't my impression when I Skyped with her." Tim cocked his head thoughtfully. "What makes you so sure?"

"Besides the fact that she said she was only interested in using our fame? Nothing."

"And is that so wrong?"

I glared at Tim. "What the hell are you talking about? *Of course it's wrong!*"

"We used her to repair your reputation. On that score you appear to be even."

"Maybe that's how it started, but it's not—"

"We're leaving the studio," Chris interrupted. "Instead of pouting you might want to try actually talking to the girl."

"Funny, but I think I said plenty when I gave her . . . doesn't matter."

Tim shrugged. "Some girls need things spelled out. Either way, this is *your* problem. I'm taking that two-week vacation you promised to visit my boyfriend. If you do anything stupid, I will *not* be doing community service hours to help you this time. So just . . . pull yourself together, Dom."

I should have been psyched to have my vacation extended, especially because it wasn't like I had relaxed much on the cruise. But it wasn't like I would be able to do much relaxing in LA. Not with my every movement dogged by paparazzi wanting to know the status of my relationship with Holly. "No comment" wasn't exactly the answer they were looking for, but I didn't know how to change the story. It wasn't like I could just start hitting on some up-and-coming actress without breaking my promise to Holly that I would observe a relationship hiatus to make our sudden hookup seem more realistic. And just because I had been completely mistaken about her didn't mean I could break my word.

At least I wasn't the only one having a rough time. I had a feeling the photos of her tackling Santa in an elf outfit hadn't been part of her post-cruise plan. Which didn't make them any less hilarious. Jen's horrified expression alone was price-less.

I should have guessed that any embarrassing photo of Holly would have to include Jen. Even with an ocean be-tween them the two girls were inseparable. So if Holly was willing to let me renege on the seeing other people part of the agreement, Jen would know. Not that I really wanted to date anyone right now. But neither Jen nor Holly needed to know that tidbit of information.

Holly hadn't bothered to remove Jen's Skype information from my laptop, which almost made it too easy to contact her. Except it became pretty clear that finding her number was going to be the only easy aspect of our conversation when Jen answered the Skype call with a deadly glare.

"Well, if it isn't America's Worst Fake Boyfriend."

Crap.

"Uh, hi, Jen. How's it going?"

"*That's* what you have to say to me after you hurt *my best friend! SERIOUSLY?*"

Apparently, my biggest fan was no longer impressed.

"Uh . . . sorry?"

"Is that a question or a statement?" she snapped. "It better be a statement. Otherwise I will personally track you down and kick your a—"

"Statement!"

That only appeared to mollify her a little. "Do you have any idea what I've had to deal with, thanks to you?"

"Uh, no?"

"For the past four days, I've been researching art schools with Holly."

Maybe trying to talk to a girl to figure out a girl wasn't such a good idea. Jen was only confusing me even more.

"You're blaming *me* for Holly's interest in college?"

"No. I blame you for the fact that she's been obsessing

over those stupid college guides ever since she walked through the door."

"And that's my fault because . . ."

Jen's scowl made me glad I wasn't having this particular conversation in person. For someone so bubbly she could turn downright terrifying when it came to protecting her friend.

"Because you're the jerk who dated her just to score some points with the press!"

"Holly agreed to it."

"And did it ever occur to you that Holly has spent most of her life waiting for people to leave her? Because that's what she does. She befriends her grandpa's friends and goes to their funerals and wonders how long she has before he's the one in the casket!"

"But what has that got to do with—"

"Everything, you idiot! She agreed to this fake thingie with you because she thought that as long as she could see the end coming she'd be fine. But then you had to go all Prince Charming right before you *dumped her!*"

I stared at her in disbelief. "She dumped *me*. Get your facts straight."

"Yeah, but that was only because you made her think that you liked her when *actually* it was a staged photo op—"

"I did like her."

Jen rolled her eyes. "I mean romantically."

"Me too."

Her mouth dropped open and a big grin spread across her face. "Really? Oh, well . . . she didn't know that."

I raked a hand through my hair, ignoring the way it stood up in tufts as I pinned Jen with a look of disgust. "What was I supposed to do? Hire a freaking skywriter?"

"Um, well . . . that might have worked, actually. As long as you explained that it wasn't another media stunt. I mean, it *is* kind of hard to tell what's real with you."

"*I'm* not the one who started randomly dumping people." I couldn't keep all of the bitterness out of my voice. "Holly managed to mess that up all on her own."

Jen crossed her arms fiercely. "You want someone perfect? Then leave Holly alone. Because we both know that she's never going to fit into the Hollywood mold. She's fifteen pounds too heavy and she would have to change her—"

"What the hell are you talking about?" I demanded. "No, she isn't! Holly doesn't have to change a damn thing!"

A pleased, self-satisfied grin spread across Jen's face, and I knew she had tossed out that crap as a kind of girl test.

Which apparently I had passed.

But I doubted the majority of the American public would agree with me. Considering all that I had witnessed just within her own family on the cruise, I should have realized that Holly couldn't open herself up for rejection. Not when she was convinced that she was every bit as worthless as her aunt and cousins made her feel.

Thanks to me, now total strangers were also saying that she wasn't good enough to date one of Hollywood's most popular drummers.

And I hadn't said anything directly to the contrary.

There was a dreamy cast to Jen's eyes when she announced, "I have a plan, if you're still interested. If you really mean it."

I paused to consider her words. After the way Holly had shot me down, did I want to risk more rejection by following her best friend into some harebrained scheme?

Surprisingly . . . yes.

So I leaned forward and nodded.

"What do you have in mind?"

Chapter 37

Holly

"Uh, Jen? You're scaring me."

Even as I said it, I didn't expect my words to have any effect. Jen doesn't believe in vegging out until *after* the ball drops on New Year's. Then she makes lists of resolutions and feels guilty for eating a boatload of holiday chocolate.

Although this time she had something different in mind.

Jen knotted the scarf even more tightly around my eyes. "I've already cleared it with your grandpa, Holly. So you're going to wear the blindfold and be *amazed!*"

"You know blindfolds and heels don't really go together."

"If you think I'll let you stuff that spectacular black dress into the back of your closet, then Dominic Wyatt's pepper spray must have caused serious brain damage."

Ouch. I really wanted her to stop bringing that up. I already felt like I couldn't escape ReadySet, even without my best friend's reminders. The band logo was everywhere from backpacks to lunchboxes to pencils. Worst of all were the enormous billboards plastered all over LA.

The guy hadn't so much as texted me and I still felt like I couldn't avoid him.

Not that I had expected him to contact me.

That's not what you do with a fake girlfriend. And since the Christmas photos had quickly jumped from my high school to *People* magazine, his timing for distance couldn't have been better . . . for him.

Oddly enough, the photos hadn't stopped me from getting messages from the popular kids who would suddenly *love* it if I came to their New Year's bash. Because telling a bunch of strangers intimate details about my fake love life would be so much fun.

Yeah, I decided to pass.

Although Jen wasn't going to let me have a quiet night in.

"Okay, now there's another step," Jen warned as she escorted me out of the house.

"Can I please take off the blindfold?"

"Nope. Oh, good. Right on time."

I didn't have time to figure out what she meant since the world tilted as my best friend *shoved* me into an abyss. I was falling into nothingness, and even throwing my hands out to break my fall didn't make it any more comfortable to land with a jarring thump. I had no idea what she was thinking, but I could tell I wasn't going to like it.

"Jen? What the—"

"Have fun, Holly!" she yelled as she shoved my legs in with the rest of me. "Call me later!"

The car door slammed shut and a millisecond later it moved, pitching me off the smooth leather . . . something or other . . . and onto a thickly carpeted floor. Definitely time for me to invest in a new best friend—preferably one who doesn't push me into her half-baked schemes. Grabbing at my blindfold, I braced myself for the worst.

"Good to see you, Holly."

The worst I could imagine? Yeah, not nearly as uncomfortable as the situation I was actually in. For starters, I was sprawled out on the floor of a sleek limo that was probably rented out most often for the pleasure of entertaining foreign dignitaries or ridiculously expensive call girls. And that particular voice happened to belong to the one person I most wanted to *avoid*.

I flopped back onto the seat, mentally cursing my best friend, my high-heel shoes, and the rock star who had just interrupted yet another holiday.

Definitely time to play it cool.

"Well, it's, uh . . . good to see without the blindfold."

He nodded and for a moment it was unbearably quiet in the car. "So how have you been?"

"Before or after *I was abducted!*"

He grinned and my idiotic heart lurched at the familiar expression. "I don't think it counts as abduction if I intend to take you home. Eventually."

"Um." I pointed at the blindfold. "It still counts as kidnapping, genius!"

"Considering that you illegally broke into my suite, you don't exactly have the moral high ground here."

"That was an accident!"

He shrugged dismissively, and I went on the offensive. "Where are you taking me?"

"We'll get to that in a minute. Do you know how pearls are formed, Holly?"

I stared at him in disbelief. "*Seriously?* You *kidnapped* me because you wanted to give me a science lesson, Nick?"

"You haven't answered the question."

I glared at him and then rolled my eyes. "Fine. How are pearls formed, Nick?"

"It starts when an irritating foreign object slips between a mollusk and its shell."

"Fascinating," I said drily.

"It is, actually. So the irritating object—no surprise here—keeps rubbing the mollusk the wrong way. Annoys the hell out of the poor devil."

"I'm guessing that the irritant in this charming analogy is supposed to be me."

He smirked. "Naturally."

Great.

I didn't want to hear any more. The prospect of spending any longer sitting next to him and feeling this crappy had me considering the ramifications of jumping from a moving vehicle. "Could you let me out now?"

"Nope. As I was saying, the irritant keeps frustrating the oyster. It could be another kind of mollusk, but let's use an oyster for now."

"Yeah, because it's so important that we get all the details of this analogy right."

"So the oyster gets annoyed—"

"I take it you're the oyster."

"Stop interrupting, Holly. See, the oyster's natural defense mechanism is to cover the irritant with the same substance as its shell. Eventually, that forms the pearl."

I stared at him. "So you're saying what exactly, Nick? You want to smother me with a blanket?"

"At the moment, a muzzle holds some appeal. But no." He raked a hand through his hair in frustration, making it stand up in familiar tufts. "Holly, you irritate the hell out of me."

My stomach dropped even farther. So that's why he had kidnapped me. Dominic Wyatt wanted to explain his complete lack of interest in me, which Jen probably thought I needed to hear in order to get closure. Great way to kick off a new year.

"But you're also smart and funny and I miss spending time with you."

"Uh . . ."

He continued as if I hadn't said anything, which technically I hadn't.

"And, yes, you're a completely tone-deaf morning person, but—"

I kissed him.

And for the first time it wasn't a calculated decision intended to please the American public. It wasn't about protecting his reputation or trying to make the best of a bad situation. He had missed *me*. And if Nick was willing to risk a kidnapping charge he had to be interested in more than friendship.

There was certainly nothing platonic about the heat between us when he kissed me back. I had to make a concerted effort not to melt into the leather seats when I felt his lips move into that familiar grin.

I might actually have to thank Jen for being an accessory to my kidnapping.

When we finally came up for air, Nick handed me the black box. "I believe this is yours, Holly. And just to be clear: I want a real relationship this time."

I grinned back at him. "Yeah, I picked up on that."

"Good, because you have to be the densest girl in the hist—"

"*I* am a pearl," I corrected loftily. "A shimmering treasure. A rare—"

"I take it back. I didn't mean it."

My laughter died pretty quickly when he took the necklace from my hands only to help me with the clasp in the back. There was something really intimate about having his fingers brushing the nape of my neck. I shivered.

"So where are we going?"

He shrugged. "I didn't actually have a location planned out. Jen didn't give me instructions on that part. Is there anywhere you want to go?"

"You know what? I'm already there."

I slid my arm around his neck so that we were pressed even closer. "Now where were we?"

He didn't kiss me. Instead, he moved back so that he could

look directly into my eyes. "I've just got one more question, Holly."

I nodded, suddenly nervous. "Shoot."

A decidedly wicked grin replaced his serious façade. "Any chance you still have that little elf costume? Because I was think—"

I didn't give him a chance to finish his sentence . . . choosing to drag his mouth back to mine, effectively cutting him off instead.

Although I have the sneaking suspicion that he enjoyed being too preoccupied to speak every bit as much as I did.

FOOD FOR THOUGHT

1. What are some of the perks Dominic enjoys because of his celebrity status? What are the disadvantages? Do you think the advantages outweigh the disadvantages?

2. Holly's cousins are good examples of bullies. Do you think Holly's method of avoiding and ignoring them is effective? What about when she confronts them? What other tactics do you think are good for dealing with bullies?

3. Holly struggles with her body image. How does she come to better accept herself by the end of the book?

4. Holly and Dominic complement each other in different ways. What good qualities do they bring out in each other?

5. Holly and Jen are very close. How does their relationship help Holly get through this nightmare vacation? How does it hinder her?

Did you miss Marni's first novel,

AWKWARD?

I'm Mackenzie Wellesley, and I've spent my life avoiding the spotlight. But that was four million hits ago. . . .

Blame it on that grade school ballet recital, when I tripped and pulled the curtain down, only to reveal my father kissing my dance instructor. At Smith High, I'm doing a pretty good job of being the awkward junior people only notice when they need help with homework. Until I send a burly football player flying with my massive backpack, and make a disastrous—not to mention unwelcome—attempt at CPR. Just when I think it's time for home schooling, the whole fiasco explodes on YouTube. And then the strangest thing happens. Suddenly, I'm the latest sensation, sucked into a whirlwind of rock stars, paparazzi, and free designer clothes. I even catch the eye of the most popular guy at school. That's when life gets *really* interesting. . . .

Chapter 1

You probably think you know me . . . and I understand why. You've probably read about me on AOL or heard Conan O'Brien or Jon Stewart reference me for the punch line of some joke. It's okay if you haven't. In fact, I prefer it that way. But let's be honest: The whole world knows about Mackenzie Wellesley and her social awkwardness. Except maybe some people in Burma and Sudan . . . but you get my point.

The thing is, despite all that's been said about me (and there has been a lot), only a handful of people actually understand how I was able to go from a boring high school student to a pop culture reference in the space of a week. That's why I am even bothering to explain. Don't worry: This won't be one of those stupid celebrity autobiographies where I describe my sordid past and complain a lot—my past isn't all that sordid, and that's just lame.

Let me start by saying that I've never hungered for the spotlight. My younger brother, Dylan, was always the one who craved The Big Moment. You know: catch the football in overtime with a few seconds left on the clock to score the winning touchdown. The very idea of a stadium full of people watching me makes me want to hurl. That's probably due to my elementary school ballet recital. I remember every detail perfectly. My mom was in the audience cradling a baby Dylan in her lap as I leaped across the stage. I was craning my neck, searching for my dad in the crowd, and worried that he wouldn't show up. That's when I glanced into the wings and spotted him right behind the curtains . . . making out with my dance instructor.

We have the recital on tape. You can tell when my world imploded by the way my brown eyes expanded and my shoulder-length brown hair whipped my face as I looked from my dad to my happily waving mom. But it gets worse—so much worse. I was frozen while all the other little girls twirled and flounced around me. I stumbled out of formation and—blinded by the stage lights—I tripped on the sound system cable and went flying right into the curtains, which promptly fell down and revealed my dad sucking face. That's when I decided it was better to be invisible than to fall on your face in a ridiculous pink tutu.

Freud would probably say that's why I suffer from a fear of crowds and attention. And in this specific case I think Freud might have a point. I've been paranoid ever since that damn recital—and the divorce. I avoid the spotlight. I guess you could say that I strive for anonymity. But I'm fine with my geekdom—totally cool with the fact that I never get invited to parties. I fill a certain niche at my school, the local nerd, and it's a role that I've gone to a lot of effort to create for myself. And while, yes, a normal day for me means three AP classes, it really isn't so bad. Definitely stressful, but I like it—especially because it'll look great to financial aid committees who decide on college scholarships.

So, yeah, I'm happy with my life. I've got friends, a job, and an awesome GPA to propel me into a solid university . . . or at least I *did*, until I became famous.

And keep an eye out for the next book,

INVISIBLE,

coming in July 2013.